Chris Wilson

is author of three previous novels, *Gallimauf's Gospel*, *Baa* and *Blueglass*. Until 1988 he had an academic career, completing a doctorate on humour at the London School of Economics, researching at The London Hospital and, for ten years, lecturing in Communications at University of London Goldsmiths' College. He now writes full time.

CHRIS WILSON

———

Mischief

Flamingo

An Imprint of HarperCollins*Publishers*

Flamingo
An Imprint of HarperCollins*Publishers*
77–85 Fulham Palace Road,
Hammersmith, London W6 8JB

Published by Flamingo 1993
9 8 7 6 5 4 3 2 1

First published in Great Britain by
André Deutsch Limited 1991

Author photograph by David Meek

ISBN 0 586 09203 X

Set in Palatino

Printed in Great Britain by
The Guernsey Press Co. Ltd, Guernsey, Channel Islands

For my brother David

My Love is of a birth as rare
As 'tis for object strange and high:
It was begotten by Despair
Upon Impossibility ...

As lines so Loves oblique may well
Themselves in every angle greet:
But ours so truly parallel,
Though infinite, can never meet

ANDREW MARVELL

One

It's an unlikely story, I concede. We have this much in common, at least — our lives have not been easy. It's the secret bond between us.

You look a sorry skinful. Forgive my mentioning that, but the shimmer of your youth has dulled like tarnished silver.

Ecstasy disdains your call, despite your heavy breathing. Out of tact, I say no more. Least said soonest ended.

Little changes. But your glance in the mirror surprises and saddens. A weariness betrays you, skulking behind your forced, transparent smile.

Perhaps you need some fun — to take you out of yourself. It gets so cramped and claustrophobic, when you're stitched up so tight in a skin.

I'm sorry. I seldom mean to cause offence. It's just I've an unfortunate appearance, and mischievous manners. They're a wilful lot — my manners — and take liberties when I'm not watching. My personality is just as bad. He's got a mind of his own.

I have this habit of imitating people. It can cause annoyance, that habit. Please do your best to ignore it. Don't assume I'm laughing at you. So sniffle away to your heart's content. Scratch it, if you fancy. But don't mind me if I copy. I'm just a fool and a simpleton. You'll find I try your patience.

Forgive my language. I'm not at home with words. You're so clever with your ifs and buts, shoulds and woulds, your possessive case, your past perfect and future simple, notwithstandings and hereinafters. Left to my own devices, I'd merely grunt and gibber.

My life has been a struggle to understand you, to fathom the human heart. Mischief has been a special interest of mine. Oh, mischief! Wilful child of rhetoric and desire.

It's a difficult tale to swallow. I don't suppose you'll believe me. There's a lot of suspicion about, have you noticed?

Here goes.

My father had no part or pleasure in my creation. I was found, not conceived, by my parents.

I was the small, improbable discovery of Dr Robert Jay Duckworth, a zoologist. He found me by the Cobija river, near Guajara Mirim, in the Province of Abuna, in Brazil, close to the Bolivian border, on the afternoon of 16th August 1949. This is as he told it.

He was collecting specimens. I was lying on my back, in the steamy shade of a rubber tree, swaddled in matted banana leaves, gurgling moistly, fixing him relentlessly with my sulphur-yellow eyes.

Dr Duckworth's specialism was amphibians. But he sensed no alternative to collecting me — though I lay beyond the narrow cul-de-sac of his competence. Clearly, I was abandoned. He'd been pottering close by my hiding place for several hours, and had seen no one but his botanist companion — David Wright-Morris, also of the Department of Biology, University College, London.

He stooped down. Tentatively he fingered me, grazing my lips. I commenced to suck upon his finger with a desperate passion, then howled against his dryness.

Hope leaves a lot to be desired.

He unpacked his rucksack and mashed for me a mixture of banana and condensed milk, which he spooned into my voracious mouth. He and Wright-Morris waited in vain for my mother's return. At dusk, they rode back to their camp at San Antonio do Boa. Dr Duckworth tucked me into his shirt-front and buttoned me tight to his chest. I smiled contentedly up at him, he reports, whilst leaking into his lap.

The Mayor of San Antonio do Boa, and its only householder, was affronted by the very sight of me, and probably by my smell.

2

He denied paternity with huffy plausibility. I was not a human child, he explained, but a baby Indian — Xique Xique, he thought from the colour of my eyes, or perhaps an Azul, judging by my swaddling. But more likely a Xique Xique, considering my hue and smell.

The Major advised I be returned whence I came, and left on my former spot. He cautioned against peeling an Indian from its rind of place. These Indians were another species, he said. Shiftless wanderers who perched in trees, innocent of roofs and culture. But they were possessed of memory and would retrace their steps and find me, in the fullness of their time.

At Principe da Beira the chief of police, the doctor, and the rubber planter disowned any kinship, or concern for my fate. They were appalled that a civilised man should carry such a thing as me in his luggage. The store owner volunteered to dispose of me discreetly, without pain to himself or to me.

Dr Duckworth appealed to higher authority by sending a letter by messenger to the Provincial Governor at Corun.

Was it appropriate, Dr Duckworth enquired, for foreign visitors to have to foster local foundlings? Did the Governor suppose that he could care for this child forever?

Irony doesn't travel well in translation. The Governor obligingly returned a certificate of adoption naming himself as godfather and the good Dr Duckworth as my legal guardian. The Chief of Police delivered the document to my new father, levying a fee of fifty escudos. He meant to make Dad pay heavily for causing such heedless trouble over a small unnecessary animal.

If possession were nine tenths of the law, Dr Duckworth had inadvertently gained the missing tenth. He had the complete portion of my paternity. And I was his — a humid, howling package of life. So, I became a human being.

There I lay burping in the balance of his motives, oblivious of the tussle between convenience and humanity. He could have lost me no doubt, as my natural parents had done. He might have passed the parcel on. But he knew my dismal fate without him. He had seen ranchers in Juruena hunt Indians on horseback, and burn their huts by night to clear the land. It was expecting too much of me to take care of myself. The locals could not see me as a human. To cast me from his life would be to despatch me from mine.

'I think he's yours, Duckworth,' observed David Wright-Morris.

'Ours, don't you mean?'

'Oh, no,' said Wright-Morris. 'You bagged the bugger. You can keep him. Besides, I'm only the botanist. Mammals are your concern . . . but God knows what the Dean will say when he sees what you've collected.'

At the orphanage at Queimadas, the Jesuit missionaries flap and flutter about me, curious as magpies. They smile with rapt delight as my father tells his story. There is sighing, loud exclamation, and the laying of hands on brows. They marvel at God's handicraft. It was miraculous and ordained, they declare, that in the depth of the rain forest a man in want of a son should chance upon such a boy in need of a father. It is indeed fortunate, they observe, that the plump Dr Duckworth is blessed by the Lord with the means and money to care for me. And I was now no longer an orphan they observe, pointedly, since he is now my legal guardian.

Nor could Dr Duckworth find anyone else to take me off his hands.

So I gained a kind but reluctant father and, on reaching England, a perplexed mother. Mrs Mary Duckworth was forty-five. She must have been bemused to be delivered a first child so late in life, and with less that nature's customary warning. Father had sent a telegram as he embarked at Recife —

'Due Portsmouth November 18th on SS Joao Pessoa. Collected much. Five new species. Three Frogs. Two toads. And one child. Congratulations. You now mother. Expect arrival of baby son. Sorry short notice. Suggest call him Charles after Darwin. Please make arrangements. Wright-Morris sends regards. Me well. How you? Love etc. Robert.'

I should introduce my name — though it is a misleading label. I was christened Charles Xique Xique Duckworth, on 3rd December, at St Mary's, Upper Street, Islington. It is an item of our family lore that the vicar remarked upon my duplicated middle name — suspecting some satire on the participants, gathered together in the eyes of God.

I learned all this much later in life. Despite the contrary evidence of appearances, I believed until the age of eleven that Robert and Mary Duckworth (bless them!) were my natural parents.

My appearance, a tirelessly indiscreet companion, is extrovert — unlike my character — and always insists on provoking remark. People always stared at me. They still do. Children are often hushed to awed silence at the very sight of me. It's not that I frighten them. I'm more a surprise than a scare.

Now, in my prime, I slouch six feet nine inches tall. It used to please me, being three full inches short of the freakish.

My arms and legs look long in proportion to a compact, barrelled trunk. My fingers and toes are long and pencil fine. My elegance has been favourably likened to that of a gibbon.

A broad high forehead is accentuated by the paucity of my hair. All I have is a sparse cover of wispy black down — as though I've suffered a radical crew-cut.

Offsetting this harshness, I've a wide-eyed amiable gaze; made curiously compelling by my crocus-coloured eyes. My nose is delicate if snubbed, with flared almond nostrils. Thin lips guard a tight porcelain smile. The effect is of youthful distinction. People often flatter that I look much younger than my years, for I've a hairless face, unruffled by wrinkles.

I've been blessed with a good complexion. My skin has a translucent pearly sheen, betraying a map of veins beneath.

Doctors often suppose I'm jaundiced, for I've that hennaed hue people earn from hepatitis or by buying a fake suntan from a bottle. But my liver's fine. Orange-brown is my natural colour.

Whilst I'm not conventionally handsome, my looks are extreme and striking. I interest women, turning many a head in the street.

I'm best in motion, for then I've got the lithe, liquid pad of a puma.

I've got a rare agility. Even now, approaching my fortieth year, I can bound a pillar box from a standing jump. It's a natural skill.

At school, I broke the high jump record by three and a half feet. The Xique Xique would have thought nothing of it — being an athletic sort — but at Stoneham School it caused a stir. I'd have competed seriously, but I learned early to evade attention as best I could.

I cannot claim to be an expert historian of my infancy. I was asleep for much of the time and my mind was then untutored. This much has been reported to me by my parents, perhaps muffled by their diplomacy to avoid abrading my rawest feelings.

'What's this?' asks mother, when she first spies me. I am an irregular item of hand-luggage; lying in the makeshift cot of father's leather holdall. I am wrapped in a stained sheet and sucking on a leather strap. The taste is thick and salty.

'A baby,' says Dr Duckworth, dogmatic in his diagnosis.

'An orange one!' she chuckles. 'So it is.'

'It's your son,' says Dr Duckworth. 'Don't you like it?'

'My son?'

'Goodness gracious, woman . . .' Dr Duckworth chides, 'surely you got my telegram. This is our child.'

Mother lays her chill hand on my brow. It is our first touch.

'He's got a fever,' she sighs, shaking her head till her cheeks quiver, 'and a very sickly colour.'

My eyelids flutter open. I regard her with my calm yellow gaze.

'But he's a darling, isn't he!' She clutches me up and rocks me in her fat freckled arms. I inhale her savour of hot garlic butter.

The family doctor examines me. He expresses bemused concern.

'He's running a temperature. He's underweight. He's jaundiced. The pulse and blood pressure are way too high. Yet he does seem a happy chappie. . . .'

He is surprised that my placid façade belies such a turbulent metabolism. He examined all my nooks and crannies, reporting certain irregularities — including my hairlessness, the colouring of my pupils, the length and flexibility of my limbs, the position of my Foramen Magnum, the wide sutures to by bulbous cranium, my weak brow ridge, my small jaws and cartilaginous cheek bones. Oh, yes, and the high location of my unlikely penis.

'He's an unusual little . . .' the doctor pauses '. . . baby,' he declares. 'It's hard to know what to make of him. If he reminds me of anything, it's of a seven-month foetus. It's as though he's come into the world a couple of months too soon. . . .' He looks at Dr Duckworth with wry pity. 'He's *your* son, is he?'

'Yes,' concedes Dad, 'and no.' Already, he's started apologising for me. 'I adopted him in Brazil.'

'Ah. . . .' the doctor's brow smooths at a puzzle solved. 'A foreign body? A native, eh?'

There are many monochrome photographs of my childhood, for Dr Duckworth was a keen amateur photographer. The earliest snap is of me lying, eyes closed, knees drawn up to my belly like a trussed duck, displaying myself on the fireside rug. A foot rule lies before me to show the scale of my tiny being. You can see every interval on the ruler, while I lie blurred beyond the focus.

I was a slow developer. I'm told that I did little worthy of remark in my first two years of life. Indeed, I can't recall doing anything at all. But I was known as a paragon of lethargy. As though possessed of a blissful secret, I lay on my back, snuffled and smiled.

'We thought you were retarded,' said mother.

'You were like a jaundiced slug,' said father. 'Sickly, yellow, fat, sticky and slow. And tacky to the touch.'

Having delayed my development, like a hibernating animal awaiting a propitious season, I woke brisk and eager at the age of two.

I began to speak for myself and plead my special case.

If I've often felt fully Duckworth, I've never considered myself entirely English. I don't like to carp. This country has been my home for four decades. It's provided me language, education and home. But if the English have a foible — as I believe they do — it is an intolerance of difference, an expectation that others should match their mould.

I am tall. I am orange-skinned. My eyes are yellow. This has earned me disdain and distrust.

Dogs, despite their lack of cultural achievement, offer us lessons in affability. And I'd always prefer a friend to a man who can compose a string quartet — however skilful his counterpoint.

To look at them, you'd suppose a bishop and a pimp have more in common than a Dobermann and a Yorkshire Terrier. But you just can't get them to mix. The dogs at least would pause for a yelp or a sniff.

And if you were to offer me a choice of companion between cocker spaniel and professor of moral philosophy, I should, without a second's hesitation, select the spaniel — and find him the more amiable, accepting and open-minded companion. Never mind if I always had to buy the dinner. It's the company that counts. This isn't empty banter; I've spent my time with both.

I admire enthusiasm and spontaneity. I find both in plenty in dogs. Dogs have played a large part in my life. There's empathy to it too. Like me, they've been thrown into the deep end of human affairs they cannot fathom. We have strayed, dogs and I, from our kin.

My mother and father contrived to overlook or ignore my oddness. I was their only child. They were late and innocent parents. And Dr Duckworth, as a zoologist, was accustomed to the dizzy quirkiness of life. Compared to that species of Nematode worm that needs to wriggle inside a German felt beer mat before it feels at home, a two-toed sloth or magnetotactic bacterium, I must have seemed a dully orthodox item. It takes a lot to startle a biologist.

Early in life, I displayed strong enthusiasms. I was besotted by the dark, by holes, by hiding things and watching people.

Left to my own devices, I'd sidle into the shade — furtively discreet as a mole. Mother would find me under the sofa, in the cupboard beneath the stairs, in the oven, stowed in a cardboard box. I'd be there in the dark, watching life through a crack or crevice, on the outside looking in, observing my adoptive family.

Holes entranced me. I'd clamber into the sink or bath, lower an eye to the plug-hole, and gaze endlessly into the dark, dank,

8

gurgling tubes. Or I'd hoist myself into the chimney and perch precariously within. Neither of my parents were followers of Freud, and I was left to feed my whims. Dragging a chair behind me, for use as a ladder, I'd patrol the home, switching off all the bulbs, tugging the curtains closed, at war with the dazing glare of light.

In the morning, I'd listen for the postman's step in the street. Scampering to the hall I'd watch the mysterious slit in the door blink open, and witness, enthralled, the birth of letters — which I'd seize, to hide in dark places, beneath pillows and under mats. Till I was found out and forbidden.

Also, I was fond of climbing — to the top of cupboards, above doors, up curtains or drain pipes, inadvertently causing consternation or damage. Frequent falls and breakages did not dissuade me, until Dr Duckworth did — by explaining I made him unhappy.

His frown would pierce me with shafts of sorrow. His glare raked me with miseries. Cross words made me vomit.

Sympathy has been my Achilles' heel. I can't abide another's discomforts and pains. They become my very own.

It is a physical affliction that became apparent early. I share in the suffering and injury of any other being I like.

When the grocer's dachshund broke a leg, I developed a sympathetic limp. Once I saw a child kick an unwary cat on the rump. Promptly I developed a bruise on my buttocks and we made a dismal din together, what with the caterwauling and my wails. I could not sit with any comfort for two days after.

I found myself particularly prone to the pains of my parents, who were the beasts I loved the best. If either Dr or Mrs Duckworth contracted a cold, then so would I. In the evening in the sitting room, we'd sniffle and snuffle in concert, bound together by mucus.

As mother entered the menopause, I quickly followed, as far as I could with masculine tubes. It's hard for men fully to understand the discomfort and disorientation in being ambushed by attacks of hot flushes, dizziness, headaches and melancholia.

With my father, I shared chronic low back pain, prostate trouble, and impairment of my short-term memory.

9

I must have seemed a delicate and sickly child. Dr Foster soon railed against my frequent visits to his surgery, slandering me as a precocious hypochondriac. Once, I remember, he bellowed at me, shaking a stern finger. So, I burst into tears and retched in his enamel tray of surgical bandages.

To this day, the sight or scent of a doctor makes me queasy. I've always been a sensitive soul, you see.

I believe I know your secret.

Two

You may have read of me before. I used to be K 77 — no, not an obscure work of Mozart, but one heart throbbing for another. I had an anonymous celebrity amongst the friendless and forsaken, and those flesh-eaters who fed on them, for I used to advertise my desolation in the lonely hearts column of a well-known London magazine. If that literature is to your taste, if you enjoy reading the plaintive pleas and muffled howls of the unloved, you might recall my advertisement, which ran unchanged for two full years in every issue:

> Skinny, nervous, yellow-eyed, copper-skinned, vegetarian man, with wince, stammer and slouch, seeks similar, preferably female, for intimate and profound understanding. Colour photo appreci-ated. All genuine letters answered. Box K 77.

I decide it's best to be honest, to avoid misleading all the decent people. I haven't intended any double-meanings, but folk can always find them lurking in the shadow of an adjective or burrowed clandestine in a noun. My frank and guileless declaration earns me four or five replies each week, but they are never addressed to my quest.

The letters tell of exotic rites and rituals from the Far East of Loughton or Tropics of Crawley. I get canvassed by erotic constituencies I've never guessed at. You have to admire the dazzling deviousness of desire. And there's a measure of mischief, too. You'd be surprised how many passions can dance around the point to celebrate the prick.

Folk are uncannily ingenious in reading my invitation. Many

offer to come in fancy dress, play charades, or do their party tricks. They hear unspoken supplications, see invisible signs, sniff the whiff of pungent cravings.

In truth, I seek the most elusive of partners — a being like me, another Xique Xique. I seek a woman as wife, but would delight in embracing a brother.

This is misunderstood. I'm pestered by the whims of pale people. Pink as spam and quite as tasty.

Men are the gross majority. My stated preference for a woman is read as declaring a taste for men. I am a Rorschach inkblot, in which every man can see the beckoning leer of his lusts.

I get invited to suck this, lick that, dress myself in leather, or lodge my fist up a fundament. One man promises I may enter into his marriage, through a private portal of his wife's — whilst he films the comings and goings. One kind soul says he'll take me to the Coliseum to see *Carmen*; another promises to thrash me, after binding me in barbed wire. Some say they'll piss on me. I don't doubt it.

Ah, mischief! Each to their own. It's a fool that aims to please everyone. I don't try.

The women are more reticent; preferring to meet before pledging.

There's a convention of photography that a portrait should show the face of the sitter, but in a few of the snaps I get sent, the camera slips to a lower focus. A few imperfect strangers — too vain or cautious to disclose their faces — send me wide-angled, technicolour, intimate surveys of the lie of their leering pudenda. But you can't trust someone by the blind, bearded smirk of their privates. I'd rather look a party in the eye.

Yet eyes lie too. For often in amateur snaps, they register pink or scarlet. Some brown eyes appear a deceptive yellow, if the print is over-exposed. There's the frequent lure of fool's gold.

Grasping such a teasing image, I flush like a retina caught in the flash. Perhaps I clutch a Xique Xique in my molten palm?

But the phone-call or meeting scatters the petals of hope. Her eyes are never crocus-coloured. Her copper hue was burned upon her in Sicily, Cannes or Naxos.

I was never to find another like me, not through the personal columns. Though the pursuit was not without interest. I took some twisting turns, down some dark, damp passageways in the labyrinth of desire.

Sometimes, sex with a stranger can assuage loneliness. Other times it fuels it.

My plight loans me the chance of solitude or bestiality.

In women I clutch consolation.

To the limits of my vision, I see across to the implacable stare of the Georgian face of Hermit Street, and backwards to my youth. The gauze twitches in the window of Mrs Groggarty's lounge; and a curtain in my mind swishes open to the play of memory.

Two old troupers trudge centre stage. It's been a long run, they act their parts with weary resignation.

Mr Duckworth's heavy hams judder beneath her floral nylon dress as she lifts a steaming dish from the oven. The man circles the oak dining table with a cautious, shuffling step. He is a sceptical man and a scientist. It occurs to him that he must entrust himself to gravity and floorboards; that the former is an abstraction, and that the floor, though apparently solid to human vision, consists of more or less nothing, being a yawning space hewed by the push and shove of electromagnetic forces. Then a trusting smile lights his face. He realises that the ground can support him. For, at the subatomic level, he is insubstantial too. Here's a man who knows more about amphibians than he does about his wife.

This is marriage. Though they stand side by side, they are in different worlds, in separate sealed minds. Alone together.

In her kitchen Mrs Duckworth is working her alchemy. Raw and commonplace staples — egg, flour, haddock, cheese, milk — are transmuted into golden, steaming treasures for the sacrament of supper.

Dr Duckworth sniffs the air. He knows what's been going on. Certain gaseous hydrocarbons have been oxidised in the bunsen burner of the oven to heat the striated musculature of certain marine vertebrates, which his wife will mix higgledy-piggledy as 'fish', to stick in a pie, the mere smell of which makes him wince, courtesy of some involuntary gastric spasms.

He sweeps his right palm over his thinning hair, as if to erase the bald spot. Perching on a single foot, like a crane, he rubs a brogue toe against a tweed trouser leg.

'Where's Charlie?' asks Mother. 'Hiding again?'

It is the drama of their dinner. I'm beneath the sink, in the dark, peeping out through a crack in the cupboard door.

'Fish pie again?' says Father, peering down at his plate, tapping at the crust with his fork, as if divining.

'Marjorie's Malcolm has got impetigo,' says Mother, 'and nobody came to fix the fence.'

'There wasn't a single student at my ten o'clock lecture,' says Dr Duckworth. 'Is it conceivable I'm boring?'

'And André Gide died,' says his wife, 'bless his cotton socks. There's an obituary in the paper.'

Dr and Mrs Duckworth are both kind, short, plump, pink dwarfs with brown eyes and bulbous noses. They smell of cheese and urine, much like other folk.

I, it seemed, was the oddity.

'About Charlie,' says Mother. 'Do you think that child's quite right in the head?'

'Shh!' says Father, 'the little rascal's listening — there in the cupboard.'

Even as a three-year-old, I was more attentive to my parents than they to me; for I had the leisure to watch them, whereas they had work and worries.

I had an advantage over them, by virtue of my acute dark vision. Even through the keyhole of their bedroom, with the light switched off, they were visible to me. Whereas they would enter a gloomy room and be quite unable to spy me, even when I dangled before their very eyes, clinging by my finger tips to the picture rail, or swinging upside down from the lamp-shade.

Having rested much in my first two years of life, I took less sleep thereafter. Four or five hours were sufficient. Now, I make do with less.

It is indiscreet and indelicate to mention it, but I must report that my parents squabbled — about the habits and characters of each other, and certain numbers attaching to money.

Between eleven and twelve at night, I'd hear them bicker in preparation for bed.

'Good God, woman. The milk's boiling over.'

'If you talk to your students like that ...' says Mother, 'it's no wonder they don't come to your lectures.'

'Good God, woman. What do you think I do at college? Teach people how to make cocoa?'

'It's not *my* fault you're going bald,' observes Mother, 'there's no cause to shout at *me*.'

He'd unerringly tread the sly, seventh, creaky step on the stairs. Whereupon Mother would hiss 'shh', and quite as loud. In the bathroom they'd join to pass fluids. I'd hear her soprano gargle, then the splat of spit in the basin. He would urinate copiously and mutter. Then they'd exchange positions and tasks. Father brushing his teeth with a brisk mechanical vigour — 'ch-ch-ch' — while Mother released her tinkling trickle.

Now I have only to hear the opening bars of Schubert's B flat sonata and I am transported back, infantile, my heart throbbing in time and sympathy to her molto moderato widdle.

It was a precise and invariable ritual, as if it had been a marriage vow — to love, honour, and pee in turn. His loping tread would precede her heavy footfall. Then the bedroom door would clunk behind them, rattling a pane in my window.

Father wore a vest for bed, beneath striped flannelette pyjamas — sky blue or candy pink. He'd stand, lost and bemused, groping the inside of his thigh, or scratching between his buttocks, whilst Mother undressed, hoisting her shift over her head, to release shuddering pink blancmange mounds, as if emptying a jelly mould before my apprehensive eye, which was pressed to the chill keyhole.

Sometimes I witnessed Dr Duckworth stranded upon the belly of his wife, eyes closed, his face strained in a grimace of concentration, as his buttocks dipped and rose between her thighs.

It was a wordless ritual, audible only in the rustle of her nightdress — as his urgency rasped her polyester — and his panting as he gained a terminal momentum. Odd, joyless, dutiful calisthenics, as though he'd been obliged to do press-ups.

'Business all done?' asks mother. 'And did you finish your cocoa?'

'Yes, dear,' father sighs. 'Thank you. Even the dregs.'

Then they'd wriggle apart and turn back to back.

And I felt a sad intruder to some sorry private ceremony, as I looked at them in their dim hours, when they tossed, whimpered, snuffled, shuddered, ground their teeth and snored.

So I'd watch over them in the pathos of their sleep. Or slope around in the gloom, feed potato peelings to the mice that lived beneath the vegetable cupboard, feeling the twitch of tiny whiskers tickling my cheek, as I inhaled the musty sweetness of their fur.

Or I'd curl up with Oscar the corgi in his wicker basket by the stove. He'd whine and snarl in his sleep, so I'd stroke his bristling back to soothe him. Then he'd wake, bleary and bemused, panting his gravy breath, and lick my face with his rasping tongue.

Given my irregular start in life I can count myself fortunate to have been taken on by the Duckworths. They provided all my material needs. They never thought to hit me, and were sparing of cross words for fear of having me weep or retch on their carpets, and were kinder to me than to each other.

But they lived in Islington, which was in 1953 and remains to this day a place of gross depravity, by virtue of the wickedness of several residents.

The most conspicuously vicious was a trader in Chapel Market who kept a box of writhing eels. The customer would point and pick. Then the assassin would seize the victims and slice them up; chopping their lithe wriggling lengths into bite-size pieces which continued their slimy squirm and throb. There was no scientific or religious alibi for the slaughter. It was just a trade in flesh. It was a measure of the place that folk took it for granted; that a person might have another being killed to serve as supper.

In certain shops, disembowelled sheep and pigs hung dead in the window, secured to a rail by hooks through their feet, their glazed eyes perplexedly watching the shoppers. There was no pretence of hiding this business nor evidence of shame. 'Butcher' said the brazen signs.

It was nothing to see a mother assault her child in the streets, or find grown men trading punches. I was a frequent witness to discourtesy and drunkenness. Children wept, women screamed, men roared. Cats screeched by night. Dogs wandered the streets in fear, slinking an arc around people. It was a dark place. Worse lay in the shadows.

Strangers would stare at me with naked contempt and pass unkind judgements on my appearance. Children mocked me, likening me to a monkey. When Mother parked me on the steps, kids would sidle past and gob on me, release the brake on my pushchair. They devised a game of throwing pebbles at me from the opposite pavement — scoring five points for a hit on my head, and a single point for a strike on my chest or arms. As I recall, the first to get a total of twenty was judged the winner.

Our small house, with its tight rooms and creaking stairs, was a raft of tenderness, awash in a sea of malice.

I wondered at the wickedness of the place and the wanton unkindness of people. Naturally, I became suspicious. I knew that something was amiss. There was mischief afoot.

I don't want to go to school. On this I am adamant. There'll be new people to watch, yet I worry that some may prove spiteful. I have my suspicions of people.

Yet it means so much to my parents that I learn my lessons. I cannot bring myself to defy them.

'It'll make a little man of you,' Dr Duckworth declares, compounding my foreboding. 'And please climb down from the bookshelf. You're trampling on Graham Greene.'

'We know you're in there, in the sock-drawer,' Mother coaxes, tapping the chest. 'Come on out now, Charlie. It's time for school.'

The air is hot and sour in the nursery school, lifting me from the floor by the two foul fingers of stench in my nostrils. The smell is of fish, simmering in urine. I flinch, clutching Mrs

17

Duckworth's wet palm more firmly as she tugs me down the corridor through the parting pack of children. I run the gauntlet of stares and smirks. Shrieks and squeals echo over the hammer of feet on the stone floor. All my senses are flooded, and my comprehension exceeded as I faint from the inferno.

Miss Frobisher hoists her eyebrows, fingers an ear lobe and smiles grimly down at me as she suffers Mother's muffled explanation.

'...sensitive child, you see,' Mrs Duckworth confides.

'He'll learn to fit in ...' Miss Frobisher bares her yellow teeth '... just like other children.' She lifts her spectacles off the bridge of her nose to peer at me with pitiless eyes, reminding me of the stuffed ferret in my father's study. 'Won't you Charlie?' This sounds like a threat. She pinches my cheek for good measure.

With a desultory pat to my scalp, Mother turns about. I watch her fat rump bounce beneath her skirt, see the uncaring haste of her retreat, hear the cold clip of her step. Gone. Lost. I am abandoned in the lair of strangers.

'Come now Charlie,' says Miss Frobisher. 'We'll meet the nice children.'

'Nice?' I ask. Well, you'll imagine my surprise, for I've never met nice children before. Indeed, I'd doubted their very existence.

'Of course, dear.'

'Don't they spit, then? And punch? Or call people names?'

'Of course not,' she lies. 'My children have to behave themselves. It's my one and only rule.'

'I bet you're fibbing, or joking,' I venture, whereupon she slaps my leg. She calls me a name.

If I think I can watch the dim proceedings of the natives from a cupboard, I'm quickly disabused. No sooner have I fled to a gloomy refuge in the book cupboard than Miss Frobisher drags me out by the ankles, into the glares of daylight and publicity.

I am placed between two gross, pink, snuffling children. The boy on the left pinches my thigh.

'Turd,' he whispers confidentially.

'Pardon?'

'My brother,' he promises, teasing my ear with hot bursts of breath, 'will smash your face ... if I ask him ... or make you eat a dog turd.'

Promptly, but without malice, I vomit on his jigsaw — releasing my breakfast egg to lie as glistening mucus mosaic over the farmyard scene — earning me more unwelcome attention.

As the day passes — with plasticine, threats, singing, abuse, milk-break, chinese burns and books, interspersed with vigorous bouts of retching — I begin to win the space I desire. Other children give me elbow room. They are wary of my volcanic effusions. Miss Frobisher learns her lesson too — that I will stay continent and quiet if left to loiter alone beneath the table.

My timidity can be forceful, my weakness is stern. My whims won the day.

In time, I made my concessions. I rapidly mastered the work, which was repetitious and undemanding. We assembled some facile jigsaws (there were only seven, and none of them posed a puzzle), recited numbers, listened to improbable stories (in which bears or rabbits imitated human foibles), mouthed a small repertoire of songs, filled and emptied buckets of sand, chased balls, arranged bricks in stacks. We were given coarse brushes and paper with which to paint rudimentary pictures of stick people in lurid colours. Sometimes we were required to dance to scratchy records, imitating animals, plants, seasons or elements, in time to the music. Or were invited to fall over, which my colleagues much enjoyed. Or were given tambourines to shake, drums to beat, triangles to strike till the tumult was quite overwhelming and I was compelled to plug my ears with my fingers. It was like first hearing Stravinsky's *Rite of Spring*.

We were led to understand that these various labours, though not in themselves productive, were preparation for some future work we could commence when we were wiser. We were also coaxed to like each other, which was the hardest task of all. For I was a taste the others were reluctant to swallow.

No human child, I believe, has the will or concentration to stay constantly vicious. They lack the stamina for sustained malice. But each does his best, goaded by a personal demon. No sooner had I established a tentative trust than my companion would push or tug, kick or punch, quite erasing my trust in their kindness. So, I'd be forced to gulp in the exaggerated manner of a tropical fish — to pretend I felt sick — to clear a space around me and become an island unto myself again.

Many companions made unkind observations about my physique or colour, implying some uncleanliness, or suggesting I belonged to another species. There were failures of sympathy or logic here, as if they believed I'd fashioned my own appearance, choosing to look different.

But I learned to please by accepting their assertion, making animal faces, rolling my eyes or imitating some explosive bodily noises. Farts and burps found favour, as did pig grunts and monkey squeals. Even then, I had a flair for mimicry.

And there were ties and tugs of friendship too. If another child fell and hurt himself, or cried after a fight, I was always moved to help him. So he might feel kind to me in return, and share a game or square of tacky chocolate, until prompted again to repay my smile with an epithet about my appearance.

'Custard eyes,' says one. 'Yellow bastard,' he explains.

'Shit face,' says another. 'You don't half look like a chimp.'

School would have been more unpleasant, if I'd believed myself a child and felt full sympathy for my companions. But I noticed their sorrows did not move me as much as the sufferings of a parent, dog or cat. Somehow, I felt different, and separate from them. We sense our fate early.

'Do I look funny, Dad?' I ask Dr Duckworth.

He hesitates and appraises me carefully, sucking pensively on his pipe, before exhaling an acrid smoke screen between us.

'Not terribly,' he consoles me, 'Why do you ask, you little monkey?'

I was the abiding irony of my father's life. All he had to do was recognise me for what I was. The discovery should have made him ecstatic. But he never guessed. It was left to me to discover my self for myself.

He first took me to the Natural History Museum at South Kensington when I was five years old. We must have loitered for a full hour in the Amphibian corridor. Father wanted to acquaint me personally with every last wart on the Bradcock Tree Toad. For though he had not discovered the species, he sighed, he had supplied this very specimen which now sat stuffed on its haunches, its forelimbs outstretched, its pocked yellow underbelly brazenly exposed, eyeing us indignantly through a plate of smeared glass.

'There!' said Father. 'Read the label.'

'. . . collected by Robert Duckworth, B.Sc., Ph.D., Brazil, 1949' the legend said. The same could have been said of me, I was later to discover.

'That's me,' said Dr Duckworth. I'd never seen him smirk so wide or long. It was grotesque and deeply moving. His eyes were wet and glassy. His mouth twitched in spasm. He blew bubbles of spittle as he spoke, and looked not unlike his toad.

I felt it somehow shameful that a father should need to brag to his five-year-old son.

'I'm glad, Dad,' I piped up to console him, 'that you're bald and boring. It makes you special and different. I'll always remember to love you . . . Even when mother forgets.'

For I'd heard them bicker the night before. I wanted him to know my affection was not conditional on him being companionable, or proportional to his hair.

This reassurance rendered him mute, and moist about his eyes. Silently we wandered the maze of the cemetery, inspecting the glass-eyed relics, admiring the balding pelts, broken bones and pickled fishes.

It all totted up to a single perplexity. 'Why, Dad,' I asked him, 'do people like killing animals?'

He said there was a lot to learn from dead animals. He confessed that, in a way, that was his profession — studying dead beasts.

Again, I felt sad and shamed for him. In the cafeteria I wept with desperate, quiet restraint as he ate a sausage roll. A flake of pastry kept the company of a knobble of gristle, bouncing on his upper lip.

In the Primate Section we circled, at a polite distance, the plaster models of Cro-Magnon man, Homo habilis, and Ramapithecus — which muscular, hairy, heavy-jawed fellows,

Father explained, were far distant, long dead, relatives of our very selves.

I stopped transfixed, delivered to joy, seized by the most ignoble feeling, giggling at the spectacle of these ape-like freaks who had the presumption to walk upright, who regarded us with such self-satisfied stares, as if they were off to some social engagement from which we were excluded.

I saw the likeness of these proud, furry hulks to Dr and Mrs Duckworth. There was no gainsaying the family face — heavy brow, bulging jaw, smug fat-lipped smile.

'What are you laughing at, Charlie?' Dr Duckworth tugged my arm. He looked agitatedly around him, fearful lest some curator might recognise him — the collector of several significant toads — in the company of a facetious child, an atheist in the temple of Science.

'Silly peoples,' I gurgled. In my mind's eye, I had dressed Australopithecus in father's herringbone sports jacket, corduroy trousers and brogues. I pictured him pecking my Homo habilis mother on her bloated cheek, clutching up his briefcase, spluttering that he must hurry to be on time for his lecture on the metabolism of Axolotls, which the students would all forgo.

I was moved by malice, I concede.

'It's not funny,' Duckworth scolded.

And suddenly I fell silent and solemn. I'd realised why people laughed at me — for I must look as funny to them, as they to me. And so I'd learned to forgive.

Three

I haven't forgotten you.

Can I be frank? May I be personal? I know a little about you, as it happens.

You are too dark, dense, torn and tangled. Your life is beyond your competence.

We are all our own mysteries; enigmas to ourselves. It is a wise person, indeed, who knows his own mind, respects his pancreas, or has a single encouraging word for his sphincters.

I am not disposed to optimism. Human life is comic to observe and tragic to experience. Skin enwraps much misery.

I follow a terrible trade. I'm a voyeur, an observer of life. I spy on people. I keep alert.

Once, I lived alone with Emilie. Now I live alone with my self. We have come to an understanding, my self and I.

My plight and education have led me to dismal conclusions. There are botches in the design of human life, clots to its custard flow, lumps to its texture, which cannot be smoothed away.

You are dropped into this world without your consent; fluff on the carpet of culture, awaiting the vacuum of death.

The pleasures you grasp and guzzle as children are soon soured by shame and guilt.

You are weaned from sensual delights onto the dry rusks of words. No child, I believe, has ever preferred a noun to a nipple. But each is coerced to accept the exchange. Our desires are soon bound by the tangle of talk.

Our lives are interminably brief; anxious and boring by turns.

Existence is far too short and tedious: our experience is too precious and painful.

We are told we are free to fashion our lives. But freedom is a terrible thing. Free, we have only ourselves to blame.

Birth, suffering, death. Suffering is the main part, the stuffing of the sandwich. The knack is to enjoy it.

We play an enigmatic game of ineffable complexity. None of us understands the rules. Yet to utter or move we must pretend to. Each step, each syllable, tugs us beyond our competence. For, in truth, we are all quite lost, peering out through the opaque, misted window of confusion.

I believe it would be foolhardy and heroic to be a human being — if there was the choice of an attractive alternative.

Perhaps you find me morbid? We could re-examine the evidence — just to confirm your humanity.

Imagine! You are waiting for the one you love most. No. Not yourself. Another body entirely — lover, spouse, friend, parent, child. I do not discount a pet. You might be one of those characters who marry a dog or cat, or shack up with a pair of hamsters.

Your loved one is many hours missing. So? What do you suppose?

That they have been unfortunately delayed? That they have abandoned you — because you are worthless and selfish?

No. A voice in mind whispers that the loved one has met with an accident. Your imagination, quite nonchalantly, nudges them under a bus, perhaps, or swerves their car into a lamp-post. And why? Because they have kept you waiting. Your mind is a vicious organ. It will punish them for that. Besides, it is better to kill your lover, or maim them, than allow them to abandon you for another. Then you can be a tragic bereaved figure, recipient of sympathy, cosseted by friends and family. Rather than a rejected shit.

You would — I submit for the prosecution — rather kill your lover in your imagination than believe yourself discarded. For the loss of the loved one is less threatening than the loss of love. And less damaging to your esteem.

Greater love hath few men.

Consider the probabilities, too. More folk, I submit, are unfaithful and unreliable than are killed in accidents. I know many who've followed prolifically successful careers of adultery without even being grazed by a bus.

And consider a variant of the scene. Suppose you're waiting for an electrician or a plumber. They are several hours late. Do you imagine *them* damaged or dead? I think not. You suppose they have better things to do than keep an appointment with you. You probably don't love your plumber, you see. And you reserve the vindictive violence of your mind for those you care for most. You keep your lover in mind; to kill him there.

It's a familiar complaint, a mortal condition, a human foible.

Now, if you're at the airport or train station, to meet your loved one. You keep seeing his face emerge from the crowd. But no. It's someone else entirely.

Your faculties are faulty. You see and think what you wish. For you're a glib bigot with half the scruple of a tabloid journalist, and a fraction of his wit.

But now the loved one has really come. You clutch him in your arms and smother him in your chest. Darling! Delirium.

No. Not quite. There's also a nagging awareness that something is amiss. Somehow it should be better.

And why? Because you desire an ideal. And not a person. You want them as you want them, and not quite as they are. A sorrow, that. A double tragedy — for your partner feels the same.

Take a good look at your lover. Think carefully. Is that really what you need? If so, do you want it?

Desire is a dismal enigma. Truly, you don't know what you want. And where's the bung to plug the gap?

Do you sense the void? Do you, and ache at the lack? Listen to the hollow rattle. That's the pulse of your life.

I knew an ingeniously stupid librarian in Epping who insulted the problem by collecting stamps. He was voracious, having no specialism. He merely wanted a clean specimen of each and every stamp in the world. Needless to say, he never married. He was too busy mounting stamps.

All day he stamped and issued books. Every evening and weekend he ordered his stamps. Naturally, he was a man of fierce desires and remorseless action. For there was always an infinity of books to be stamped and stamps to be collected.

He always had passion and purpose for he'd taken care to devise for himself an insatiable ambition. So desire could never call his bluff. He paid in endless instalments, as if for a mortgage he'd never redeem. He never discovered that stamps don't satisfy because he never managed to collect them all.

Whereas, the person who wants a lover often gets one: then finds himself still wanting.

But I forgot to finish the sorry story. Desire has a way of striking back, and refuses to be jilted. The librarian had a fire in his flat, consequent on his habit of grilling his socks on the cooker to dry them.

Hell hath no fury like desire scorned.

His collection of stamps was cremated. It is a tribute to his heroism that within six months, after a pious period of chaste mourning, he'd taken to consorting with antique coins — furtively at first, then flagrantly. I think he chose to love them because they too are infinite, but not inflammable or flimsy like stamps. I believe he'd learned by his loss. Tragedy had tutored him. There's a lesson wrapped in every disaster.

When I feel depressed I reach first for hope. If there isn't any left in the flat, I knock myself out with pethidine. The next day I feel better. It's my recipe for keeping content.

I digress. My early years —

Dr and Mrs Duckworth had hatched certain plans for me and loaned me unlikely ambitions.

Their confidence was alarming. Without the least consultation, they declared the facts of my life. There was no limit to their intrusions. They knew my bedtime, tastes, desires, moods and interests — and pretended amazement at my refutations and denials. They meant well, I know. But as the sole tenant of my skin, I knew my insides better.

'You must be very happy and clever yourself, Dad, to know what's best for me.'

'That's right, Charlie.' He beamed his condescension as he patted my scalp.

I heard them talk of me and plot my future, behind my back. For they did not sense me there – prostrate on the paperback fiction section of the bookcase, or hunched on the second shelf of the living room cupboard, or sprawled flat beneath the sagging sofa, tickled by the sprouting horse-hair, the strands of which reminded me of those tufts erupting from Dr Duckworth's ears and nostrils.

'A delicate child . . .' says Mother.

'Odd boy,' says Dr Duckworth, 'but clever as a lorry load of monkeys.'

'Yesterday afternoon, I found him curled up in the oven . . . stroking a mouse,' says Mother. 'No one can tell me that's hygienic.'

'I've been asking around,' says Dr Duckworth, 'nobody else's children hide in cupboards . . . or vomit if you shout.'

'He has got a delicate stomach.'

'I asked Professor Schell in the Psychology Department . . .' says Father, 'they know all about children in the Kelmsley Annexe. He said Charlie sounded like a Timid Character Type – of the Top Percentile. He says we should do something before it develops into a Sociophobic Syndrome.'

But it strikes me as perverse for my father to trust the diagnosis of a man who's never met me.

'What does the Professor suggest?' asks Mother. She mouths the title with reverence.

'Behaviour therapy.'

'What's that?'

'Sweets and chocolate,' father explains, 'when Charlie does what we tell him.'

'Not good,' Mother frowns, 'for his little teeth.'

'Or boarding school, so he'd have to learn to cope with children.'

No. I doubted I would learn that trick.

'But he's so . . . delicate,' says Mother. 'It'd kill the poor child.' Her forehead is crinkled as corrugated cardboard.

'There's Lovesgrave College. My old school. It'd make a little chap of him. There'd be so many decent young fellows to play with.' There was a treacly tackiness to Dr Duckworth's voice that made me shudder. For it spoke finality — a decision made.

So I was despatched at the age of eight — with a trunk, tuck-box, and two sets of thirty items of clothing — to my father's old preparatory school, Lovesgrave College.

Dr Duckworth had explained it to me. It was for the best. Naturally, my stomach spoke its usual revolt. He was regretful but firm.

'Will there be carrots at school?' I asked, 'Apples, turnips and parsnips?' For I needed reassurance that there would be pleasures there.

He said there'd be a range of vegetables, and opportunities too. A little chap who learned his lessons at Lovesgrave could then proceed to Stoneham. And after only six years there, was well placed for a Scholarship or Exhibition to Oxford or Cambridge. And after only three years at university, a fellow was well prepared for a profession.

This seemed a long wait, and a deal of work, to bear a burden I didn't seek.

'Then life would be your oyster,' Dr Duckworth declares.

'Oyster?' I ask. 'What's that?'

An oyster, he tells me, at lecture length, pleased to revert to some business biological, is a spineless bivalve mollusc. It lurks in its shell. It opens and closes to a daily rhythm, sifting tiny speckles of nutrient from the sea that engulfs it. If a grain of sand lodges within its soft tissues, it can ease the nagging pain, converting the grit to a pearl of beauty.

Well, I thought, I could learn to be an oyster. At least a fellow would get some privacy and shade, and make a quiet contribution.

My first seventeen years were not happy times, bar brief interludes and time asleep.

On my first night at Lovesgrave College, Arthur Reeves, who

had the next bed in the dormitory, took me in hand and briskly taught me to masturbate. It was to be the only kindness I was shown that week.

On the afternoon of the second day I sniff the cruelties that will follow. We don boots and kit to play rugby. It's all a matter of throwing, kicking, running, grappling and being trodden on. It's too popular to rank as a proper perversion. But it's a sado-masochists' charter, designed for boys of all ages to be physically intimate whilst inflicting pain. Fellows fight for the possession of balls.

I prove a virtuoso of evasion. I've a ferocious turn of speed, and when another fellow tries to tackle me, I swerve around him like a scalded cat, or bound over his head — in the manner of a kangaroo. I never seek the ball, but if it lands in my hands I flee for the try line in sheer fear. For I certainly don't wish to be laid on the ground and booted by a scrum of boys.

I also won a reputation for my cross-country running, which allowed me briefly to shed the company of other boys. Each evening in the winter term, after prep, we'd be sent on a three-mile run across ploughed fields. I'd show a clean pair of heels, to arrive back first by at least ten minutes, so I'd have hot water and first dunk in the bath, which was a privilege worth winning. For if thirty-seven boys share one bathtub of water, it gets tepid and scummy after a while. Those who got back last kept themselves cleaner by staying unwashed.

The vegetables were invariably boiled to mush. There were no bananas to be had. Courgettes were never served. I'm loath to malign a tomato, but those at school were tinned. I went two months without the sniff of a peach.

I was forced to find ingenious modes of survival. I took to sleep. The night became my day. Dreams were my wakefulness; my conscious hours were torpor or nightmare, till I could wake again to sleep. I dreamed that I was dreaming daytime and could make it go away. Oscar, my corgi, romped panting at my side down dark woodland paths. We were bathed by the glow of a purple moon.

In the doze of daylight, the other little fellows coined special terms for me — such as Fuckworth and Duckshit — celebrating my surname. But I was best known as 'Whippet', which was a pun of sorts. I was small, fast and thin; also some of them liked to whip me.

'Whippet?' says Roger Purves.

'Yes,' I concede, incautiously acknowledging the nickname, and for the very last time. Whereupon several lads shriek with laughter and flail me with their ties, taking special aim to flick me on the ears and behind my knees.

'If you're not careful,' I warn them, 'you'll hurt me.'

'Oh dear,' they say, but with scant sincerity.

Left to their own devices, as they often were, the boys would invent new games — tying a chap to an iron bedstead, and taking turns to pee on him, or tossing him in a blanket, or taking his clothes off and smearing him with boot polish (for there were no private parts at Lovesgrave), flushing his homework down the lavatory, twisting his ears, or pushing him downstairs in the laundry trolley — so shaping each other's characters. I suppose they were bored.

Naturally, a young fellow preferred not to be the subject of these attentions. And would rather not inflict them on another.

I'd become an unwilling conversation piece amongst the other boys. They lashed me by my wrists to the cross-beam in the dormitory: leaving me to dangle for some hours. It was a popular pastime called Crucifixion, which the lads had learned from the Gospels in Divinity lessons, but (for the want of nails) had adapted for themselves. I wondered why they did this. Even a fool could see it made me unhappy.

'Let me down,' I howl, 'it isn't pleasant.' But they just chuckle.

Roger Purves and Malcolm Maddox — though usually indifferent to my feelings, and hostile to each other — formed a brief coalition to lower me by my ankles from the common-room window. The height didn't alarm me, but I worried about the security of their hold on me, and their grasp of kindness.

I wept. I was fragile. My lip bled where Snodgrass kicked it. Tears only provoked more torture. Maddox trod on my testicles; on purpose, I believe. Retching only won me fresh torments.

For the fellows — turned suddenly and strangely house-proud — made me lick it up.

The evidence accumulated. I was forced to the conclusion that the boys — through some fault in their design, and deficit of sympathy — enjoyed inflicting pain.

The Red Cross knew nothing of this. The masters were curiously incurious.

'What's happened to your mouth, Duckworth? You little bleeder.'

'Purves hit me, sir, with his hockey stick.'

'It doesn't do to sneak on other boys, Duckworth.' My house-master scowls, sucking with loud distaste. 'Now tell me again. What happened to your mouth?'

'Fell, sir. Hit my head on a door.'

'See matron,' says the warder. 'And be more careful, stupid boy.'

'Thank you, sir.'

I knew I must learn some new, evasive gestures. It helped, I found, to be vigilant, absent or quiet. But in the final resort I had to pretend cruelty.

I knew what had to be done. I had observed the technique. I braced myself. I'd prepared and practised in solitude. But I wasn't sure I could act the part with conviction.

'Here's that tit Duckworth,' shrieks Roger Purves, 'Let's . . .'

'What?' say I, tugging his tie tight on his neck whilst twisting the lobe of his ear.

'Pick on Muldoon,' he gulps, his startled eyes swivelling.

Of course, I'm ashamed. I was a coward. I didn't want the sharks to eat me. I clawed my way onto the life-raft, pushing another beneath the waves. I was desperate to secure my own safety. I pretended not to see him: his arms threshing, his face in frozen scream, before he sunk.

I still feel guilty about Muldoon. He was a professional victim already, before he was called upon to work over-time, taking my turns on the rota.

He retired early and broken from Lovesgrave College. Having been tossed three times in a blanket, he could land in it only twice. We were all made to pay for his fractured skull and pelvis, from which he recovered with the souvenirs of a limp and epilepsy. The headmaster kept his promise to make us all suffer.

'Do you like hurting boys?' I asked him. For all the evidence suggested so.

He must have mistaken my appalled curiosity for youthful wit: and he promptly confirmed my supposition, engraving his taste in welts upon me.

Our letters home, written on Sunday mornings on order after chapel, were read by our house-master on the pretext of correcting our spelling.

He proved a stern editor — blue-pencilling any candid commentary upon the food and conditions, erasing any character sketches of the masters.

So. It was not until half-term that I could acquaint my father with the state of the asylum.

Alone in the shuddering compartment of the rattling train, on the journey back to London, Father asked me about school.

'Do you find it jolly?' he asks.

So I tell him. I speak frankly of the porridge, beatings, the unkind temperaments of certain boys, bartering, baths, matron's patent water-cures, rancid margarine, draughty corridors, torn sheets, dirty lavatories, censored letters.

I stay silent only about our erotic lives and the Chaplain's gentle, furtive petting. Alone amongst the masters, he loves the boys, having a fond, absent-minded way of stroking our buttocks, with a far-away look to his moon face as he ponders other things.

I knew it had cost Dr Duckworth dear to have me committed to Lovesgrave. I felt he should know quite how his money was spent, and learn of my costs too.

'Well, Charlie, I can see it's done you good.'

'It has?' I hadn't reckoned on his approval.

'Brought you out of yourself.' He beams, slapping my thigh with a heavy, humid hand. 'But what have you done to your eye?'

'Fell over,' I say.

'Of course.' Dr Duckworth is disconcerted by some wetness about his eyes. Perhaps he's recalling his own time at school. 'It's a long time ago, but when I was there we used to have midnight feasts in dorm. Do the fellows still do that? And do you chaps have pillow fights after lights-out?'

'Not that I've noticed,' I tell him.

I realise he means me to serve my full sentence. There's to be no release or reprieve — only parole of holidays.

He seems a stranger now; this balding, awkward, pig-pink, wrinkle-faced, heavy-jowled, decaying man who cannot bring himself to hug or hold me.

I squirm closer on the seat, pressing my arm into him. I lay my cheek on his prickly tweed shoulder, and sniff his sundry vapours — cheddar, perspiration, stale tobacco, must and pee.

'If I stay at Lovesgrave,' I say, evenly and slowly, 'shall I grow up to be a man like you?'

He does not reply immediately, or look at me, but with studious care he draws a large handkerchief from the breast pocket of his tweed jacket. He scrumples the linen into a ball, dabs his nose, sniffs twice then blows like a porpoise.

'That's the idea, Charlie,' he announces at last.

We sat in silence, all the way to Euston.

Four

People can be unbearably kind. Complete strangers have smiled my way as they've passed me by on the pavement; making me wince and shiver. For I felt so undeserving.

When I was nine a man I'd never seen before blocked my way down Upper Street. He held me by the lapel, imprisoning me in shadow. Then laid a half-crown in my palm.

'Buy some ice-cream,' he growled, glowering down, his face the colour of bacon.

It was an order not an invitation. 'I can't eat ice-cream no more . . .' his bloodshot eyes rolled starboard on the turbulence of desire, 'on account of my ulcer,' he explained.

He wanted no more than to eat by proxy.

He watched unblinking as I lapped away.

'Suck the last bit,' he demanded, 'through the bottom of the cone.' When I'd finished, he made me eat another. And then a tub of lemon ice. I'd begun to feel sick; but I persevered for him. When I'd licked the last smear from my lips, he patted me gently on my scalp, then melted into the crowd, bearing a beatific smile on his face.

And I can cite numerous other occasions when people have been gentle, giving and kind, without any disreputable motive.

There was a Catholic priest who once strode up to me at Euston Station. 'Be brave,' he advised, 'remember that Jesus Christ himself was despised. And never forget that Our Lady loves you.' I wasn't certain what he meant, but there was no mistaking his gentle gist.

Or there was the greengrocer who caught me stealing his

parsnips. 'Keep them, laddie,' he said, tucking two bananas into my jacket pocket, 'I can see your life ain't easy. Would you like an apple, too?'

The Duckworths fed and watered me, provided my stable and flung the fusty musty wrap of their love around me. Nobody ever paid them to do this. It was a matter of unstinting compassion. Whenever I despair of people, the thought of the Duckworths dispels the despond.

Many women have lain their sleeping heads on my pillow and trusted me with their naked treasures. One stayed to have me as her companion-lover for the best part of a year.

Emilie knew many of my eccentricities before she took me on, for better or worse. But she was a strong-willed woman. I believe she thought she could change me.

We were different sorts — miscible as oil and water. We shook ourselves to a vinaigrette. When we grew tired of the agitation, we separated out. It came to a head over Ludwig, who acted our third party.

When I was eleven I passed from Lovesgrave to Stoneham, winning the Gibbon Scholarship — open to the sons of clergymen and scholars. In the examination, I scored ninety-eight per cent in Mathematics, ninety-six per cent in English and a perfect mark in Latin. My Divinity was sketchy though. I could not recall much about the Son of God. Still, I wrote him a good reference, praising his skill as a carpenter.

I'd done enough to gain free admittance to Stoneham, where the blazers were blue not red, and the young thugs bigger and bestial. But I too was larger, properly calloused by preparatory school, cautioned and wiser.

Certain boys who lacked my capacity for abstruse learning bribed me with money, cakes or protection to do their preparation. And I won some status and immunity through my flair at rugby — once scoring seven tries for the Junior XV in a grudge match against St Aloysius.

Though not known for racial fairness — or any tolerances — the school already held captive seven black boys, two yellow chaps, and several off-pink fellows. So my coppery colour, though uniquely distinctive, shone out from a broader spectrum, and must have seemed less worthy of mention. When questioned on my pedigree, I made the hostile claim to be an Apache. Some amiable fellows spread the fiction that I was excessively dirty, but otherwise much the same as them. I was known as Ginger or Corkscrew which, whilst still hurtful, sounded sweeter to my ear than Fuckwit.

When I returned home at Christmas, largely unbruised, on the completion of my first term at Stoneham, I was able to report with candid satisfaction that I was happier than I'd been at Lovesgrave. Perhaps my acclimatisation was too thorough, for at breakfast on the first morning, forgetful of domestic idiom, I caused my father to shudder, by asking him, genially enough, to 'pass the fucking jam'.

Oscar the corgi had aged in my absence, his muzzle bleached a peppery white. His back had spread and flattened, and he'd submit for me to use it as a table. Though dogs, in their exuberance, spend their vital energy at seven times the speed of man, it was my parents who showed the worse decline. They were redder, rounder and slower than before, as if transmuting inexorably into gravid, scarlet spheres, like snooker balls, I thought.

Their minds were just as I'd left them. But they'd grown more ponderous of speech. In my absence it had been doubly declared a rule of the household that anything worth saying should be spoken at least twice.

'Exactly,' said Father. 'Precisely.'

'Too true,' said Mother, 'Just so.'

On Christmas day, we strained together to make a celebration. Father offered to play football in the garden. To repay him, I asked him about fossil amphibians and suffered a thorough account. Then we helped Mother lay the festive table.

For lunch they ate some portions of rotten pheasant, spitting grits of lead to the side of their plate. I couldn't stomach it, though its odours of putrefaction drove Oscar to a snuffling frenzy. The vegetables were fresh and fragrant, but my parents' slurps and mastications quite drained my appetite. For the first time I missed the sharp, clean company of boys.

After lunch, we exchanged presents. I gave my parents a pregnant house-mouse – whom I'd christened 'Molly'. To accompany and explain her, I'd written a lengthy treatise in a Woolworths exercise book, entitled 'Caring for your mouse: a layman's guide in easy lessons', outlining the rudiments of mouse husbandry for the novice.

'Ah,' said Father, 'Glis glis.' For he had a Latin name for every species bar one.

'She's very friendly,' I said, 'and she's going to have a family.'

Looking back, it does seem an odd choice of gift, even to me. But I was an odd child. I suppose I'd wanted them to gain a new friend, and learn the gentle, subtle consolation a mouse will award anyone who'll take the pains to court its affection.

Even Mother – though never before partial to rodents – pretended some enthusiastic surprise.

But on Boxing Day, when he thought I wasn't about, Father released Molly on the back steps. He told me over dinner that she'd escaped from her box. I didn't challenge this deceit. And there was no harm done for, within four hours, Molly had found her way back to her usual place in the larder. She seemed quite unperturbed.

For their part, my parents had presented me with a stocking full of tangerines, sundry sweets and nuts; a new pair of rugby boots; a red plastic transistor radio; and a violently disturbing book, that shook my life's foundations.

It was called *The Bumper Fun Book of Evolution*, and boasted 365 colour illustrations ('one for each day of the year'). The title was mischievously ironical. For, as the text declared, evolution was no fun: at least not for those living beings flicked by its fickle fingers, or crushed in its brutal calloused hands.

No, indeed, life is a bestial fight. The reader was warned, as early as page 5, that each of us – species or individual – stood in daily danger of being gobbled, or evicted from our environment, by a meaner, fitter type.

I knew this already from Stoneham. For each biological example in the book, there was a perfect parallel at school.

Muldoon was a dodo, now extinct. Harris and Bevins were large marauding predators. Most of the boys were amphibious, slithering to and fro between dry land and slime. Toby Jollyon, Latin master, was a coelacanth; plucky, unlikely survivor of a type long supposed gone, a desiccated titbit abandoned by fate.

Home – 23 Cloudesley Street – was a Galapagos; an island of isolation, where these two laborious old lizards could shuffle on, slow and unmolested.

Weak and small beings were cautioned to camouflage themselves. To survive and reproduce, I learned, I should have to change my coloration with the seasons, like a snowshoe hare avoiding the predacious lynx. Or else mimic something dangerous like a certain moth which displays a large unblinking eye on each wing. So a swift that swoops to gobble it finds itself eyeball to eyeball with the satanic scowl of an owl.

I found all this disturbing enough. But worse was to lie ahead for me, because pages 147-153 of *The Bumper Fun Book of Evolution* outlined the principles of heredity, illustrated by the family resemblances pertaining amongst mice and peas. This did not fool or throw me. I'd seen the act of generation – as the text euphemised it – performed both by my parents and our domestic mice. I knew that, mutatis mutandis, the principles were the same. For explanatory purposes, I could consider my parents as under-sexed mice of low fertility. Like certain peas, they were wrinkled whilst I was smooth. Nor was that the only anomaly. They were ruddy pink; I was orange-brown. They had brown eyes; mine were yellow. They were plump; I was thin. Their copious brown hair sprouted disconcertingly all over the fleshy folds; my hair was black, and tidily restricted to my crown. I was lithe in mind and body; they were ponderous and slow. They grunted and dribbled; I did not. They had broad, coarse-boned, fat-lipped Neanderthal faces. I have a high brow. My features are etched with delicacy. They reeked of their excretions. I had a mild aroma of spinach and crushed coriander.

You probably know those visual illusions. You gaze at a picture and suddenly it transforms. The supercilious duck turns into a startled rabbit. A cube twists inside out. An amiable, haggard crone becomes a disdainful coquette. Then — though you strain at the effort — you cannot reverse the picture, to see it as it was before.

So it was for me, as I gazed upon the picture of smooth and wrinkled pods. This Duckworth changed into a alien. My parents were gone in a twinkling; barged out of the picture by two grunting portly gnomes.

My skin prickled and went icy. My head throbbed as the bolt was hammered through it. It was a chill world in which I slouched alone.

I was not one of those wise children who knew their own father. As for Mother, I was uncertain. In nature, I knew, pollen gets sprinkled with wasteful abandon. The pea flower is not by temperament monogamous. Molly the mouse entertained several suitors. She wasn't disconcerted to be mounted by Izzy or Ivor, when Freddy wasn't about, and would continue gnawing on a potato. But my mother was less gregarious. Certainly, I'd seen no man upon her but Father: and he but rarely.

I could not confide this to the two pygmies who snuffled and snorted on the sofa, nonchalantly munching mince-pies. I needed to bide my time and explore my plight.

Crumbs cascade from Dr Duckworth's pulsing blubbery lips, through his plump fingers into the folds of his capacious sterile lap.

'Oooh,' sighs the goblin. 'Aah.'

'Mmm... urp,' said his consort troll. Then their dim eyes swivel towards me.

'You like that book. Don't you Charles?' says the man who called himself Father.

'He does. He really likes it,' simpers the woman I'd thought was my mother. 'He's been taking notes on it. Like Father, like son.'

'Mm.' I turn a page, my face aflame.

'If there's anything you don't understand ...' says her husband, spitting a glob of mincemeat towards me, 'don't forget to ask.'

I said nothing, feigning distraction, pressing my snub nose

deeper into the fold of the book, sniffing the acidic scent of knowledge.

I wondered if they were finally telling me something intolerably painful to speak. For, clearly, there were some facts of my life they hadn't disclosed.

We all make disconcerting discoveries about ourselves. I was much discomfited.

Some invisible curtain had descended to divide us, myself from my mother and father. I was choked. My tongue was leaden. It is difficult to confide in your parents, once you discover they are members both of some other family.

I was not their child. We were not kin. My blood was not their blood. We were not each other's.

So I thought, as Mother and Father smiled on me, stifling me with their fevered kindness.

Self-pity is seldom productive. I fight against it. But when I see another raw, suffering being, abraded skinless by the sand-paper of life, I turn molten and moist with sympathy.

There was a drunk tramp I saw, in solitary abandon with a bottle of Cyprus sherry, swaying about the vertical, on a bench in Euston Station, suffusing the already fuggy air with the sweet stench of his putrefaction. He scowled, defiant as a skunk, at the mute, sniffy passengers as they skirted his dominion.

'Gay piss yarsen,' he advised us. 'Arms good as year.'

Then he reached down below the bench, to lift a paperback between the disdainful pinch of thumb and fore-finger.

'Arf raid boox on yore sot,' he howled. 'Arno wart yar doon.' And to show so, he began furiously flicking the pages.

I walked close by him so I could see the cover. The author was Dale Carnegie: the title was *How to Win Friends and Influence People*.

'Books can be hurtful,' I wanted to say. 'I know. They've bitten me too. We have that plight in common.' But instead I stooped down to smile, and asked 'Are you lonely? Can I help?'

'Fark awf Kant,' he slurred, his face concertinaed by loathing. 'Yah broon bustard. Fark awf weir yah kimfram.'

I laid a ten pound note on the seat beside him. Then I slunk away down the platform.

'Farkan koon,' he wailed. 'Whore yeast ah gimmy manny?'

I knew just how he felt. A fellow can't help feeling peevish and truculent when he peers down to find a chasm of isolation quite surrounds him.

You know a being's really needy, when they fling your help back in your face.

As with strays like Ludwig, whom I found slinking by my dustbin, shivering as he crunched some rancid chicken bones that Emilie had already gnawed clean. The splinters of bone must have pierced his palate, for he was dribbling froths of blood as he gobbed.

His hollowed ribs heaved. He had less belly than a whippet. His black eyes glinted his hatred. He raised a jowl to me in warning, even as he chewed.

I bounded back into the flat, returning with Emilie's bacon. He wolfed the rashers in one convulsive gulp. Then he bit my outstretched hand.

But the next night he returned. And whined at the sight of me.

'Hi, Ludwig, boy,' I said. For now I knew his name. I'd call him after Beethoven and Wittgenstein, whose cheeriness and gratitude he shared.

I'd believed myself Duckworth. Now that tether was torn.

Words failed me. How does a person address himself when he discovers he's a quirk of nature? How does that beast talk to his parents who are not his parents, but only his kindly keepers?

By what means, and with what rights, does an exhibit cross-examine its curator? And why has he been so wilfully mislabelled?

I didn't mount a frontal attack. I preferred to try the sly.

'About mice, Dad?' I ask. 'If both parents are white, what colour will their babies be?'

We are sprawled on the hearth rug, before the spluttering gas fire, playing Happy Families, holding our cards close to our chests.

41

'White,' he declares decisively. 'And do you have Master Bun the Baker's Son?'

'No,' I say. 'So they can't be brown, then?'

'You must have him,' he stares at his cards, and waggles a finger in his ear to excavate for wax. 'Because you must have one Baker to ask for another. And you asked for Miss Bun. And I've got Mr and Mrs.'

He was often slow on the uptake like that. I've tricked him by asking for a card I already have – to make him disclose his hand.

'Why will the baby mice be white?'

'Genes,' he says vaguely. He still hadn't worked it out. 'The children will look like the parents.'

'Can I have Mr and Mrs Bun?' I ask him. 'So . . . if you and Mother are pink, why am I orange?'

'Ah! . . . Yes!' he hands me the two cards, his cheeks and neck shot scarlet, 'People aren't quite the same as mice. They arrange their family matters differently.'

'And I've got yellow eyes,' I say. But still he will not meet them with his own. 'And I'm only eleven, but already my metacarpals are longer than yours.'

He lays his cards face up on the floor. 'Aren't you tired of this game, Charlie. . . . Let's ask Mother if she'll make a nice pot of tea.' He glances sadly at me and shrugs, 'Perhaps she'll give us both a slice of Victoria sponge.'

'And the tips of my phalanges are still cartilaginous,' I say quietly to his stooped, retreating back.

I've got him on the run. There's no reply but the click of the door behind him.

It took twenty-five minutes for Dr and Mrs Duckworth to conspire to make a pot of tea. I heard long silences between the throb of their muffled voices. I knew they were discussing me.

When they came in, Father bearing the tea tray, against domestic custom, they announced they had something to tell me. I could see it was a special occasion, for there were napkins and Battenberg cake.

So they told me more about myself – all, that is, that they knew. That my parents came from Brazil where they lived in a forest. That they were good people, called Xique Xique, who lost me when I was a babe. So Dr and Mrs Duckworth had adopted me, because I was so lovely. They loved me dearly, they said. Both gave me a hug to prove it.

They'd always wanted a son like me, says Mother.

'Just like you,' Father agrees.

'But wouldn't you have preferred a proper child?' I ask. 'A normal person.'

'What?' asks Mother.

'What do you mean?' says Father.

'Who am I?' I wailed.

'You're a very nice boy, Charlie. You're our son.' He sounds bemused by my enquiry and sincere in his reply, 'Who else could you possibly be?'

I said I'm not certain. Although I have a theory, I cannot quite believe it.

I ask them their intentions. I want to know if they mean to keep me on.

They promise me that they will. 'You're one of us,' they say. Yet the thistles of doubt were sown.

Abed that night, I remembered the story of the Ugly Duckling. Tears welled up in my crocus-coloured eyes. I tried to visualise my parents. I wondered what manner of person my mother was to abandon me. I pondered which of my deformities or inadequacies had prompted her desertion. I supposed she must have found it impossible to love such an oddity as me.

Five

Sometimes in my solitude I run a finger down my spine and count the knobbly vertebrae. I have my reasons. It is a terrible thing to be so alone. Or my skittery yellow eyes startle themselves in the mirror, as they appraise my orange skin. For in my mind, at least, I am forever pink.

I don't doubt your sincerity. I fear it. You're usually right, as I've heard you remark.

Only the lazy need ever be wrong. There's a rhetoric for every occasion, a justification for any unreason, if you'll only make the effort to find it.

I read about an American who, in his bare-handed vigour, for seven years in succession, outperformed the entire population of Norway at murder. And why? Because he sincerely believed, as you often suspect, that other people need teaching some manners. He was always meeting rudeness. People kept disagreeing with him — in general and in the particular. Garage attendants refused to clean his windscreen, waitresses kept him waiting for his coffee, hitch-hikers would spill ash on the carpet of his car or decline to give him a blow-job.

Was he guilty? The jury believed so. He did not. After all, as he'd shown so often, people are dispensable and disposable. He called them trash. And the way he discarded them, crumpled and broken by the roadside, only proved his point.

He denied that he took his victims' lives. They were all due to die anyway, he insisted, for life's a fatal condition. He'd just rescheduled their debt to mortality, by advancing their final payment. There was some moral tuition to his actions too. Death's a kinda leveller, he said. It teaches humility, and warns folk not to get uppity.

And he wasn't incurious about his victims' feelings. Sometimes he'd crack open their skulls with a tyre lever and ponder their gelatinous brains. He wanted to see how their minds worked. He needed to know what went on in their heads that made them so unreasonable. It was his way of getting to know them; his way of saying 'Hi! How's things?'

Some said he was mad. But I thought he had all the sanity of a politician defending a tarnished record.

I've always admired that in people. It's hard to get them ever to concede that they're in the wrong. However odd their conduct seems, it's dignified by some laudable purpose.

Some Cambodians – having studied a French philosopher called Althusser – thought to protect their country and hit upon a striking solution. They disposed of a million of the people with deft blows of their machetes. This maintained the revolution; and cost no more than a quarter of the population.

Althusser later strangled his wife. We said some cutting words about the men with machetes. But circumstances change: it's best to forgive and forget. Both have returned to what they do best. Althusser is back, writing unusual ideas. The Khmer Rouge have forged a coalition with the anti-communists; again, to protect their country.

I suppose we become idealists because ideals are cleaner, finer things than people. For principles are precious, pure and brilliant; whilst people are dull and sordid; more plentiful than rabbits. Well, ask yourself! Which do you prefer – Truth, Art or your neighbour? And if one had to be sacrificed to preserve the others, which would you discard?

But justice and truth pose awkward questions, and demand ruthless answers. Sometimes only the bold dare answer the summons – to toss reactionaries from windows, or radicals from helicopters: place burning tyres around the necks of gossips to solicit their silence; or fix electrodes to the genitals of the taciturn to coax them into speech.

Your own contribution, if smaller, is important. The personal is political. Every little bit helps.

It's a glib and shallow mind that needs electrodes or machete. There are so many domestic utensils to hand. You can make friends and family wince with words; you can conduct a purge by gossip; looks can kill; you can imprison a soul with threats; and promises, promises, ensure compliance. It's all a matter of good-housekeeping, aptitude and will. And being in the right, as you are so often. You're a credit to your rhetoric and will follow it down its corkscrew twists, right to its spiky, bitter end.

When Bonker Harris held my head against the jamb of the Junior Common Room door, then slammed that door closed, so crushing and splitting my nose, I did not guess what would come of it, for I was quite distracted by pain and blinded by spurts of blood.

Often men have broken my bones and damaged my corpus. Like many victims I signal my availability for abuse and attack. It's as if I wear a placard around my neck; 'Hit me, please' it says.

I am misshapen, mystified and misplaced. Naturally, then, I incite and entice. And my sympathy bears a portion of blame. I am prone to smile at those in trouble, which they tend to take amiss.

I speak too candidly, and out of turn. Being attentive to people's flaws and foibles, I tend to point these out.

My habit of imitation doesn't endear me to folk. I sniff with snufflers, hop along with the lame, stutter with the hesitant, slur with drunks, snigger with sneerers. I take on the accent and intonation of those around me. Some take strong offence at this. They often fly into a Paddy, if they think I'm taking the Mick.

I do it, I suppose, from empathy. No sooner have I glimpsed a compelling face than I start to stare. Then I'm sucked into the person's world and ways. It's an inadvertent and amiable mannerism that others misconstrue.

At school some masters called me insolent whenever I followed their lessons by adopting their quirks.

'Duckworth, what are you doing?' demands Mr Toby Jollyon, hurling his copy of Caesar's *Gallic Wars* to the ground. His left cheek twitches regular as a metronome: for we both have an involuntary tic.

'Doing, sir? Nothing, sir.'

'You're winking, boy.' He scratched that part of a nose where I felt an irresistible itch.

'Am I, sir?. . . . So are you, sir.'

'Precisely, boy.'

I mistook this for a test of my observation. 'Oh yes, sir,' I volunteered. 'Sixteen times a minute.'

'Are you being funny, boy?' We flush in concert.

'Me, sir? No, sir.' But I was, I suppose. For the other boys were sniggering behind their texts. Naturally, then, I laughed with them, suckered again by sympathy.

Neither he nor the class could be convinced I meant no harm or hurt.

'You're a nasty child, Duckworth. What are you?' said Toby Jollyon, digging a finger deep into his cheek to arrest the spasm that empowered his tormented, twitching eyelid.

'I'm a nasty child, if you please, sir.' I winced.

'Write it down a hundred times. Then you won't forget it.'

Because I was shy, ugly and gawky, and most offensive to those very souls I liked best — like my jerky Latin master — I didn't think to make a friend at school.

So Fartzmann came as quite a surprise when he took to limping behind me; sounding his stalking presence by the scrape of his surgical boot.

'Hello, Farts,' I turn to face him, for I don't want him to hack me with his walking stick. He can get vicious if he feels a fellow holds him in contempt. 'Hop along. You'll be late for supper if you drag your feet.'

Sometimes I've this uncanny inadvertent knack for the exactly hurtful phrase; then I'm disabled by remorse.

'Sorry, Farts. I didn't mean that about your foot.' I make my lame excuse. 'It was a spastic thing to say.'

He falls in by my side. We trudge along the gravel path towards the refectory.

'Don't like that name . . . Farts,' he spits it out, 'My friends call me Bruno.'

I didn't know this. We've been in the same dormitory for six months, but I've never seen him with a friend. I wonder what his disclosure means.

'You can call me Bruno,' he says, 'but Charlie....'

'Yes, Bruno?'

'For fuck's sake, stop limping. Or I'll clout you with my stick.'

Bruno was two years older than me and clutched at maturer tastes. Behind his locker he kept hidden two bottles of brown ale and a magazine called *Skin and Sun* showing naked men and women playing tennis and picnicking on a beach. He told me he could ride a motorbike, and knew sixteen different ways to wank, and three positions for having sex with a woman (in bed; standing up; in the cinema). When he left school, he confided, he was going to find a job that involved sleeping with women — like being an osteopath, writer or sculptor.

We shared our stigmas and isolation. Lacking conversation, we often sat together in silence, smiling sporadically to celebrate companionship.

So this is the flavour of friendship, I thought, both bland and oppressive. Perhaps it's a taste that grows on a fellow.

His jam was my jam. My buns were his buns. Our secrets were ours. I jumped and ran for him. He'd stand lamely by the track and shriek me on.

'We won again. No sweat.... We aren't even out of breath,' he'd pant. His morose face would crease to a grin. 'Half a mile in two minutes two. And we can go much faster than that, can't we Charlie?'

'I'll say,' I'd say. For, in truth, I always held myself back. It was enough that Bruno always won his race, by streaking ahead in the final straight.

He loaned me his foul mouth, and threatened fellows with his lethal boot.

'If you pick on Duckworth again, I'll give you a good kicking in the balls.'

'Right, Farts.' Bevins blinks and shuffles back.

Between us, Bruno and I had enough wit, agility, malice and

48

temper for two. It was just a matter of sharing what we had, having agreed a division of labour.

But the federation of our talents was to suffer abrupt partition. Harris crushed my nose in the door. When Bruno got to hear, he want after Bonker with his walking stick, parting him from some teeth. Other chaps joined the fight, broke Bruno's stick, unlaced him from his boot, strung him upside down in the cricket net and split his duff foot open with a spade, before they scampered back from the playing fields to be on time for prep.

It had the crisp, fatal timing of a farce. As I was discharged from Casualty, Bruno was admitted. By the time he was well enough to limp again, the headmaster had expelled him.

The friendship of boys is a beautiful, brutal thing. I didn't want people to fight over me: I feared that the love of me would only bring my partner pain and disgrace.

At school I spent my pocket money on books, nuts and vegetables. I read a deal of biology and animal stories — *Pooh Lorn of the Elephants*, *Tarka the Otter*, *Animal Farm*, *Moby Dick*. Two books left a deep impression in the soft tissue of my mind; one was about a man who woke up to find himself turned into a giant beetle, then discovered his family were noxious insecticides; the other was about a man who thought he was half wolf and so suffered some unhappy confusions.

At school, I'd always swop with the other boys. My sausages or meat for their vegetables.

A carrot is a near perfect thing, an exquisite confection, comprising delights of aroma, colour, texture and taste. Parsnips are marvels too, of course, but I defy a man to better a carrot. When I couldn't afford to buy my own, I'd steal them from the local allotments. I loved best those immature nubile growths, lithe, lush, gorged with sweet and innocent juices. At that age I was just a glutton and lacked discrimination. A carrot was a carrot. Tiana, Kundulus, James Scarlet Intermediate, Chantenay Red Cored or Bericulum Berjo — they were all the same to me. Now, as a connoisseur, I can tell a Nantes Tip Top from a Mokum blindfold, just by sniffing the fragrance of their leaves.

Flesh means nothing to me. Keep your blood. I'll sup on sap, and gorge on tubers.

Aside from literature and vegetables, I most enjoyed Sammy, the groundsman's yellow labrador. The colour of his skin meant nothing to me, mind. I'm no racist. I'd have gladly romped with russet, roan or black. But he being the only dog I met daily, we came to find fondness, and passed from there to intimacy. I confided to him my sorrows; he trusted me to see where he buried his bones.

In summer, we'd flop together in the long grass behind the cricket pavilion. I'd scratch his back, he'd lick my ears or watch me, delighted and delirious, with those maudlin brown eyes. When it was cold we'd pace the boundaries of the fields, so he could raise a leg to demark his dominion with squirts of pee, overlaying the lingering claims of intruders. There was no secret I would not whisper behind the flaps of his retentive ears; nor did he withhold any aspect of his life from me. For he was candid, kindly and affectionate. Being shameless himself, he was quite unshockable. Golden times together. Every dog has his day.

'Just be yourself,' he seemed to advise. 'Dog as you please. Raise a leg. Follow your wet nose. Sniff it out.' For he moved amongst people with an amiable assurance, presuming their acceptance, conceding no deference. Rank meant nought to him. He was a reflex democrat. Why, if the mood took him, he'd think nothing of sniffing the headmaster's crotch, attempting sexual congress with Matron's leg, flopping down on Jollyon's fastidiously folded sports jacket, sprinting onto the pitch to field the ball during a senior cricket match, or snaffling the chaplain's beef sandwiches.

'But people are used to dogs,' I'd say. 'There are lots of labradors. But I've never seen another person that's the like of me. Everyone says I'm odd. They jeer and sneer.'

'Nonetheless, you're better than most,' said his languid lick, and the waggish sweep of his tail. 'And chuck me a stick,' said his yelp, 'to pass the time of day.'

Books have arrested me at various times, then imprisoned me in their knowledge.

When I was thirteen, I first read the works of Louis Bolk in the school library.

Bolk was the first biologist to assert that a human being is an under-developed ape, retarded by glandular problems. There's more reason to this than first greets the sceptical eye.

It was a family business amongst the Bolks — calling other beings retarded. Louis's brother Julian had made some intimate observations on amphibians — remarking how some of them just never grew up. Not to be out done, Louis took a peek at people.

He was forcibly struck by the similarities between adult humans and monkey embryos. Like an unborn chimp, you have a large, bulbous cranium, small jaws and teeth, muted muzzle, minimal brow ridges. The hole in the base of your skull — Foramen Magnum — is centrally placed, so your skull faces forward, as in baby baboons. The sutures to your skull, those gaps between the bones, closed only in adulthood, allowing your brain to grow.

A baby's long bones are softly cartilaginous, like those of a fourteen-week macaque monkey foetus.

A woman's vagina is not without interest, for it points ventrally. This enables her to enjoy sex lying on her back — if she chooses — which is a convenience denied to other apes, who must suffer some furtive jerky business behind their backs. Monkey embryos have such ventral placement of the vaginal canal, but it rotates backwards before birth.

I suppose we've all lain in bed or bath pondering our protuberant, unrotated, nonopposable big toes and wondering what they were for. Rest assured, they do their best. They earn their keep. For they help us hold ourselves upright and come in handy for walking. An embryonic ape starts off likewise but soon steps out of it.

I could say more, but I rest Bolk's case. In so many ways (twenty-one) you resemble a retarded ape. If your mother had been a chimpanzee, she'd have found you a raw, feeble, unfinished thing and quite a liability. For you take so long to grow up and insist on suckling so long. Some of you just cling to childhood. It's years before you'll pick your own fruit, earn a living, or present yourself for puberty.

Since your hormones govern your development, you're best described as an immature ape with slovenly glands. Your body struggles to grow into a chimpanzee's, but is too sluggish ever to finish the course.

But being slow, you're cute. As you dawdle, so you learn. Within a year you're good at grunting. By eighteen months you're up and walking, brighter even than a chimp. Slow you may be, but you get better as you improve.

People, Bolk submits, are that species that has paused to explore those possibilities that lie latent in the juvenile monkey. There's a deal of potential to this — which is why, in a zoo, you are on the more spacious side of the bars, occupy the larger cage, make the more telling observations, and have the louder, longer laugh.

Slow as a person, I resisted the pains of self-discovery. It took weeks for the truths to register and rouse me from my doze. Though I knew that Bolk was knocking at my door, I delayed answering his call.

Humans are retarded chimps. I was a retarded human: soft fingered, baby-faced, almost hairless.

I'd hidden the book in the theology section, so no one else might find and read it. Each evening after prep, I'd return to the library to study this gospel.

I wanted to learn. But I did not want to know. I needed the truth of my condition. Yet I feared to find it. Probably, I knew already.

Six

If you ever feel the urge to confirm your humanity, you couldn't do better than consult J. Hardwick-Montague's *Morphology of the Hominids* (University of California Press). Turn to pages 156-63. There's a checklist of human features. I knew this posed the test I must take. I set myself for a searching examination.

One Sunday afternoon, in the winter term of 1965, I locked myself in a labatory cubicle with Hardwick-Montague, mirror, pencil, paper and tape measure. Then I stripped to the buff to take the test.

I passed the early sections of the exam with flying colours, for I had all the right credentials — the correct tally of fingers and toes, upright posture, and an ability to lie and laugh, weep and sneeze. So far, so good. I couldn't be an orang-utang, chimpanzee, gibbon, gorilla, mandrill or marmoset. But I'd known as much already.

Then the test became more intricately discerning. I had to calculate the ratio of toe to foot length, map the distribution of my bodily hair, examine my teeth and vertebrae, and measure several portions of my skull.

This eliminated several possibilities. I found that I could not be one of those primitive proto-people — like Cro-Magnon Man, Ramapithecus, or Homo habilis.

It was most reassuring. By default, I supposed, I must be a person. So I turned the final page of the exam with an exultant confidence.

I'd been over-optimistic. My orange, hairless body was not that of a Homo sapiens. My limbs were too long (in proportion to my spine). I lacked that class of teeth called Incisors, that you use for tearing flesh. My eyes were an inadmissible colour. My hair-line was inhumanly high. I had two vertebrae too many. And my penis (a kinky item, having corkscrew twists) was not like that of man.

I felt very cold in my misshapen nudity. Also, very disconcerted.

And yet I'd feared as much. Always, I'd sensed some separation — knowing I didn't belong. All my life I'd been aping the human.

Now I'd found myself out. The higher the monkey climbs, the more he shows his tail.

Life and school were never the same beyond that moment of revelation, when the beast was born.

People seem different when you know they belong to another species.

Boys will be boys. But I wouldn't.

Hope springs eternal in the human heart. But my pulse had a different drummer.

Not Duckworth but swan. Lost amongst aliens. Found by myself.

I sniffed the air. I gagged on the human reek. I heard the jibbers and grunts on the other side of the thin oak door.

I knew I couldn't hide in the lavatory for the rest of my life. But I couldn't decide what else I should do.

We all make disconcerting discoveries about ourselves. We all believe our problems are unique. But mine was truly a singular fix, an entirely personal pickle.

I have more than one singularity. I've known most forms of isolation. It has been my lot to be abandoned, forsaken, deserted, despised. But to find you aren't a human being really takes the biscuit. I considered my sorry prospects — a lifetime of monkeying with myself.

I was desperate, tearful and fearful. I didn't know where to put myself, for I didn't know where I belonged. My bestial heart fluttered my befuddled fluster.

*

The morning after my revelation, I woke early in the dormitory to the dawn choruses of groaning boys and chirruping birds. A shaft of light bent across the boards, over my bedstead, down the blanket, onto my face, dazzling my blinking yellow eyes. There was something I must remember – an important matter, concerning my condition.

'Yes,' I recalled, 'I am not a person. My being isn't human.'

I'd mislay then recover this truth through the subsequent days. It was a boomerang I couldn't discard, forever returning to clout my head when I thought I'd thrown it away. I'd find myself watching boys play cricket. Then I'd remember that, as an ape, it really wasn't my concern.

When Jollyon demanded I rise from my seat to recite the Indicative Active of *parare*, I hesitated, poised on the brink of mutiny. For Latin verbs weren't monkey-business. I had more pressing demands on my mind.

Yet I did not say so. Instead, I stood up and coughed, before chanting the liturgy, eager as a human puppy: '*Parabam, parabas, parabat, parabamus, parabatis, parabant*' I said. As if it really mattered.

Not an hour passed but I was snared in some such contradiction, disowning my bestiality, aping the human. In English lessons I was asked to understand the plight of the Ancient Mariner; and deny my sympathy for the albatross. History required I accept the fraudulent claim that it was people who discovered America.

My eyes were opened to stunning hypocrisies. We watched Hitchcock's film *The Birds* and were asked to suppose that swarms of sparrows would peck at people. And yet it was the pheasant season, and we were served boiled bird *ova* every breakfast, and chicken for Sunday lunch.

In the papers much was made of the attempted assassination of General de Gaulle. Harold Macmillan caused an outcry when he sacked seven of his cabinet. But when the vet slaughtered the litter of eight kittens that mewled beneath the cricket pavilion none but the victims turned a hair. I pondered the possibilities. People fashioned special places for other animals — zoos, farms and abattoirs — but none struck me as pleasant.

I considered writing home —

Dear Mother and Father,
As you may know — but forgot to tell me — I am not a human being (but an ape). Education is wasted on me. Boarding school is no place for a beast (like me). Please come and take me away. Don't worry about people seeing me. I promise to keep out of sight. I'd be no more trouble than a Cocker Spaniel (and quieter than a Jack Russell).

Much love,
your very own
Charlie. XXX

Suppose Dad knew already? There was the enigma. He wasn't very observant; but he was a biologist. I supposed he'd gain a deal of credit at work, and get his name in the papers, if he were to discover a new species of being, cousin to the human. But, then again, he'd look foolish if the specimen was his son.

Perhaps I wasn't as blatantly bestial as I'd thought. Snoddie, the biology master at Stoneham, hadn't spotted me for a wrong 'un yet — though he'd taken me for games and prowled round me in detention.

'You're a strange boy, aren't you Duckworth? An odd colour, eh?' he'd observed. Yet at least he hadn't quizzed me on my zoological classification.

'I'm bizarre, sir,' I'd confirmed. 'Everyone says so.'

'It's nothing to be proud of, boy.'

'Oh, I'm not proud sir. I'm a disgrace to the school.'

'Are you trying to be cheeky, Duckworth?' He'd lowered his face to mine, rolling his bloodshot eyes. I could smell the rancid oils oozing out from his scarlet skin, and whiff his whisky breath.

'Honest, sir. Truly, I wasn't. It's just that I've got unfortunate manners. That's what the headmaster says.'

'And do you know what distinguishes us from the animals, Duckworth?'

'An upright posture and language, sir? The use of tools? Shame? Vice, sir? Marriage and war? A soul?'

He shook his head. 'It's manners, boy, and our capacity to deceive. Perhaps you'd better practise.'

'Thank you, sir. I'll bear it in mind. You're too kind.'

'That's better,' he chuckled, cuffed my ear and turned away. 'Lying brat,' he slurred beneath his boozy breath.

Snoddie was tipsy; and father myopic. Perhaps I was charmed and had lucky escapes. Or else there was the play of stupidity and arrogance here. A being who could speak, learn trigonometry, play rugby, sneer and laugh, must perforce seem human. Because people — people know — are the cleverest beings of creation, the ornamental cherries on the icing of God's cake.

It doesn't occur to people that another being could mimic or outperform them. There lay my protection — in the stupidity of the wise. Camouflage isn't needed when the predator is blind.

Learning as much, I became brazen. I had a compulsion to confess.

'I'm an animal,' I told the chaplain. 'What should I do?'

He nodded sadly. A rosy flush suffused his face, as if he'd guessed already. He'd heard the sorry tale before.

'Do you play with yourself?'

I nodded. I had no friend now Fartzmann was gone.

'Then you're beastly, boy,' he observed. 'The devil finds work for idle hands. Aren't you ashamed of yourself?'

I conceded that I was, very ashamed.

Later, I realised we'd been talking at cross-purposes. He'd confused a pleasure and a problem.

Nor were the boys more understanding.

'I'm a beast,' I howled one night in the dorm.

Maddox broke the sudden, shocked silence. 'Beast!' he sneered. 'Fucking weed, you mean.'

These were desperate days for me. I gained new and beastly mannerisms, to declare my new identity. Digging my nails hard into my arms, I'd gouge out long weeping furrows of skin. Alone, slouching over the playing fields at dusk, I took to howling against the dark.

The headmaster, Dr Beresford, must have heard. For I was summoned to his study to answer for my misdemeanours.

57

I stood before his desk; he sat back, arms folded, bald and spare as a skull, watching me over half-moon spectacles. His ulcer made him wince and grimace. I took this for a smile, grinning back pleasantly.

'This isn't the first time, Duckling, I've had reason to speak to you.' He interlocked his fingers. I heard a snapping of bones.

'No. I'm Duckworth. A duckling is something else entirely.'

'That's your excuse is it, boy? Not being something else? We're all not something else, Duckworth. But it doesn't give us the right to. . . .' He paused, shaking his head in exasperation.

So there we came to the nub of the problem. And he was right. Everything considered, I'd have to take responsibility for what I was — not for what I wasn't.

'Sorry, sir. But I didn't think. . . .'

'Exactly, boy. You didn't think.'

We eyed each other in silence. He scowled. I swallowed, gulping back a nascent howl.

'So?' he demands. 'Why do you do it? Scratch and make those noises?'

'I'm a beast, sir. An animal.'

'That may very well be true, Duckworth. But while you are a pupil at my school, you will behave like a human being.'

'I will, sir? How do you know, sir?'

'Because I say so, boy.'

'I can see your point of view, sir. . . .'

'Thank you, Duckworth.' He beamed without humour at this concession.

'But I can't quite agree with it, sir. . . . I've got my character to consider.'

'Then that's *your* misunderstanding,' he threatened me with a flash of teeth. 'You don't have to agree with it. It doesn't have to agree with you.'

'No, sir?'

'No. Because you are a boy, and I am headmaster. You will obey me. As to your character, your parents have entrusted it to me. . . .'

'Yes, sir?'

'I'll look after it for you. You may collect it at the end of term.'

'Thanks, sir.'

'Remember, I am in charge at Stoneham, Duckworth. If I say a thing is so, it is.'

I considered this. 'So if you said Tuesday was Wednesday, it would be Wednesday, sir?'

The auditor examined the candid account of my face. To check for fraudulent conversion. I gazed back piously.

'Yes, Duckworth. At Stoneham it would be Wednesday, if I said so. The rest of the world could believe what it liked.'

'So if you announced at morning assembly that Maddox was . . .' I paused to ponder the possibilities, '. . . a mole, then he'd be a mole. And have to eat worms.'

'Exactly so, boy – and dig tunnels. I think we understand each other.'

'It's a very important job you do, sir. A bit like God's, sir?'

'Yes, Duckworth,' he agreed wearily, 'but with power come responsibilities – for the welfare of beasts like you.'

'I must pretend to be a human being, sir, even though I'm an animal?' I asked. 'So I must behave like a person?'

I was impressed by his cynical nonchalance in the face of my confession. I suppose in his time he'd met many beasts in boys' clothing. A variety of animals pose as humans. I supposed the school needed the fees.

'Indeed, Duckworth. Don't forget it.'

'Would you take a pig as pupil at Stoneham, sir? If his fees were paid?'

'Indeed, Duckworth, I often do. We also take little monkeys, vermin and brutes.'

'Thank you very much, sir. It's quite a reassurance. And, sir . . . will you turn Maddox into a mole, please?'

'No, boy. I won't.' He snapped, rustling some papers to dismiss me.

So, Dr Beresford squared the circle. I was a boy like me, like the others. He showed how my square peg should fit the round holes of his school. It was the first time I'd conversed

59

with a philosopher of his persuasion. His frosty manner told a chilling truth.

We are snared by rhetoric, defined by our descriptions. Mind and language impose themselves on reality. Language is not the vehicle of thought, but the driver. Our vocabulary dissects reality, our grammar reassembles it. There are as many separate worlds as systems of representation. Reality, insofar as it exists, consists in competing conspiracies.

People like you can speak with confidence. We apes are different, liberal beings. We lack conviction, and restrict ourselves to jibbers. We have our theories, but we don't believe them. When we itch, we scratch — ourselves. The monkey knows well enough not to seek the remedy in another's fur. When we get hungry, we slaughter fruit.

You are fond of pairs and oppositions. Colour bemuses you. It's too rich a diet. You prefer a monochrome vision — black and white, good and evil, true and false, hot and cold, dos and don'ts, them and us, male and female: you and I. The sophisticates amongst you will strain your wits to juggle threes — thesis, antithesis, synthesis: id, ego, super-ego; medium, large, family-size; father, son and holy ghost: yes, no, uncertain.

There lies the problem with astrology. You know there can't be as many as twelve different sorts of people. Even psychiatry doesn't name as many.

And there's a yawning chasm at the centre of the system. For it forgets to name the enemy and tell us who to blame. Even Scorpios can be OK — if you believe astrology.

Unless difference is inferiority, there's no currency of credit. Without an enemy, we're left with no one to hate but ourselves.

No one but young children would ever believe me — that I wasn't human.

Stoneham School declared me a boy. My psychiatrist thought me neurotic. Nor would my lover understand me, when her time came.

A fellow doubts his sanity, when no one else will accept his identity or take him at his own valuation.

Not a day passed but I heard the looming tread of a new horror, striding toward me to stamp on me, and smear me underfoot.

Society makes so few concessions to its inhuman members. Those that aren't skinned or eaten get imprisoned as pets. My juvenile mind pondered my legality. The law, I supposed, would afford me the same protection as a domesticated animal. I would be no more responsible for my actions than a cow, cat or dog. But woe betide me if I caught rabies, or bit someone. I came to think of vets as a class of assassins, who might accept a contract on my life. Zoos repelled me. I saw each as a possible prison.

Much stigma attaches to animals. Apes get a poor press. They're supposed to engage in sexual malpractice and display loutish manners — like television celebrities, royalty or rock musicians. It's wilful slander — for people loan monkeys human depravities. I daresay Her Majesty's Government wouldn't seem so sweet, sage and sanitary if you caged them, gave them straw for bedding and tossed peanuts through the bars.

It is true that mountain gorillas — like rabbits — eat their own dung, but only when food is short and the weather chilly. And you read much worse about people in the Sunday papers. Anyway, there was a well-known international statesman who drank his own urine, and nobody thought much the worse of him.

Marriage would pose a quandary. It would require an indulgent wife to take me on, and tolerant in-laws to embrace me as son. And even with such good fortune, I doubted that the Church would bless the union — which would amount to bestiality.

It's a clever monkey that owns its cage. Like lunatics, the inhuman are denied possessions or a vote at elections.

Knowing as much, I resolved to stay mum. And thereafter hold my secret tight to myself; disclosing it only to those who might need to know, to properly understand me, in order to love me, should they care to, which I thought unlikely, yet still possible, especially if I ever found another of my kind, which chance I was loath to discount, for it was to become my quest and mission.

Seven

Together with my travelling companion, a tin trunk into whose tight black hole I'd sometimes retire for seclusion, the parcel of my person was posted back and forth, to the timetable of the scholastic seasons, between Stoneham School and the residence Duckworth, 23 Cloudesley Road, Islington.

I counted neither phase as holiday, neither place as home. For I was a fugitive imposter – neither child of my parents, nor boy of my school. I knew no kin and belonged to no place, being singular and my own. Some days I felt too orange to be seen. I'd hide myself away.

I should like to say that the kindliness of my adoptive parents seemed preferable to the cruelties of school. Yet it wasn't so. It was painful to witness the misery and decay of those I loved best. Age dealt harshly with the Duckworths, who in turn were unkind to each other. They seemed to find diminishing pleasure in their conspiracy of marriage. At night they took themselves to separate bedrooms. The harvest of their intimacy was a bitter fruit of insult and recrimination.

'I should have married Freddie Leyton,' I heard Mrs Duckworth confide to her spouse.

'I wish you had,' her husband observed. 'Can you pass the mustard?'

'He did very well for himself.'

'I'll say!' Dr Duckworth agreed, 'He married Dorothy Hodgson.'

'If it wasn't for the boy . . .' Mrs Duckworth sighed.

When I kept them company to act as buffer, they'd

practice selective deafness and route their remarks through me.

'Charlie, ask your father why he's put his tank of toads on the kitchen table.'

'Dad, what are the toads doing there?'

'Feeding on Drosophila flies, Charlie.' He'd smile at his wit.

His few triumphs were domestic now. He'd still teach his wife a lesson or two, if no one else.

He wouldn't be promoted at College, he knew. Students shunned his classes. Junior colleagues humiliated him, writing clever books behind his back. No more was he invited to address scholarly conferences. His toad had been withdrawn from display at the Natural History Museum. Even his hair had tired of his head. He sported supernumerary chins. His breath came heavy after the briefest walk. He was worn out and ground down. Neither fate nor his talents would award him the distinction he longed to deserve.

I was moved by sympathy for him and sorrow for myself. Supposing I told him? Perhaps we could work some alchemy together, transmuting the mix of our miseries to shared joy. For it had occurred to me that his failure could be resolved by my dilemma. So that his solution could be my salvation.

I could gain the credit for being myself, he could have the fame for discovering me. I trusted him not to deliver me up to a zoo. Perhaps we might travel the world together, displaying my person and his eminence. We could stop off in Brazil and search out my long-lost relatives. Father might deliver the lectures; I could field the questions. We could be a famous double-act — professor and performing ape.

'Dad, supposing you discovered a new species of human being? A cousin to Homo sapiens, like Homo erectus or Neanderthal man.'

He exhaled slowly, beaming at this fantasy. 'I'd be famous, Charlie. Like Leakey, Oakley or whatsisname. They'd make me a professor at Oxford or Harvard. The young chaps at work would be jealous.'

'You'd like that?'

'I'd say.' He was warming to the prospect.

'You could call it Homo Duckworthensis, I suppose.'

'That's the idea.'

'Let's look for one, Dad. If you want to be famous.'

'Where, Charlie?'

'Here,' I said, 'here in the sitting room.'

'Sh!' he tip-toed in laboured parody of a circus clown. 'You look under the sofa,' he winked archly, 'I'll look behind the curtains.' And he did look there; as if it were all some farce.

I thought I'd given a broad enough hint already, hazarding my future, offering myself up. You can take a horse to water, I realised, but you can't make him think.

'I look at it this way ...' I tried to nudge his wits. 'Humans have evolved from the apes by some mutation that makes them grow up slowly. Bolk says that anatomically people resemble embryonic monkeys.'

'Who's this Bolk chappie?' His brow furrows, his voice goes peevish with suspicion.

'A famous embryologist.'

'Odd,' says he, 'I've never heard the name. I'll ask the young fellows at college. It's clever of you to know his work.'

'I read a lot of biology,' I said.

'Yes,' he sighed, wistful, 'soon you'll know as much as me.'

'Anyway ...' I persevered, trying another way through to his wits. I knocked at the front door. 'Listen, Dad, if another species emerged, perhaps they'd have evolved further in the same direction — and develop even more slowly. Have a longer infancy, less hair, childish face, cartilaginous fingers, and so on. They might even pass for people. So it'd need a biologist to spot them. What do you think?' I couldn't have said it more clearly — short of affixing a label (Homo ridiculus) to my lapel.

'If it's all the same to you, Charlie, we could do it tomorrow instead — look for another species.' He sunk into the sofa; his head dropped, he closed his eyes. 'I've been on my feet all day. I'd like a little snooze.'

He hadn't the wit or will to discover me.

It was only three in the afternoon. He was only sixty-three, but he must have had premonitions. He'd been preparing for years, practising to be a dead thing. His hardening arteries were strangling his heart. In seven months he'd be gone: in a stroke.

Seven people gathered to bury him, like a bone, in Mill Hill. We mourned him briefly, till distracted by tea and ham sandwiches. His cousin Ernie was the life and soul of the funeral party, doing an impersonation of Norman Wisdom.

*   *   *

We became much closer, Mother and I, after Dad died. Sometimes, in maudlin reverie by the fire, she'd call me Robert, confusing father and son.

'We'll have supper soon, Robert. I've bought some nice cod.'

'It's me, Mother,' I'd reach out and pat her plump shaky hand. 'It's Charlie. And I'm vegetarian, remember?'

'You look so like your father, in this light,' she'd say, 'it's quite uncanny.'

It was sentimental short-sightedness. If my appearance wouldn't disabuse her, nothing would. I was well over six feet tall, orange-skinned, lanky and gangling, with a sparse thatch of black hair. Still, at seventeen, I had the wide-eyed look of an eleven-year-old. It was a feat of will to see me as a bald and wrinkled gnome.

She'd begun to display that forgetfulness that was to become her forte.

'Whatever happened to Freddie Leyton?' she'd demand, out of the vacuum of an hour's silence.

'You never married him,' I'd remind her. 'He married Dorothy Hodgson instead. Now he's a borough surveyor in Leicester.'

'Your father never liked him,' Mother observed. 'They were best friends. But your father never really liked him.'

'Have you written to School, Mother?' I asked. 'You can't afford the fees on Father's pension.'

'Can't I?'

'No,' I said. 'And it's better if I stay at home now.'

'Is it?'

'Much better,' I said, 'I really don't mind.'

'What'll you do, Charlie?'

'This and that,' I promised. 'And look after you.'

I'd got two precocious 'A' levels. I didn't need to stay on. I had lots of books to read at home, and my own congenial company.

I'd devised a definite plan for my future. I knew there were going to be further changes to my being. I reckoned on becoming mature; on experiencing something akin to puberty. I'd resolved to wait for this before I took myself to work or university.

I awaited sexual maturity with eager anticipation. There'd be so many new things to do when I got there, I reckoned. And perhaps it would make me look more human. It might render me less orange or award me supplementary hair.

I'd estimated my arrival at around the age of twenty or twenty-one, judging by my past development. For I'd worked out my ratio of retardation at about 1.33 recurring. My species — whatever this was — seemed to take about a third longer than the average human to reach any developmental milestone. Accordingly, I'd supposed my gestation at about eleven months, and my probable life span as being over a hundred years.

With that expectation, I felt I could afford to dawdle. I've never known that frantic headlong rush to death that humans feel. Perforce, I've been patient.

Mother and I soon established a tranquil modus vivendi. I replaced my father in most mundane respects, quite as if Freud had written our script. I took over his study, library, papers, toads and bedroom. I adopted his expressions and mannerisms of absent-minded distraction. Mother would have to call three times before I could be coaxed to meals, which I ate with the nonchalant ingratitude expected of me.

'If you knew how long that took to cook, you'd show a little appreciation.'

'Mm.'

I let my dirty clothes fall where she could, after a diligent search, uncover them. Two days later, they'd reappear on my father's chest of drawers, washed, folded, tainted by reeks of cooking, yellowed by her scorching iron.

'I don't run a laundry, here,' she'd lie.

Like my father before me, I'd stall over those domestic chores she designated man's work. As he'd often explained to me, it is foolhardy for a man to erect a shelf, mow a lawn, or paint a door. You run the risk of hubris and over ambition. There may be ladders involved. Best leave well alone. Don't court your fall. Life's difficult enough, without defying gravity by parting from terra firma.

'Have you fixed the plug yet, Charlie?'

'I'm working on it,' I'd say. 'I'm doing a feasibility study. It shouldn't prove a problem, except for the wiring.'

'Bath plug.'

'Ah,' I said. 'I'll see what I can do. Is it a big job?'

'You sound just like your father.'

'Thank you, Mother.'

On Wednesdays and Saturdays, I'd sullenly scuff my heels behind her to carry home the shopping – just as he had done.

If I didn't stop her sometimes missing him, I filled the space he left behind and spoke his silence. I did this in honour of him and as a kindness to her. It suited me well enough at the time.

People have sometimes had cause to ask me: 'What makes you so fucking superior?'

And, of course, I can't tell them – that having taken longer over each stage of my development, I'm a more finished specimen; that I lack human spite and anger; that I am more sympathetic than most, and kinder; that I have no interest in cheating people; that I have an inhuman sensitivity; that, unlike them, I have acute sight.

Instead, I stammer, 'Sorry,' before I slink away.

As for your problem – that sense of nagging unease – I think there are several causes. Perhaps you fear you'll be found out. Caught in the act. Exposed. So everyone will know. And detest or deride you. A shame that – the disgraceful part of you.

The morning post is always a worry, don't you find? Amid the harmless or friendly items there might be the message you fear. 'This is your past. I have caught up with you at last. Now you must pay.'

Even though you've dismissed it from mind, there's the dim, flickering fear it will return. It will dog you for life. And whilst we're on that subject, shouldn't you return those whatsits you borrowed? They're years overdue. It's not a solution, is it? Trying to forget them.

Now you're grown, you are no longer terrified by the dark, you merely feel anxious. So, as you enter a room, you switch on the light, to banish the gloom, the worry of what lies hidden — in the folds of your curtains, or mind. You fear your home, because you fear your self. That part banished to the dark.

Torturers know this. They never name the ultimate threat. You devise that for yourself. Your hell is in you. It is a portion of yourself.

It's worse when you're tired or ill. You've less energy to hold it at bay. Your anger leaks out in petulance. Worse can slither out behind it. Hence your sense of foreboding.

You resemble those people you dislike the most. You loathe the mirror of their look. You have my sympathy. Self-loathing is your hateful burden.

But there's seldom a need to hate people. Most do it better for themselves. You are anxious. You torment yourself with fears of poverty, failure and illness. You're frightened you'll meet yourself in the dark. You're the sort of person that scares people like you. It's characters like you that give people a bad name.

Dr Duckworth was more confiding and loquacious in death than he'd ever been in life. In his papers he disclosed much about himself that I hadn't known before. He had been poet, diarist, adulterer, collector of pornography, debtor and fraud.

His diary for 1956 was bound together with a bundle of letters from Sandra Symonds. These documents, his laconic notes and her literary effusions, told both sides of their affair.

'Oh, Robbie, yesterday in your office when we pledged ourselves...,' — she declared, her hurried looping handwriting careering diagonally down the purple page, drawn by the eccentric gravity of her lopsided passion – 'and you took me there, on the lino, I knew as never before that whatever our differences of age and background, our love. . . .'

For his part, Dr Duckworth had nonchalantly entered, under June 2nd, 'Invigilate exam 10.00. Return scripts. Research Committee, 3.00. Sandra S, 5.30. Twice. Lucky rascal!'

Her subsequent letters gained in tidiness and control as they lost in lyricism and warmth. The final missives were no more than memos, briskly contrasting her morality and his, to his disadvantage.

On July 7th, he was moved to confide to his diary: 'SS. Won't be told.'

I was proud to learn that others had loved him too – FG, AK, LB, DN-S, and B McK – as he must have liked them, in his fashion. 1958 was his Annus Mirabilis, judging by the swarms of exclamation marks dotting his diary; small memorabilia of passion.

In a much fingered manila envelope I found six photographs of young women, who must have been his conquests. His taste was for chubby blondes. Their expressions were of bewilderment or awkward shyness.

In his collection of photographic erotica, blondes were also to the fore. So I wondered why he had chosen a dark-haired woman as wife.

Financial strains between 1955 and 1963 had forced Dr Duckworth to dispose of inherited stocks and annuities. His bank had repeatedly written to advise him not to write further fictions on their cheques. Two court orders for debt had been registered against him. I believe his wife knew nothing of this.

There was a folder on me in his cabinet, filed under 'S' for Son, containing no more than my birth certificate, invoices for school fees, and termly reports. 'Charles is a shy, timid and surprising boy,' Dr Beresford had written. 'He must learn to take more part in school activities. He is very prone to tears, and has to be discouraged from howling. If he applies his talents, he might develop into a competent scholar or distinguished high-jumper. He has a most unusual sense of humour. We have

69

cause to dissuade him from mimicking the masters. His fees are over-due, again.'

In another file, Dr Duckworth had collected together, in order of receipt, seventy-four rejection slips for his collected poems — 'Sighs amid thighs'. He had underlined in red ink the epithets or adjectives editors had tossed to him in qualifying their regretful rebuffs of his work — which was also his life. 'Banal', 'candid', 'unsuitable at this moment of time', 'derivative', 'heartfelt', 'inept', they said.

Of Dr Duckworth's two hundred and sixty poems, this is the one I best remember —

> As I grow weary, bald and fat,
> I wonder at time, then ponder that.
> In the mocking mirror I reflect
> wrinkles, waste and disrespect.
> The child within grows testy and tired.
> For Hope's resigned; ambitions retired.
> Farewell Faith, goodbye Joy,
> The maids have scarpered my employ.
> Prudence and Chastity serve instead.
> Frosty partners for my chill bed.
> Oh, the years that made flabby my corpus,
> have only withered and wasted my purpose.

I realised that there was something missing here — besides talent, and a terminal rhyme — in the epitaph he wrote for himself. There was missing a pleasure in life and sense of success. It made me weep for him. It made me review my own plight.

He was a failure as scholar, poet, husband and adulterer. If a human failed at the human agenda, what hope was there for an ape?

I vowed I would be more than man manqué. I knew I must find my own kind. I pondered where to look. I slouched down St John Street towards Finsbury Library. Somewhere, hidden in the non-fiction section, lay my kith and kin.

Eight

I fell into the quicksand of self-absorption. Perhaps, you know it too. The harder I struggled, the deeper I sank.

I pondered who I was and why.

'I ... I ...' I thought, 'I ...'

How I tired itself out. And there was no escaping the remorseless, insistent screech of that impersonal pronoun.

'I' did its best to describe 'me'. Yet they were merely phantoms: a spectre confronting a spook.

I pondered how it was that I had an orange skin, yellow eyes and curly penis. Why was I so miscast?

Those who've studied the evolution of human kind look to the past and the ground. They dig around for dead bits, gnawing upon old bones.

It's as if Nature completed her task, exceeding her ambitions, when the first Homo sapiens stumbled forth, sly-eyed, sniggering and snuffling, wondering who to eat for breakfast.

The scientists' stories are of the emergence of their own heroic species. They never think to look around for their living cousins, like myself.

I read assiduously through the standard texts on physical anthropology, human biology and palaeontology. But there was never a report of a thing resembling me.

And I never saw my likes in the streets of Islington, on cinema or TV. This was discouraging. A fellow felt alone, and prodigiously odd. He supposed himself a mutant or alien. Whenever he counted his vertebrae, the number was always the same.

You doubt your own judgement. You suppose yourself mad.

And — sanely — you worry that others will notice. You are an enigma in search of solution. Doggedly, you search again. Somewhere there must lie the explanation.

'Xique Xique' said my name. Near Cobija and Guajara Mirim, Dr Duckworth had told me.

I took myself to twenty London libraries, examining every book I could find on Brazil, scouring the indexes for likely clues.

But I couldn't find my kind in literature. It is dismal to be a nameless thing, beyond the clutch of language, lacking a proper noun.

Then one day I was given my clue. It was terse advice, daubed in white on the window of an Indian grocer's in Penton Street.

FUK OF KOONS
BROWN BASTIDS

I was stirred. I was shaken. I had an inkling of profundity. There was more to this than met the eye. It spoke more that it said. Somewhere in there, I sensed, was a splinter of kindly advice.

A dormant egg suddenly hatched to a maggot, and began to wriggle deep in my head, munching a path through to conscious mind. It nagged away in me.

It was something to do with spelling. But I didn't know quite what. You can't force it. It comes in its own good time. You can do no more than relax and wait.

It took me by surprise as I lay in the bath, absent-mindedly numbering the bumps of my spine.

Somewhere ... in an orange book in Holborn, perhaps ... or a brown one in Kentish Town ... my eye had flicked over what I sought. And yet I'd passed it by. Because of the spelling.

'Zika Zika' it had said.

Two weeks later, retracing my steps, I found it again.

The book. And within it, the word.

I discovered a man who may have been my father.

He was in Swiss Cottage library. He lay, purple bound, in Boaz's *Amongst the Tribes of the Cobija*.

*

Boaz reports that the Zika Zika were a tree-dwelling tribe of thirty or forty members. He camped beneath their trees, attempting to address them through a megaphone and observe them through binoculars. Whilst Boaz and his party slept, on the first night of their encampment, the Zika Zika had descended to pay a shy, sly visit. For, on waking next morning, they found that a latrine trench had been dug for them, a pile of assorted fruits had been left, and the barrels of both their rifles had been bunged with compacted bark. Nothing, he recounts with approval, was stolen.

Next night, Boaz records, he lay awake and waiting. But there was no further visitation until the fourth day. Then a solitary male climbed down through the foliage, sat on his haunches, held his hand to his face, observing the visitors through the gaps between his fingers, snorting as he wept.

I leave Boaz to tell it. . . .

Having already established that these were a timid people, I knew that I must match their tact and cause no fright or apprehension, as might be caused when stone age man greets modern culture, and for the first encounter.

The man stooped over two metres tall, naked except for a loin cloth which was woven of matted plant fibres. On his chest and cheeks was a intricate pattern of whorls, painted in green and purple grease.

Knowing no other appropriate protocol by which to address this representative, of a tribe that had never witnessed such a man as me before, and who probably knew nothing of the manners and accoutrements of our culture, I chose to reciprocate and mimic the man's own gestures.

I approached until we were ten metres apart, then squatted, placed my hands to my eyes, watching him through the spaces of the digits. He lowered his hands. I lowered mine. He replaced his. I replaced mine. And so on, in an extended game of 'peek a boo'. He split his mouth to show his teeth, in the manner of a contrived smile. I did likewise. He shrugged his shoulders. I shrugged mine.

For fifty minutes, we followed this pattern, in a most exhaustive and, ultimately, tiring fashion. He initiating, I

73

imitating — sticking a finger up a nostril, scratching a thigh, gasping, grunting, chuckling, clapping, counting our fingers and toes, sneezing, balancing on one leg, touching our toes, folding our arms.

It had soon occurred to me that we were no longer engaged in an elaborate show of politesse, but that he was systematically assessing my behavioural repertoire; that he was investigating me. This suspicion became confirmed as his actions, and implicit demand for imitation, became increasingly demanding.

I made no attempt to match his backward somersaults from a standing position, or to rotate through a full circle whilst standing on one hand. I lack the suppleness to wrap my feet around my ears.

He repeated these gymnastics and then observed my passivity with some bemusement. I shook my head. He shook his.

At that moment, it seemed, he had returned the initiative to me. It occurred to me that whilst he could better me with some crude calisthenics, I could blind him with the resources of culture.

So I reached into my trouser pocket, withdrew my cigarette lighter and flicked it aflame. He reached down for two twigs, rubbed them together peremptorily and then tossed them away. I lit a cigarette; he put a finger in his mouth and gave a burlesque portrayal of an infant suckling. Then he withdrew the finger and tapped it with the palm of his other hand, as if punishing it.

For such a moment, and for my own recreation, I had brought with me a gramophone. I was intrigued how tribal man would comprehend the magical technology of a disembodied voice.

I told Alfonso to play a record. The first disc he came upon was of the Count's 'Vedro, mentr'io sospiro' from Mozart's *Marriage of Figaro*.

This tree-dwelling stranger listened entranced, jerking his head to the melody. He closed his eyes, looked heavenward and sucked in his cheeks in rapt attention. When the gramophone had wound down, he commenced an uncanny imitation, mimicking both the baritone and some instrumental effects, slowing and slurring towards the end in faithful copy of the machine. Though I've heard better and more conventional renderings at the Opera house, I was astounded by his facility. For a musical novice, hearing Mozart for the first time, he showed extraordinary understanding and mimetic talent.

Rotating an imaginary handle on his navel, he signalled, agitated by impatience, for us to wind the gramophone again. It seemed he had grasped some rudiments of the mechanics of the machine. Alfonso played the other side of the record – Cherubino's 'Voi che sapete' – whereupon the man astounded us with his sweetly expressive mezzo-soprano voice.

We clapped him and called 'encore'. He clapped and echoed us.

Then, flicking his fingers just as I often do, he spoke to us in colloquial, but entirely lucid, Portuguese.

'Alfonso! Quick!' he called, in an eerily exact copy of my voice. 'Pronto, dickhead!'

Alfonso stumbled forward some paces towards the man, then stopped abruptly, looking foolish.

It was several seconds before I understood. These were frequent phrases of mine. The man must have overheard my witty and good-natured banter.

'Pronto yourself, son of a whore,' the Indian then declared, sotto voce, before spitting between his feet, perfectly parroting Alfonso's sour tones and surly manners.

We became aware that this ambassador of the Zika Zika was not only a sagacious observer of life, but an accomplished parodist, and satirist too.

So too were the rest of the tribe. For that evening, as we sat around our flickering fire, about forty voices serenaded us from the heights, with a corrupt but moving rendition of 'Deh vieni, non tardar' into which they had woven an improvised chorus of 'Pronto, fuckface, son of a whore.' We were left in no doubt that they were singing directly to us, and from their hearts.

Figaro – for so we named him, in respect of his deep affection for Mozart's music and Da Ponte's libretto – never left our sides for the duration of our stay beneath his people, encamped in their shade.

It was a cause of shame and regret that, while Figaro acquired words and phrases of Portugese within mere days, we never learned any items of his own language. For he never mouthed a syllable, save in our tongue.

'Speak Zika Zika,' I demanded.

'No words,' he said, shaking his head sadly, pointing up to the chorus hidden above. 'Silent persons.'

Here, I suspected him of circumspect deceit.

He often looked up to the heights, trickles of tears coursing down his cheeks, abandoned in mute melancholy. But most of the day he would follow us, assiduously attentive to our every action, swearing softly in Portuguese, scratching himself whenever we did. And if I or Alfonso stopped, turned our backs and unbuttoned ourselves, to observe a routine call of nature, he would fumble with his loin cloth and urinate too.

If I ever playfully clipped Alfonso's ear, or slapped his face, Figaro would strike himself in the same place, then howl at the imagined pain.

'You — Figaro — go back. Bring other Zika Zika,' I proposed to him. 'We give cigarillos and brandy.'

'Only Figaro,' he shook his head adamantly. 'Other sons of whores stay. They live. Figaro dead meat.' He sniffed back some tears, stumbled forward to point out our breakfast tin of corned beef to emphasise his meaning. For he had an opaquely aphoristic turn of phrase. 'Figaro stink. Like you. Dead thing.' He sniffed at his arm-pit then spat on the ground, as if disgusted by a taste.

'Zika Zika give you small person,' he locked his fingers and rocked his arms, as if nursing a suckling child.

'Baby?' I asked.

He imitated the cry of an infant.

'Yes,' I replied, 'that is baby.'

'Baby,' he nodded. 'You want baby. To make you good. Or better dickhead.'

I was startled that the tribe should think to give us a baby. Many tribal cultures have gift ceremonies, donating or trading animals, brides, foods, ornaments or valuables. Yet I had never before encountered a tribe that gave away its babies. I worried what I should do if this eventuality arose, and pondered what the Zika Zika might seek to extract in return. For there is no gainsaying a ritual gift without causing deep offence, perhaps precipitating violence. Field-workers do not forget certain salutary precedents. Bratowzki was decapitated by the Assai for declining to copulate with a Shaman's wife. Parry-Jones was speared through the throat for his insult of spitting to the ground his first mouthful of a meal of human afterbirth — a compound gesture which, in the eyes of his Serengiphitti hosts, pithily said: 'I curse your children. I place a hex on their parents. May your entire people wither like yam in a drought. I pollute your land, and wish upon you seven barren harvests.'

76

'Eleven moons make baby,' Figaro observed, 'Big work for fat person.'

'Nine moons,' I corrected him.

'Eleven moons,' he insisted, 'Zika Zika take longer. Make better.'

Some primitive people have suppositions, biologically inaccurate notions of procreation. Some even deny any causal connection between intercourse and pregnancy.

'You have woman?' I asked him. For I was eager to hear some account of their sexual mores. I cupped my hands to my chest, as if cradling breasts.

'Woman.' Figaro savoured this new word, closing his eyes in some reverie of reflection.

'You have woman?' I repeated.

He scrutinised me with some amusement. 'Womans have Figaro,' he sighed, 'make big work.' And he extruded his tongue, jerking his hips in imitation of lazy copulation. 'Two days. To make woman happy. Then Figaro sleep.'

'Figaro many women?' I asked him.

He wrinkled his face in perplexity. 'Every woman,' he said, 'Everyman with everywoman. Makes baby.'

Not for the last time, I realised he was wilfully misleading me with some unlikely misinformation.

'Baby come two days,' he promised. 'Then fuckface go,' he proposed. For he was of the adamant conviction that we had come for no other purpose than to gain a Zika Zika child. I was unable to convince him otherwise.

'I want to meet Zika Zika.' I said. 'Make friend.' I clasped my hands together and smiled.

'No,' he shook his head in alarm, 'Fuckface steal babies.'

It is hard to gain the trust of a man who is of the adamant conviction that you have come to steal his children. 'Tell Zika Zika come,' I pleaded.

'No.' He made a circular stirring motion with one hand, then tapped it with the other. 'No come speak bad people. Zika Zika stay clean.'

He had the notion that Alfonso and I were pollutants who might cause his people harm. When I explained that we were good and kind, he slapped his ears, in jocular disbelief, as if we were teasing him. . . .

77

Figaro, I like to believe — I choose to believe — was my father. At the very least, he must have been on intimate terms with my mother. Certainly, we have a character in common.

Sorry, I'm quite ignoring you. These are my concerns, not yours. You've got problems of your very own — which stem from your vision and intelligence, both of which are well known. I feel I know you well enough by now to tender certain observations.

Nature has favoured you in so many ways. Your talents are beyond dispute. I believe your reputations are well deserved. A personality like yours deserves mention. Your integrity and generosity are noted. You're every bit as honest as your conscience will allow. It's to your credit that you try hard to help others. Only, often, you have to be harsh to be kind. You can't please everyone. There are so many people to disregard in this life. Sometimes you don't know where to start.

You are prey to certain anxieties and gripped by vague foreboding. You are nagged by discontent. You want something but cannot clutch it. You fear something, but can't name it. People of your age and background often feel so. It's an effect of your age and situation, but current circumstances can't help.

May I confide? Some people — I neither name nor blame them, for it's your dispute not mine — hold you up to ridicule. They sneer at you behind your back; mocking your pretensions, deriding your abilities. They make more than passing mention of your character. They name certain popular vices.

It has occurred to you on more than one occasion that you are infected by a fatal illness. Often you feel lethargic and irritable. Sometimes as you raise a glass, you wonder if you drink too much. Your weight has sometimes caused you concern, as has the plight of the starving. You know you should take more exercise.

Purchase provides only brief relief. New clothes, books, music, gadgets, household furnishings are not the things you really want. Sometimes when you've got it home, you can't remember why you bought it.

You are slowly decaying. This natural condition alarms you. You do not want to be an autumn leaf. You'd prefer endless, seamless youth.

So often your choices in life seem forced. It is a position that chess-players call Zugzwang. You can only move to your own disadvantage.

Your erotic life leaves something to be desired. Out of tact, I'll say no more.

Trust means much to you. Your few infidelities are brief excursions, scarcely serious. If you bad-mouth one friend to another, it is only to pepper your conversation. You protect others' feelings. The only things you say behind their back that you would not address to their face are hurtful observations. When it comes to the crunch, you are married to your mistake and devoted to your foibles: faithful as the best.

You consult your past to plan your future. You are deferring life. The present is a waiting room for a train that may not come.

Others withhold the consideration that you show them. Too often they take you too much for granted. They complain you complain. Which is true. And unsurprising.

Naturally, you are anxious or angry. There are certain people you despise. It's the way they go about their business; their transparent lies; the way they cheat and connive; amongst themselves, for those bastards stick together. They deserve what they get — if it isn't pleasant.

Still, at least you're harmless. I had a neighbour once who killed his car. People had said he was a villain, but I'd never seen a sign of it until he shot his Alfa Romeo.

All Sunday morning he'd been stripping and cleaning the carburettor and rummaging in his manifold. But to no avail. Whenever he closed the bonnet and turned the ignition, the car just gave a wearied wheeze, like a chronic bronchitic groaning in bed.

'Trouble, mate?' I asked as I passed him. His name was Len, I should tell you. He said nothing. I could see from his scarlet cheeks and corrugated brow that this wasn't a man at peace with the world. Anyway, silence was a form of politeness in Asylum Road.

'Stupid bugger,' he told a piece of cowling, as he hammered it into the pavement.

Late in the afternoon, I heard a shot outside, and a tinny retort of metal, like the sustained ring of a cymbal. I rushed to the window. There was Len, confronting his obdurate car. Aiming a shotgun from the hip, he fired the second barrel into the sprinkling can of its radiator.

'Now will you start, you bastard?' he howled.

But it didn't. He was too angry to see — that he was locked in a logical fallacy. It was sheer anthropomorphism. You can't murder an inanimate object in the same way as a person.

As Figaro before me, I find myself alone amongst men.

Boaz told a story he didn't understand —

... If I ever awoke during the night I found the sulphurous eyes of Figaro upon me, alert and unflinching, reflecting the dancing sparks of our camp fire. I never saw him sleep. I never looked at him without finding his gaze fixed upon me. Despite his amiability and desire to please, he watched Alfonso and with an unblinking vigilance that, in exceeding curiosity, amounted to distrust.

'You've met white men before?' I guessed.

Figaro curled a corner of his upper lip, spitting a vivid imitation of the sound of rifle shot. He pointed to our plugged guns. We had not cleaned out the barrels, being confident that they would still fire through the loose packed filling.

'Bad men,' I said. 'Zika Zika fight?' I threw a mock punch at Figaro to show my meaning.

He shuddered and his eyelids flickered closed. 'Zika Zika no fight. No fire. No....'

'Anger?' I suggested, wrinkling my face to a grimace of detestation.

He was alarmed. 'No anger,' he said, speaking softly, with pity for us all — his people and mine. 'No anger. Dead meat,' he observed.

Frankly, we had grown tired, Alfonso and I, of this self-serving and unsubstantiated catalogue of the goodness of his kind. I was irritated enough to challenge his unlikely claim. So I slapped him hard, twice about each ear, then smiled. 'Really?' I enquired, 'No anger?'

Yet, good as his improbable word, he showed no ire. With an abject rolling of liquid eyes, he whimpered softly and shook his head. He rose to his feet, slunk away from the warmths of company and fire, to find another resting place beyond arm's reach. Though he sat with his back turned to us, he watched me − unblinking − over his shoulder. But he must have smarted with resentment, for he commenced a monotone wail. Above it, and above us, we heard an agitated chatter. Then the whine swelled in volume as the other Zika Zika joined him in the nagging wail, till our ears rang with this single lacerating note of despair.

We barely slept that night. We kept our rifles to hand, lest these unpredictable natives thought to mount a surprise attack on us. . . .

I was seared by fear. I can't call it a premonition. Whatever had happened, had happened two decades before.

I wailed, loud and plaintive.

'Take care Figaro . . . Father. . . .' I shrieked.

But it was a futile warning, to a paper phantom, twenty years too late.

'You!' hissed a librarian. 'Show some consideration.'

Nine

It was an odd way to first meet my father.

Figaro smiled up at me. The sweet, warm scent of him wafted up from the pages. We were joined, across those barriers of Boaz's prejudice, twenty-one years, the Atlantic Ocean, and the land mass of Brazil. We were one flesh, one blood, one colour, one character. Here was my kin. I wept on the pages, which rose up in wrinkled ridges where my tears had run. My kind, my family, my own. I was not alone in this. There were others like me.

Only, we were continents and two decades apart. Yet, now I knew how and where to look. Soon, I believed, we should meet.

I rang the Brazilian Embassy; three times from the public phone in the hall of Swiss Cottage library; being told to put my enquiry in writing, I'd change my accent; only to be connected again to the same sluggish voice. He spoke in a hush, as if careful not to rouse a sleeping baby.

'We cannot reply to requests by telephone,' he replied. 'We cannot say informations,' he whispered.

'It's important. I'm Brazilian ...' I said. '... like you. I need to contact my family. It's urgent.'

'Write,' he soothed. 'Our administration is not amenable to spoken confidences,' he confided, then the line clicked dead to show so.

I wrote that day, explaining that I was a native Brazilian of British adoption. My natural parents belonged to the Zika Zika — or Xique Xique — tribe. Their last known address was c/o the Cobija Basin, in the Province of Abuna. Could the

Embassy please contact my relatives on my behalf, and forward the enclosures — a ten shilling note and photograph of myself? Would they ask my relations to phone me promptly, reversing the charges? In conclusion, I expressed a sudden patriotic hope that the Brazilian football team would win the forthcoming World Cup.

For ten days I did not leave the house, for fear of missing my parents' phone call. I calculated the time difference between England and Brazil, and kept South American hours. On the eleventh day, supposing my letter hadn't been delivered, I rang the Embassy again.

'Our administrations are properly bureaucratic,' a voice consoled me, 'all correspondences receive a corresponding retort according to their urgencies.'

And, sure enough, seventeen days later I received a reply, returning my ten shillings and photo, assuring me that Brazil was populated by Brazilians. There was no such tribe as the Xique Xique in the country, nor any such surname in the metropolitan telephone directories. They endorsed my hopes for the football. Rivelino had recovered from his ankle injury, they reported, but Tostão still had double-vision which affected his shooting. They enclosed a colour poster of the team. They hoped I would pay a touristic visit to my homeland.

I replied by return post, asking for information of the whereabouts of Professor Roberto Boaz. Meanwhile I wrote to him, at The Institute of Ethnic Affairs, São Paulo — his address of twenty years before.

I visited University College library, saying I was the son of Robert Duckworth, formerly of the Biology Department.

'Dr Duckworth . . .' the librarian relished the name, awarding it a derisive infamy '. . . owes us *twelve* books. They're ten *months* overdue.'

'Oh,' I flushed. 'He's nine months *dead*.' I spoke up for him. I said that he was a fastidious man about books and punctuality, but had been distracted by his demise.

She softened at this. Taking it for a full explanation, allowing me to visit the anthropology section, where I scoured the shelves for mention of the Zika Zika.

There, I found stark news of my paper family, in two paragraphs of Salvador Perez's *Ethnographic Survey of Pando, 1956* —

Amongst those tribes eliminated by the road-building and development of plantations, were the Azul, Pequos, and Zika Zika. The Pequos were devastated by influenza and gonorrhoea, against which they had no resistance. Those Azul that survived the fire-bombing of their villages, joined the work-gangs, serving as labourers or prostitutes according to their sex.

The Zika Zika (see Boaz, 1946) alone posed any resistance, albeit of a passive form. They presented themselves collectively to the rubber plantation at Cobija, ceremonially gave over two babies, then enacted an elaborate mime, mimicking and apparently satirising the new settlers. Sitting beneath the trees that were to be felled, they refused to move. These attempts to humiliate the planters, and prevent the deforestation, were quite unsuccessful. Many were crushed by trees. The rest were shot.

So what Swiss Cottage had given me — my kith and kin, my paper paternity — University College took away. I vomited on Perez. I retched all along the corridor. I stumbled out, weeping, down Byng Place into Malet Street. The traffic could stop, or not, as it cared. Horns blared, tyres screeched, cars collided around me, all the way home. I spent two days asleep. Mrs Duckworth could not coax me to eat or speak for a week.

I've never felt so lonesome.

It's not your fault. It is not the fault of people. The scorpion stings; the piranha bites. They know no better. It's the way they're fashioned. Few of us choose to kill, but sometimes we care to be cruel.

I didn't know what I should do in life. But I believed it must involve impersonation; that to defend myself I'd have to gain a human faàde.

You must understand that I simply don't have your facility. You sneer, smirk, loathe, envy, spit, snort, swagger, snuffle without effort. It's the way your bodies are built. It's already reflex to you. But I've had to strain to gain your easy manners; to mimic your accomplishments.

Alone with Mother in Cloudesley Road, I began the long

haul of my education. I apprenticed myself to your image. I was determined to act the impressionist, to appear human, if not humane.

Two years I took — and did nothing but observe you. I read novels, poetry, psychology, anthropology and philosophy. I heard you on the radio, watched you on television and in the cinema. Every day I'd read the *Daily Mirror* and *The Times* from cover to cover, to learn of your doings. Not a day went by without my being bemused by news of some further human quirk or foible. You seemed infinitely ingenious and perverse — publishing Braille editions of *Playboy* and *Mein Kampf*, biting ferrets, clouting each other over the head with artificial limbs, fornicating on unicycles, shoplifting by secreting groceries in intimate recesses, making egg-timers from a loved-one's ashes, competing to swallow a record number of razor blades, manufacturing decaffeinated coffee and artificial grass, suing the Baptist Church for Acts of God.

At dusk, I'd bolt from the house and wander the streets of Islington, hugging the walls, slinking through the dark. I was a shadow slouched in your gloom. I feared your stares and smirks.

'Stop that ape!' I imagined the cry of the policeman, the clatter of his boots on the paving and arresting screech of his whistle.

I'd wait outside public houses at closing time till a likely drunk emerged. Then I'd slouch behind him as he weaved a raucous route home. It was thus I learned to act inebriate. Sometimes, I'd copy him from twenty paces behind, to perfect the art. And when he turned to regard me, I'd turn too, as if watching a third party further along.

'Are you taking the piss?' he'd shriek.

'Are you taking the piss?' I'd echo, shaking my fist at a street lamp.

'Come here, ya fucker,' he'd call. Then so would I.

Drunkenness was one of the easier human aptitudes to copy, being a grotesque exaggeration of the everyday. Mostly, it's a matter of being intoxicated in charge of a penis; operating an ego without due care and attention; wielding opinions with intent to cause harm. Or bragging without licence or insurance. And vomiting has always come easily to me.

On Saturday afternoons, I'd slouch through the crush in Chapel Street or Exmouth market, the collar of Dr Duckworth's mackintosh turned up around my ears to shade my face, to learn how to be offensive, argue and shout abuse. Despite the many overtures, I wouldn't be lured into the frank exchanges, but listened assiduously to detect the rules to this game of derision. I soon worked it out. I've always had a quick eye for people's flaws and foibles. As I wandered the streets, I'd try to devise an insult tailored to each person as they passed.

In the Odeon or Rex on a Friday evening I learned the courtship rituals of adolescence, taking care not to seem to stare at the grappling couples. I observed how to unbutton a blouse, unhook a bra, the polite way to insinuate a finger around a gusset and wiggle it inside a vagina, how to trap a girl's thighs apart with a strategic leg, and coax her hand to your lap.

I kept a keen eye to the fine grain of everyday skills – practising my smoking, swaggering, snuffling, spitting, swearing and sniggering till they shone with the patina of perfection.

My mother remarked on my social polish.

'You sound like a spiv, Charlie.'

'Thanks, Ma,' I'd say; 'you live and learn, if you duck and dive. Are you going to stir your butt and make another pot of tea?'

But there was a deal of human foibles I couldn't comprehend. I thought that psychology textbooks might lift the skull, to uncover the wrinkles of the human mind. For they had promisingly portentous titles, like *Man and Motivation* or *Emotion*, or *Human Personality*. But when I flicked their turgid pages I found more accounts of mice in mazes than people in perplexity. It wasn't till I chanced upon Freud that I sniffed the stuff I sought. He confirmed my very worst suspicions about the state of human affairs. Then he exceeded my fears.

You're probably familiar with Siggie's slanders. You deny his painful truths. He predicted as much.

Your mind is torn between lust, destructiveness, morality and connivance. Consciousness is but the tip of the mental iceberg. There's a mad, bad, blind backseat driver, wrestling for control of your steering. You are profoundly sick. It is normal to be sick. Lasting contentment is not to be had. Happiness is a mirage. You don't know what it is you want. And, anyway, if you did know you couldn't have it. Yours are vile desires. So you quite disgust yourself. You are a species of irrational liar. You pass your life in a state of high anxiety.

Well, I take it with a spoonful of salt myself. Only it let in a chink of light through the curtain of confusion, and showed me your shadow.

Take forgetting, for example. I'd always thought you were lying when you said you couldn't remember — owing money, getting drunk, or acting stupid. Now I see it's true. You're always rewriting your past, deleting the inconvenient, like a patriotic historian shredding the discrediting documents.

And there's the way you pick on the dog, when your argument's with gravity or God. And that habit of always finding your own faults in others. Like calling pigs greedy because you eat bacon and pork. Or calling animals savage because you shoot them. Or clutching any splinter of rhetoric that you think can show you're in the right.

First I'd practise on Mother. If she was convinced — by my belching, or the way I slurped my tea — I'd test my new skill outside home.

'Why have you started spitting?' Mother demanded.

Of course, I didn't know *precisely* why and when to spit or swear. My performance was showy but shallow. I lacked inner conviction. Until I gained the proper motivation, I'd remain a hollow man.

I studied Stanislavski's books on acting. To play a part, the great man argued, you have to live and breathe it. It takes a deal of feeling and commitment.

So I took a candid yellow eye to myself. I didn't spare my feelings. I numbered and named my flaws and inadequacies. Three big ones, I thought: anger, envy, and pride. I'd mastered sloth, covetousness and gluttony already. Lust, I reckoned, would come with time.

Of course, I was discouraged. It seemed a lot to lack, a deal to learn. Knowing is one thing; doing's another.

I engaged my quizzical orange face in the mirror. 'You must be proud of yourself,' I stammered. My eyes seemed unconvinced by my words.

'Why?' I asked, but couldn't answer.

'You're clever,' I advised myself.

'Only in comparison to people,' I realised.

'Doesn't it make you angry? The way people sneer at you?'

'Well . . .' I thought, 'I can see their point of view.'

'Eureka!' I told myself.

'Exactly,' I agreed.

I'd been going about things in a contrary fashion. Instead of learning I had to forget. Rather than doing, I had to inhibit.

My sympathy needed snuffing.

Psychologists, I'd read, had a trick for getting people to forget. They'd make them count backwards by threes.

'97, 94, 91, 88, 85 . . .' After twenty seconds of that, you quite forget what you were thinking before.

'Take your feet off the table, Charlie,' said Mother.

I could see her point of view, so I distracted myself by counting.

'Take them off, I said!' she shouted.

Yes, indeed. She raised her voice to me.

'What's the matter with you?' I asked, '. . . 22, 19, 16. . . .'

I swear she slapped my ear.

And I'd cracked it. 'You stupid, cow.' I said, 'Slag, Slut. . . .'

For I felt within me a still small flame. It was orange, hot and acrid. It flared upwards from my belly to my chest. The muscles of my neck tightened. My teeth clenched. A misty gauze clouded my sight. Through it I saw the face of Mother, rendered vile and squalid. Hideously wrinkled, leering, vicious. The cow, the hag.

Then the veil fell, and my body relaxed. I'd come. I'd done it. The first time is always special. You never forget it.

'Oh, oh. Aah. . .' I sighed. 'I was angry, Mother.'

'It's nothing to be proud of,' she said.

'Yes, it is,' I protested. 'It's taken me long enough to learn.'

When you've had it once, you want it again. And you know how to coax and nurse it. Make it grow. You feel the power possess you. You think you can fly. It's as though nothing and no one can stop you. The fever has you.

For a while, I couldn't get enough. I'd take myself to my room and play with myself. Sometimes I'd do it six or seven times a day — angrify myself — just for the sensual thrill of it; the sheer naughty novelty. I learned all sorts of ways of doing it, and keeping it up for longer. If I stopped myself just before I got there, I'd come on even stronger after. When I did it really well, I could punch dents in the plaster wall or splinter furniture.

Of course, I kept it a secret from Mother. I knew she found it disgusting.

It's all very well, doing it for yourself, at first. But after a time you want to do it with another person. To prove yourself, to know you can act the man.

I took myself to the streets, to pick up a likely partner. But now I'd found my pride, and would look people in the eye, they often averted their gaze. Although I was thin I was taller than most. Small people backed away. The runts.

'Why don't you go home?' a young man asked me. He scowled as he loitered pinkly. 'Back up a fucking tree. Where you come from?' He was shorter than me, but he'd have to do. It was the only invitation I'd had all day. I hoped I wouldn't hurt him. He had a crew cut and wore a government-surplus parka. His face puffed out in a smirk. He gave me a yellow-toothed smile, gouging a finger in his right nostril, as if something compelling had got up his nose. Perhaps I'd read him amiss, and he was only trying to be friendly.

'Say again,' I asked. For I hadn't been counting.

'Fuck off!' he explained. 'Coon,' he observed. 'Cunt.'

'Perhaps you'd care to rephrase that,' I advised, 'because, frankly, it doesn't sound friendly. You're demeaning yourself.... And you're insulting me, black people and women.'

I thought I should warn him. I could feel the warmth of my anger, like hot soup in my belly. It was all quite thrilling. 'I think you're trying to ridicule me. I'm not without pride,' I bragged.

'Piss off, Paki.'

I was inspired. I knew just what to do. I spat on his suede boot. The left one. It came quite naturally. The occasion seemed to demand it.

My recollection is misty. Though I do remember a deceptively amiable nodding motion as he jerked his forehead onto mine. From later examination of the variegated − black and purple − bruises to my ribs, chest and testicles, I concluded that, after nutting me, he'd kicked me as I lay stunned on the ground. This was also the custom at Stoneham School. English society is divided by class, but certain manners are held in common.

Mother sobbed at the sight of me; my bruised face and stumbling gait.

'What happened?' she wailed.

'I got angry,' I muttered, 'but not angry enough.'

'See where your temper gets you,' she wailed.

'Don't worry,' I said. 'It's only human.'

'Who did it?'

'A fellow in Milner Square,' I said. 'I can see his point of view. He didn't like my colour.'

I try to learn by my mistakes. It was to be a long time before I sought another fight. People are better at anger than I am. I must respect my limitations. I try to turn them into virtues.

But what I lacked − and needed to gain − was a sense of direction. For my anger. I needed an enemy; to sustain and focus my hatred. A mantra to summon up furies, to get me in the mood.

There were so many enemies on offer, so many tried and tested brands − blacks and whites, capitalists and bourgeois, class traitors, the proletariat, hippies and straights, Muslims and infidels. Christians and heathens, Jews and goyim, men and women, exploiters and exploited, Zika Zika and assassins, human and inhuman.

I selected sensibly.

Gradually, I learned not to see the other's point of view. Invariably, it was Mother's. She often began sentences with 'Should . . .' or 'Would. . .'. When she wasn't musting me, she was oughting something awful. Slowly but surely, I learned to find offence.

We both became sulky.

'What's happened to you Charlie? You used to be such a nice boy.'

'I don't know what you're babbling about,' I'd explain. 'Why don't you shut your face?' I'd advise. Then, I'd rush out, before her tears could flow to affect me.

Adolescence is a difficult time. Neither parent nor child seems to understand the other. It's part of growing up; or growing old. I'd read about this in psychology books and learned to act it out in the conventional human fashion.

'Aren't you going to carry my shopping?' Mother would wail.

'Why should I?' I'd ask, spiky with reason. I'd heard this rhetorical device on television. It seemed to serve most occasions. It's a fine ploy of infinite versatility. The other party is briefly silenced by outrage. So you've got time to prepare a proper disregard for their feelings. Then I'd get distracted by something — so I couldn't hear her talk of her age or arthritis. It helps if you hum to yourself, I find.

I was making fast progress in gaining humanity. All I lacked now was conviction.

I had this theory, you see. If I could perfect my pose as a person, I'd earn your indifference. And so secure my skin.

Ten

People have occasionally had cause to ask me: 'Why do you
hate Brazilians?'

'Don't talk to me of Brazilians!' I say. 'The bastards.'

They aren't questioning my hatred — which they consider an
admirable sentiment — but its target. They think I'm frittering
away the gold of rage on an undeserving cause. For we live in
an age that reveres anger.

'We're angry,' they pronounce with pride, 'so our cause must
be just.' It's a confidence they share with wasps and rabid dogs.

Anger is seen as the hall-mark of sincerity. And amiability is
facetious, a kind of moral feeble-mindedness.

In truth, we need an enemy. It's part and parcel of being
human. It wasn't an effort to find mine. They'd extinguished
the small flickering flame of my species; just to plant some
rubber trees.

I've never met any Brazilians. I know nothing about them,
except that they're a nation of assassins with a fabulous flair for
football. It'd be unfortunate to find a foe that you met on a daily
basis. There'd be so much bickering. Someone might throw a
punch. So, I'll stick with Brazilians, thank you very much.

Just don't defend the bastards to me. When I feel the need to
get angry, or redirect some venom, I tend to think of Brazilians.
They make me most indignant. And they never answer back.
You should try them for yourself.

I worry about your short blunt-sightedness. So many people seem
purblind. It wouldn't be wide of the mark to call you a bigot.

I knew of a child who thought that no one could see him when he closed his eyes. He hid by placing a pillow over his eyes. You too confuse the world and your sight. You think things are quite as you see them. The world disappears when you sleep.

Your headlights are dim and misaligned. They cast a gloomy light on the winding verge, and you mistake this dull beam for truth. You believe it's showing the way. But it's following you ahead, shifted by the twitch of your fingers.

It must be a curious prospect to behold, from the blinking human perspective, craning your neck, wobbling between five and six feet from the ground, squinting out through the two peepholes of myopic saucer eyes. You see the panorama of your tunnel vision: all the way to the blurred horizon.

It's perception of sorts. But an owl would starve with your acuity. For it requires a sight more vision to arrest a mouse.

You'll have noticed that you see the other person's point of view more often than they see yours. It's because you're a specially sensitive and sympathetic person. And you have a better sense of humour than most. Yet some things just aren't funny. Though people make jokes about these things, and laugh at them. Sometimes you complain about this. But they don't understand. Because they're insensitive.

You're more honest than most. People remark on it. Whenever possible, you avoid lying, preferring to speak a partial truth — so maintaining your integrity. But often you have to deal with deceitful people. If they make your bed, you must lie in it.

There are a lot of fools about. Have you noticed? Other people make mistakes because they're clumsy or stupid. But when you trip up the floor's at fault.

To celebrate my twentieth birthday, I took myself to the zoo at Regent's Park to see some distant relatives who'd been banged-up behind bars. I swear they were as innocent as you — but that's another story.

The pandas seemed poignant. Often, it's the endangered species that are the most reluctant to breed.

In the monkey house I watched my cousins, and pondered the conundrum of carnal desire.

You've got plenty of your own kind — in a variety of sizes and colours, in both of the popular sexes. You've no business flirting with monkeys. It'd likely strike you as distasteful to have a sexual liaison with an orang-utan or lemur.

Nor did I feel the merest murmur of desire at seeing those baboons, chimps or gorillas, stark naked though they were. Their copious body hair rendered them repugnant to the fastidious eye of my desire: their gargoyle faces repelled me. To my mind, the swollen purple buttocks of a baboon are more grotesque than provocative. But each to their own. The gibbons have elegance, wit and charm. They make fine, if fickle, friends, but I could never fancy one as a lover.

Yet bestiality was my only option. There were none of my kind to be had. The Brazilians had weeded them from their garden, to clear the ground for some rubber trees, because they wanted some latex.

A lady chimpanzee eyed me with anxious contempt. She split her thin lips and chattered, scratching at a furry thigh. I turned to look at the other spectators on my side of the bars.

I watched a chattering huddle of schoolgirls, all in their grey skirts and purple blazers — twenty-one variations on a pretty theme. My gaze skittered between their giggling faces, up and down their lithe lengths. There seemed something indefinably attractive about some. Perhaps it was the delicacy of their hairless faces, the refined restraint of their gestures, the sheen of their smooth stockinged legs, the curvatures of calf and shin, the swerves of hips, the hillocky chests, the twitching fine fingers, pursed lips, fluttering lashes.

Yes, indeed, I realised then, confronting the full choice of the monkey house, women were prettier than any other apes.

Perverse and bestial as it was, I'd take my chances with women.

Two girls, having turned their backs on the chimpanzees, were now examining me. They tittered. I winced my smile. They heaved, convulsed by laughter.

'Please, Miss,' says one, pointing me out to her teacher, 'What's that? Has it escaped, Miss?'

I developed irrational yearnings for the girl who served at the sweet counter in Woolworth's. My sweetheart; Mary McIlvaney, who marshalled her marshmallows and macaroons as she eyed me with disdain.

We had height and a stoop in common. She was the Venus of the store with her yellow translucent skin, sunken-cheeked stare, tangled raven hair, narrow hips, slender-legged slouch. The surreptitious swerves to the stripy pattern of her uniformed chest discreetly whispered her gender. She was woman; all woman. Often she'd discern my gaze as I loitered behind the toiletries to relish the long question mark of her bowed profile. Then, she turned her back on me, straight and fine as an exclamation!

She had one imperfection, I'd noticed — a brace to her buckled teeth. It looked as though a dentist had repaired her smile with paper clips. This only enhanced her beauty, stirring my empathy. For I was flawed too. It was a further facet we held in common.

Within six days of first seeing her, we were on conversational terms. Only a moat of confectionery kept me from her sweetness.

'A quarter of pear drops, please,' I said. Nothing ventured, nothing gained. Faint heart never won fair lady.

'Red or yellow?' said she.

'Red.' The hue of passion. 'And yellow.' The tint of her fair skin. Pear drops the shape of tears, or topsy-turvy hearts.

She fingered each last one as she shovelled them into the bag. Then she licked glistening grains of sugar from the tip of her little finger.

'Anything else?' she asked, averting her eyes.

Yes! That was the nub of it.

I coughed. 'You . . .' I said, 'I'd like you. . . .'

'What?'

'To give me some delight.'

'Turkish?' she asks. I nod, too tongue-tied to tell the tortured truth.

That night I waited outside Sainsbury's to follow her home. Down Upper Street, she twice glared over her shoulder, to tell me she'd seen me. But at the corner of Theberton Street she paused to chat.

'Sod off . . . boggle-eyes,' she said. I wasn't abashed or discouraged. Courtship often starts through teasing.

'Oh,' I sighed, 'you're beautiful.'

'You ain't,' she joked. I smiled. It was a transparent deceit, since we looked so alike.

'I do love you,' I confided. My hands were wrestling each other. Shyness made me shivery.

'Piss off,' she quipped, quick-witted. 'I don't want to be seen with the likes of you.' It was an elegant irony, given our similarities. 'People might think we're together.'

'So?' I asked.

'Look at yourself!'

Well, my eyes being central to my face, I couldn't see my head. But I looked down the length of body from chest to feet. It was a vertiginous perspective — down the canary yellow woolly jumper Mother had knitted me, which stretched to my knees, along my cavalry twill trousers to the six inches of naked shin, leading to Dr Duckworth's paisley socks and split brogue shoes.

My clothes, I thought. Perhaps she doesn't like my clothes. But when I looked up to ask she was boarding a number nineteen bus.

I needed to look more stylish, I reckoned. I'd guessed as much from television. It was another paradox of human courtship. It helps to be fashionably clothed if you hope to undress with a stranger.

Now puberty was completing my design, I needed to look presentable. I'd spurted, gaining two inches in height and twenty pounds in weight. I stood far taller than most men, and thinner. My limbs exceeded their clothing, so my wrists and ankles were much to view, counter to fashion.

Tiny prickles of hair had sprouted around a private part with the furtive stealth of seedlings. My pubis had gained the stubbly look of an unshaven chin. To this day, it's the only natural hair I wear, except for the thin cover of down on my scalp.

I began to conjure depraved and unnatural thoughts of women.

I imagined them naked. In my reverie, I touched them. And I believed they guessed as much, for they'd snigger or scowl when I stared at them. However eagerly I beamed my availability, none accepted the tacit proposition. This was a chasm I had to bridge — the yawning divide between desire and attainment, theory and practice.

I dogged Mary McIlvaney again, to voice my ardour.

'Do you like my denims?' I asked, 'And Chelsea boots? Aren't they fab?'

'Better,' she conceded. 'They make you look more human.' She leaked a tight reluctant smile.

'And my jacket?' I asked.

'S'good.'

'Well, look. . . .' I summoned the courage to ask her. 'Why don't we have sex together? I'm free most evenings.'

Her face took a tour from bewilderment to loathing, via ridicule and contempt. 'Fuck . . .' she explained, 'off. Freak.'

And I was to follow her injunction; for the bus queue began to take an interest in our conversation, gathering around us, a curious crowd.

Later I recognised my mistake. Mine was the crime of candour. I'd unzipped my purpose. It was dangling out for all to see. You live and learn.

I had other distant, unspoken passions: for Betsy Lewis, whose limp reminded me of Bruno Fartzmann: for Anne Bagshot, whose hare-lip only amplified the radiance of her smile: for Pauline Smith who walked everywhere alongside a black labrador called Jet, on account of being blind.

Like likes like, like as not, you'll have noticed. There's a narcissism in mating. So often you see the same weasel face, toadish build, Rottweiler self-confidence in both halves of a couple. It had been evident in the Duckworths. Discount his baldness and her blue rinse and you saw two versions of the same wrinkled gnomic face. Waking bleary eyed in bed, they must have wondered who was which, and whose turn it was to make the tea.

Reason says we should complement one another. Then the actor could marry an audience, the scientist could woo the experiment, the gambler could court an uncertainty, Father Christmas could shack up with the greedy child. But too often self-love has its way. Attraction tells us to duplicate, and seek another version of our deficient selves.

For my part, I was drawn to tall, slender women, with sallow skins, and deformed or missing parts. But such beauties proved rare, precious, and prickly as roses.

In my sentimental reveries, I thought a blind woman might suit me best. She wouldn't take offence at my appearance. We'd be sympathetic and kind, share a dark vision, and take delight in the guide dog. We'd see each other's point of view. But Pauline Smith resented my several offers to lead her across Rosebery Avenue. She'd just frown, her glassy recessed eyes swivelling, saying she didn't want the other side. Jet knew the way, she'd mutter. And the dog was trained to ignore me, and disdained the chocolate I proffered.

'Shouldn't you do something, Charlie?' Mother folded the newspaper with a loud intentioned rustle. She briskly patted her dimpled knees, announcing her irritation, and peered over the tortoiseshell frames of her reading spectacles. She was always trying to make me do things. Often she made withering comments, contrasting my age and attainments, implying I might take a job or enrol for some course of study. I'd learned to recognise and fear this mood of hers. She'd invariably sew some hurtful observations into conditional sentences.

'If you don't ...' she'd say, 'I shan't. ...'

I'd give her the benefit of the doubt, by ignoring the subordinate clauses — which were always packed with imperatives, threats, absolutes, nows and this minutes.

I knew I'd be lost, tossed in the blanket of life, lashed to the rafters of culture, if I ever conceded to her views.

'Well?' she'd enquire. 'What are you going to do?' she'd ask, demanding some prompt response.

'I'm reading,' I explained, 'about the psychology of adolescence. I'm learning about identity confusion.'

'Do in life,' said Mother. 'Shouldn't you do something in life?' She folded her arms, which invariably spoke a warning or told of disapproval.

'It says here that adolescents are often confused, lethargic and lacking in purpose. They need a *moratorium*, a period of indecision, before they select a path in life.'

'You're twenty years old, Charlie.'

'Doesn't time fly?' I observed. 'When you're busy.'

'You should be making your way in the world.'

'I'm a late developer,' I protested. 'To be frank, Mother, I'm still reeling from the trauma of puberty. And it says here. Look. . . .' I passed her the book, pressing a finger to the crucial passage. 'Some people don't get a clear sense of purpose in life until they're in their thirties or forties. It's dangerous to force or rush life's choices. Early commitments can be catastrophic. That's what Coleman says.'

'So what are *you* going to do?'

'I thought I'd read. And listen to the radio. Watch some television. See some films and buy some new clothes.'

'How long will that take, Charlie?' She mouthed my name as if it were some shameful infection. She'd narrowed her eyes unpleasantly, giving me a harsh critical scrutiny – as though I were some eyesore.

'Two or three years at most,' I bargained. 'Until I find a purpose.'

'No,' Mother said. There was a curious tone of finality that I'd never heard harshen her voice before.

'No?'

'No,' she announced. 'It's work or college for you.'

'That's not a very nice thing to say.' I thought my wail might soften her. 'It's not a very pleasant choice.'

'Tough,' she said.

'When you say *work*, do you mean *employment*?'

She simply nodded, indifferent to the enormity.

'And by *college* . . .?'

'I mean college. Studying for exams.'

'But that's work too!' I whined. She'd been trying to sucker me with a bogus choice.

'Yes,' she agreed, but wouldn't yield to the pleadings of my mobile face.

'Supposing . . .' I proposed, 'just for rhetorical purposes, I decided not to do either.'

'Rhetorically speaking,' she smiled, but it was a cold unforgiving smile, 'I wouldn't give you any food or pocket money. Things have got to change around here.'

'You could give me grated carrots, at least. And a handful of raisins,' I suggested. 'They're cheap and easy to prepare.'

'Nothing at all.'

'That's intimidation, Mother!' I wanted her to be clear about the ethics of it all. 'It's a threat. Against your own son. It's abusing power to get your own way.'

'Exactly,' she confirmed. 'It's blackmail.'

'It's immoral.'

'Yes,' she agreed. 'I think it will work. Now go and clean yourself up. We're going to have a visitor.'

'A visitor?'

But we didn't have any visitors, except those men who called to read the gas or electricity meters and stayed for a cup of tea and slice of cake, and made pleasantries about Pakistanis, and predictions about the weather.

'A friend,' said Mother, smugly, brushing fluff from the front of her cardigan. 'I met him playing bridge. He's my new partner.'

Bridge. Partner. Dangerous connections. All manner of things could scamper across, and invade our quiet regime.

Dr Cadogan was to enter our lives, his aquiline nose the fine edge of a wedge to divide us. He would disturb Mother's equilibrium and mine. He'd tinker with our emotions.

When a fellow's own mother turns on her only son, naturally he's upset. If she acts the domestic tyrant and denies him even bread and water, of course he feels hurt. He's done his very best to help her, yet she slaps him in the face.

I counted backwards by threes. I blew the bellows of grievance on my small ember of anger. I howled at her that she was acting like a Brazilian, but at this she only snickered.

I'd made every possible allowance, exhausted every avenue,

stretched the elastic of reason, tortured my understanding, in denying and opposing her point of view. Now I would have to face it. Even a person would understand. My childhood was over. I'd have to leave the nest. It was time to face my fears and confront people once again. So I applied myself to my future.

'I've been a parasite, Mother,' I said. 'A tape-worm. It's a wonder you've put up with me so long.'

'You're not that bad, Charlie.'

'Can I stay until I go to university?'

'University?'

'Kniggle,' I said. 'Psychology. They took me without an interview.'

'That's wonderful.'

'It is,' I agree. 'If they'd seen me, they wouldn't have had me. Now I can learn all about people ... And, Mother, I hope you'll be very happy. When you marry Dr Cadogan.'

'Who says we're getting married?' She flushed. One hand fingering her new pearl necklace, the other smoothing her pristine blouse.

'I do.'

'Would you mind?'

'I'd like it,' I said, stalking for an apt sentiment. 'I'm not so much losing a mother as gaining a pathologist.'

I kept out of the way when Dr James Cadogan called in the evenings. I wasn't bothered by the way he kicked off his shoes to slither into his slippers, his claim to my armchair, or his familiarity in calling me 'son' and Mother 'Mary', or his habit of changing the television channel without asking, or even his revelations about the natural history of corpses. What most alarmed me was his curiosity about me. He'd give me stealthy sidelong glances as though he'd chanced upon an interesting specimen. I believed he'd ask to lay his cold callipers on my cranium, or examine the recesses of my mouth, or tap the joints of my fingers, if I gave him the least encouragement. I believed he'd like to see me dead – not from malice, but so that he could then examine me thoroughly.

'Have you always been that colour?' he asked one evening at the supper table.

'It's my skin,' I explained. 'I eat too many carrots. The carotene builds up in my skin.'

'Perhaps you should see a doctor. Just to check your liver....'

'It must be very interesting,' I observed, aiming to distract him, 'working with dead people. You must meet all sorts every day.'

Home had become a dangerous place to stay. I ran a high risk of discovery. I'd invested too much in passing as a person to care to be defrocked.

Eleven

There were no prefects at my university. The teachers were known as lecturers; but this was an honorary title which didn't commit them to talk. They weren't allowed to beat students, or place them in detention. Indeed, there was no discernible discipline at all. It was a change from home – where I'd been made to rise before mid-day, then make my bed, and wash-up after meals; or Stoneham School – where Christianity, games, sadism and desperation were all daily compulsions.

Everything was optional: even choice itself. We were no more required to attend lectures than to take drugs. Both were left as matters of personal discretion. We could study or get drunk, or do both together, or neither, quite as we chose. If a lecturer wouldn't take 'no' for an answer, and persisted in demanding that a busy student write an essay, then a model answer could be purchased for two shillings and sixpence from the students' union.

Days passed. Nobody called to wash my dirty clothes or feed me. It dawned on me that the University of Kniggle cared not a jot for my comforts. Yet self-reliance was a small price to pay for the greater freedoms.

From the start, I fell behind with the work. Perhaps it was a practical joke, but at enrolment I'd been given the wrong time-table. So I followed the second year philosophy course for the first month of term.

When I eventually tracked down my personal tutor, he was drawing attention to himself, hammering on the side of the cigarette machine in the coffee bar trying to coax an outcome. I mentioned to him that I'd been dallying with philosophy. He wasn't surprised. People and time can easily get mislaid or confused at university, he said. He led me into the strobe-lit fug of the student bar. I bought him a succession of drinks as he told tales about his colleagues. The University of Kniggle had appointed a gardener as professor of physics, then sensibly rejected a physicist for the post of gardener — all through a mix-up of letters in the personnel office. My tutor also told me — with some lack of loyalty, I thought — that a Principal Lecturer in the Theology Department claimed a full-time salary from Upsala University, but actually spent his time running a turkey farm in Suffolk.

'So what are the rules at university?' I asked. 'Nobody's told me yet.'

He crinkled his forehead and scrutinised the scummy surface of his beer, in the blinking light. 'Enjoy yourself. Don't take your lecturers too seriously. Avoid the Vice-Chancellor. Never eat the meat pies in the cafeteria. Screw around. And always give the impression you know what you're talking about. Otherwise, it's up to you.'

'Nothing else?' I suspected him of teasing. I believed he was withholding crucial truths.

'It's enigmatic,' my tutor told me. 'It's all an endless game of concealment, revelation, discovery, false-revelation. Shall we have another pint?'

'What do you mean?' I asked.

'Lager,' he said. So I got him another.

'You think I'm your tutor,' he explained, 'because I said so. Life's like that. We claim identities, make promissory gestures, act out roles. By and large, we have to take each other on trust.'

'For instance?'

'Stand up,' he demanded, so I obeyed him.

'There!' he said. 'You do as I ask. You take me on trust as a reasonable person, who'll only make reasonable requests. Can you lend me five pounds until Thursday?'

'Are you a reasonable person?' I asked, handing over the money.

'Not when it comes to finance,' he conceded, stowing the

note in his back pocket. 'So don't lend me money again. You probably can't afford it.'

'Are you my personal tutor?'

'Yes,' he promised.

As it turned out, he was. Paul Walster, Social Psychologist, author of *Enigma and Identity*, libertine, junkie, absentee, joker. He was a good scholar and a bad man. I couldn't have found a better teacher.

My room was a cell, ten feet by nine, on the fourth floor of a grey and gold hall of residence of neo-Aztec design. The bed was nine inches shorter than my person, the ceiling three inches higher. I had wash-basin, cupboard, book-shelves, desk and waste-paper bin as standard issue. It was the custom to mask the white walls with posters of Mao, Che Guevara or Jimmy Hendrix; and to play the lamentations of Leonard Cohen on a box gramophone. But I painted the walls black and tacked a blanket to the window in lieu of curtains. An electric kettle was essential, to make the coffee that was offered as a pretext, to coax the company of women students, who had heard the offer before and invariably declined. This coffee was drunk alone and black. For the milk curdled in its carton beneath the radiator, then incubated a blue-green mould, reminding me to replace it. My neighbours — above, below, beside, behind — engaged in loud carnal congress from midnight until four in the morning, before commencing a second shift between ten and mid-day, in rhythm to the Rolling Stones or Pink Floyd, the insistent bass of which they overlaid with squeals and grunts. I often sensed I was missing out.

My door was always open. Being less attractive than other men, I planned to compensate by making myself more available. Any girl who made the sincere effort to search me out would find me in, I vowed. Two coffee mugs always stood ever-ready, pre-powdered, as I sat on my bed, hunched over my book, dressed to impress, chicly dishevelled, in the dark, awaiting the knock of the nymph, who would call for sex. If only I were patient. And kept faith in human lewdness.

I often spoke to my fellow students, before and after lectures. Several times I'd start a conversation only to find the other person had passed on, taking advantage of the punctuating pauses of my blushing stammer.

'Is this ... chair taken?' I'd ask. 'Or 'Can I ... sit here?'

'Saving it for Sarah, man,' they'd say, or 'I'd rather you didn't,' or 'Sure, I'm moving anyway.'

Often, I felt a superfluous thing. But the contact meant I never passed a weekday entirely alone.

Whenever there was a day of action or strike, sit-in or stay-out, about American Imperialism, or Fascism in the Faculty, or in Solidarity with the Oppressed, or for Comrades Against Exams, or to Legalise Cannabis Now, I'd lurk thereabouts, on the edge of the throng. Whenever there was a storm in a tea-cup, I perched myself on the rim. I enjoyed the agitation, but didn't stir myself. There was always a deal of talk of the working class, revolution, bourgeois individualism, orgone therapy, and repressive tolerance — and the exquisite fragrances of musk and patchouli from the women who pushed past me. Sometimes their fingers touched me; or I felt the warm brush of an arm. Or I'd get asked for a cigarette.

I joined an Encounter Group, to meet new people. We said non-verbal hellos with our feet, smiled and were honest. Only it could turn nasty. Once, we were told to wander round the room, accost a stranger and tell them the four things we most disliked about them. I told the girl that I didn't like her earrings or the way she scowled at me; but otherwise, I said, she looked perfect.

'One,' she replied briskly, 'you're a bourgeois reactionary. Two, you're an ugly creep. Three, your kind are responsible for the war in Vietnam. Four, you've got a murky aura. And there are snakes coming out of your ears.'

When I got back to my room, I gazed a long time in the mirror, then wept. I couldn't see how she divined so much in my face, glimpsing such discredit. I decided she'd confused me with President Nixon. I believe she'd been taking acid.

Hate was different in those days. It was impersonal. As was love. You loved the idea of love, not individuals. So screwing around was fidelity. Monogamy was meanness. Jealousy was illness. You hated the sin not the sinner. Everybody could be redeemed, if they only made the effort, and wore a tie-dye T-shirt. You only had to renounce bourgeois conventions and reactionary ideals, promise not to bomb Vietnam, and dress cool. Salvation was cheap and easy. The economy was booming. Capitalism was in crisis. The revolution was days away. Consciousness was changing, and it wasn't just the drugs. They paid you grants to abuse them. You bit the hand that fed you; until it gave you more. Property was theft. Incoherence was clever. Intoxication was lucidity. It was sane to be mad, mad to be sane. Mao and the I Ching had it right, man. Fascism was just bad orgasms. It was a fine time to be young at university. Only, still I was missing out — sitting alone in my room in the dark.

Everything comes to him who waits. One night a woman crashed through my door, and sprawled at my feet.

'I'm drunk, John,' she moaned.

'Hi,' I said. 'I'm Charlie. I'm sober.'

'Shit! I'm in the wrong room again.'

'It depends on your point of view,' I explained. 'I've been waiting for you for five months.'

'Wow ...' she considered this, her eyes swerving in her swaying head. 'Sorry I'm so late, man.'

'Better late than never,' I sighed. 'Would you like a coffee? Or would you prefer to have sex?'

She said she'd rather vomit. Good as her word, she crawled across my floor and hunched, heaving and shuddering, over my wash-basin. Juices gushed from her mouth and gurgled down the drain.

When she slumped with a sudden thud, her limbs flung limp like a rag-doll's, I lifted her up and laid her upon my bed. She was strangely flimsy in my hands. I pulled the blankets over her and drew a chair alongside, to watch a woman sleep.

Her black hair coiled in glistening tendrils across my pillow. Her oval face showed its shapes in shadows; the shallow hollows of her cheeks, the black split of pouting lips, the oyster grey curves of eyelid edged by inky lashes, the straight charcoal line of nose to its fine-etched tip, flared soot nostrils.

She whimpered, drew a finger to her mouth and sucked. She

twitched and shivered, twisting on her side, her hip arching up beneath the blanket, pulling cover from her naked feet. Her toes curled before retracting from view again, into the hidden warmth.

She snuffled, scratched and stammered in her sleep, tossed in the storm of nightmare. Twice she shrieked, indecipherably. Often she tugged the hem of the blanket with clawed fingers, shrugged and jerked, as if fighting for position, against an invisible bedfellow, nudging and pushing for advantages of angle and warmth. She was not alone with herself.

By dawn she'd soothed, and her face gained colour. Her tresses were no longer black, but a lustrous tawny with titian tints. The face a confection of browns, from petit beurre to bourbon. The gold lozenge of nose-tip took the biscuit. Her twitchy lips were smooth and shiny as the icing on chocolate éclairs.

Alas, I saw no flaw. I wondered if I could love her.

Her eyes flickered open, then widened as she took me in.

'Where?' She whimpered. 'When?'

'Here,' I said, 'now.' Wherever, whenever we travel, it's always the same. We can't get away from that time, place or ourselves.

'How . . .?'

'Drunk,' I said. 'Crawled in.'

'Yep.' She agreed, shaking her head, wincing. She raised the blankets and observed she was still clothed. 'We didn't then?'

'No.'

'Good,' she said. 'I don't know you, do I?'

'No. I'm Charlie. This is room 427.'

I made her a strong black coffee. She sniffed noisily between sips. I gave her due warning; that I probably couldn't love her. Because she seemed perfect. I needed someone flawed, I explained, to feel infatuation. She told me that she didn't mind. We'd be friends instead, she said. 'My name's Jenny. . . .'

After that she was quite shameless — coming to sit with me in the cafeteria. We'd smile, have conversations, make jokes. She'd introduce me to her other friends, who'd eye me with bemused concern, wondering what I was and quite where I belonged.

'This is Charlie,' she'd say, 'he's my friend.' For she was quite brazen and unrepentant. 'He's into vegetables in a heavy way. Look . . .' she'd giggle, lifting a tomato from a neighbour's salad. 'What's this, Charlie?'

I'd sniff and finger it. 'It's an Ailsa Craig,' I'd announce. 'Note the bright colour and glossy sheen. It's an early maturer. There's a pleasant tartness and a witty after-taste of pumpkin.'

'Magic!' Jenny would gurgle, beaming with triumph, 'You tell 'em, Charlie.'

I'd arrived. I was a social animal with a reliable, regular friend. She was a high-yielding companion, a hybrid of sister and confidante. There was a strong tang of mischief to her. When I told her I wanted to have sex with a woman she wasn't a smidgin shocked. She promised she'd ask around, and see who she could dig up. I told her I'd always wanted to go to a party. She said she'd take me to one.

There are certain contradictions in your beliefs. You are generous: you want to keep what you have, and gain some more. You are talented: you fear that your deficiencies will be exposed. You are kind: you inflict hurt with deliberation. You do your best: often you can't be bothered. You're honest: you connive and lie. You're optimistic: except about the future.

My tutor, Paul Walster, said you're a tissue of lies. A fiction. A game of consequences, scribbles, social graffiti.

He told me a likely story, about a man being introduced to a woman.

'Your Majesty,' said the Ambassador, 'this is Professor Zuckerman, the distinguished psychiatrist.'

Zuckerman smiled at the woman and stroked his moustache: 'Interesting . . .' he mused, turning to the Ambassador. 'The old dear thinks she's a queen, eh?'

'Sir. . . .' the Ambassador protested, his face blanched, 'this is Queen Marie of Romania.'

'Aha,' Zuckerman chuckled. 'A folie à deux, then. You must think you're an diplomat?'

'I am, sir!'

'Well . . .' says Zuckerman, 'if you'll believe that, you'll believe anything. I wasn't born yesterday.'

He was wrong about the queen, as it happens. But he did have a point. We are what we are through social consent. It's all a matter of negotiation. Picasso believed himself a genius. So did Dr Duckworth, and his uncle Arthur. Some can convince us: others cannot. You can't decide what you are. You negotiate. Your identity needs ratifying. It's a matter of social agreement. You may think you're clever, but what matters is whether you can act the part.

A psychopath escaped from an asylum for the criminally insane in Indiana. A few days later he presented himself for interview for the post of Senior Medical Advisor at a State Penitentiary and, having given a good account of himself, was promptly appointed. He must have been competent at the job, because he got caught only when his photograph appeared in the local press. It's all a matter of appearances.

There are a lot of false doctors about. Remember that when next you visit a surgery. Ask to see your doctor's certificates. Don't be fobbed off with a snarl. For medicine's one of those professions that a clever scoundrel can pick up quickly. It's one of those non-technical trades that just requires dexterity, confidence and intuition. I daresay anyone who can fix a washing machine wouldn't be bemused by the internal fittings of the human abdomen. So all manner of do-it-yourself enthusiasts chance their arm at surgery, or lend a hand at gynaecology.

For instance, there was a Dutch labourer called Henry de Vries who, having renamed himself Baron David James Rothschild, was appointed by Queen Juliana of the Netherlands as her psychiatrist. Because she needed her head examining.

Then there was Ferdinand Demara who, christening himself Dr Joseph Cyr, became a Surgeon Lieutenant during the Korean War, pioneering some original techniques in cardiac surgery, winning citations for his patients' pains. After he'd been de-gowned, he worked as a psychologist, sheriff, theology instructor and prison warder. His imagination and initiative always met the challenge, awarding him all the qualifications he needed.

I've made quite a study of imposters, since it became my own profession. Demara cheered me. In comparison with his

110

achievements, it seemed sheer humility for me to claim I was a mere person. Nobody needed to challenge me on that. It was such a humble identity – being human.

But then the psychotherapists set off a craze for it.

'What do you do?' I ask someone at a party.

'Me?' said the other, 'I'm working on being a real *person*.'

'Any luck ... so far?' I'd ask.

'I'm more together. With myself. With Joannie too. I feel more *integrated* and *whole*.'

'It's interesting,' I'd say, emboldened by booze. 'I'm a monkey myself.'

'Yeh? Are we talking Chinese astrology or metaphor, man?'

'I'm talking identity.'

'*Identity*,' the other nods. 'Identity's where it's at. Hey, Joannie. Meet Charlie. He's into Rogers. He's working on his monkeyhood.'

'Really?' says Joannie, not unimpressed, 'Does that take you back before Re-birthing and Primal Scream?'

'It's Nowness. It's Existential. It's Being.'

'Yep?' asks the other, 'Is that expensive, man? Are we talking a residential course?'

There was a lot of psychology to learn for my degree, but little to learn by it. We learned learning, memorised memory, saw to perception, and attended to attention. Yet I rarely felt emotion. Motivation never moved me. Much of it concerned rats, mice or pigeons. Sometimes there were monkeys; reared in darkness; with electrodes stabbed into the privacy of their brain; given electric shocks whilst strapped into a harness. This could be very poignant – hearing how one cousin had tormented another. It was hard not to feel partisan. But we were always encouraged to view events from the human perspective.

This wasn't ever objective. Yet it was deemed properly scientific. Suppose a psychologist chops chunks out of a cat's brain, you'd never suppose *him* the beast. You'd try and see his point of view, and follow his intricate reasons.

Or if a psychologist administers electric shocks to copulating rabbits, or lifts a male rat from a female's back before it can ejaculate, you'd not accuse him of intruding on private business, or acting a prurient prude. No, we'd struggle to grasp his point of view, to reach a scholarly conclusion.

I found it hard to grasp at first. Inadvertently, I got into trouble.

'Holzinger gave a Rhesus Monkey an electric shock every time it ate a banana,' Dr Jobson told our seminar group. 'Why do you suppose he did this?'

'Was he a sadist, a psychopath?' I asked. It seemed a rhetorical question, but I wanted to make a contribution.

'Duckworth,' Dr Jobson declared, his ice-blue eyes unblinking, 'don't be a smart-arse. Not in my seminars.'

'But look at it from the monkey's point of view. . . .' I protested.

'The monkey doesn't have a point of view,' he snapped. There was this prevalent view in psychology that animals didn't have pleasures or feelings. There were only things that happened to them, and things they did in reflex reply — stimuli and responses. I knew better. Though I didn't say so.

I tried again. I tried to think human. I put myself in the psychologist's place. 'Perhaps Holzinger wanted a doctorate,' I suggested, 'and thought he could get on in life by electrocuting monkeys. He probably had a family to feed. Perhaps he was trying to make a contribution. To science.'

'And what do you suppose he discovered?'

I returned to the ape's perspective. It wasn't difficult. 'That the monkey developed an aversion to bananas. . . then to all food. Then it died of starvation.'

'Good.' Dr Jobson gave me a brief conditional smile.

'Good?' I protested. 'It was murder!'

Twelve

I did it, at last, at eight seventeen pm on the 23rd of May, 1970, with a little help from a friend. I remember it well.

It was quite a relief, a weight off my back, renouncing my last innocence, mislaying my virginity — which had so long outstayed its welcome. And I did it with a woman, just as I'd always wanted. It was barely bestial. It didn't feel like an unnatural act at all. I do recommend it — if you enjoy meeting new people, and aren't queasy about human excretions.

'Have you asked anyone, Jenny? If they'll have sex with me?'

'Look. . .' she sighs. 'I'm not a procuress. It's awkward — asking "Anyone want to fuck Charlie?"'

'I suppose so,' I said. 'Only I do still want to try it. I feel I'm missing out.' She could see I was disappointed.

We were sprawled languid on my bed, an ear to the Grateful Dead, sucking a joint in turn, our saliva mingling on the cardboard tip.

I laid my head in the warm tacky vale between her breasts, then poked my nose through a vent in her blouse, laying my snub upon her flesh. For I'd grown to relish the warm savours of her skin. My twitching nostrils snorted her perfumes of fried squid and gruyère. I stroked her thighs. It brought tears to my eyes. She shivered, patting my scalp with a tentative hand.

'Look!' she said. 'Maybe I can help . . . I could show you how it's done. Just to set you on your way.'

I sprang bolt upright. 'Would you, Jenny? That'd be jolly decent. You're a real chum.'

113

'As an act of friendship,' she declared, 'just this once. I'm not going to make a habit of it.'

'Oh, no.' I conceded, 'I'd never expect. . . .'

'First,' she advised, 'you take some clothes off.' She pulled her blouse over the static storm of her hair. 'This is how to unhook a bra.' She showed me the catch, displaying the long knobbled groove of her spine. 'There!' she swung around.

'Then, these must be your breasts?' I guessed.

'You can touch them. Gently.'

'It's odd, Jenny, I feel as if I know them from somewhere. I've got this strong sense of déja vu.'

Really. It was as if I'd met them before. There was something particularly poignant and reminiscent about her nipples.

'You have to take your trousers off,' she advised, unzipping me. 'You really only need to take one leg out. But we'll take our time and do it properly. . . Are you nervous?'

I said I was quite excited. I could feel it coming on. There was a frisson in the air.

We got delayed awhile. She showed her surprise at some aspects of my intimate anatomy.

'Your . . . !' she said. But words failed her, '. . . . thingie!'

'What?'

'It's got twists — like a corkscrew.'

'It goes straight,' I reassured her. 'Look!' I said. 'Up!'

It rose up, stern and self-important as a parson in the pulpit. 'Down, boy,' I said. And down it flopped.

'Hey!' she gulped. 'How did you do that?'

'Mind over matter,' I said. 'It does as I tell it. It's a civil servant.

'Do it again.' She was giggling now. So I did, just to please her. Then she tried, and it obeyed her too — rising and falling to her command. I could tell it had taken a liking to her.

'You could do a stage act,' she advised me.

'Look,' I said, 'it's not a stand-up comic. Aren't they all the same, give or take a bit?'

114

'Not yours,' Jenny said. 'What else can it do? Salute the flag? Dig for oil?'

I'd done my research. I knew what was what. But I didn't tell Jenny. She seemed to like acting the expert. Anyway, there's a world of difference between theory and practice, reading and doing. So I knew I had a lot to learn.

I don't want to breach a confidence, but it happened this way —

First, I inflated the ventral column of my corpus spongiosum, as well as the dorsal cylinders of the corpora cavernosa. Soon a mucoid secretion glistened on the glans. Her nipples went erect when I skimmed them with my tongue. I stroked her labia minora, then moved a moist digit over her angulus clitoridis. She stroked my bulbus corporis cavernosi urethrae. I put a glob of saliva on my index finger before touching upon the glans clitoridis itself.

After that, we were well on our way.

It went wet in her ostium vaginae. I put downward pressure on her bulbocavernosus, rubbing at three second intervals. There was a full dilation of her circumvaginalvalvenous plexus and a heavy transudate. She was fully invaginated. Then we started.

I was acutely aware of what we were doing. I wanted to savour everything and commit it to memory. In case there wasn't a second occasion.

I hadn't expected her to be so hairy in so many places, or quite so fleshy. There was rippling subcutaneous fat beneath all her pink folds and swerving surfaces — but unevenly spread, forming substantial hillocks and mounds, especially on her hips and chest. It made her spongy to the touch, in places.

Yet it didn't put me off in the slightest. No, indeed, I found it strangely endearing.

The raw, pungent smells of leaking juices were oddly compelling. Usually, human excretions smell less inviting.

In the end we both had some pubococcygeal spasms. Jenny first: three bursts at two second intervals. Then I followed quickly, spilling inside her. It was then that my orgasm commenced. Though the spasms lasted no more than two minutes, they were more intense than ever before.

'So that's a fuck?' I shuddered, when I'd quite finished quivering.

'Yes,' she agreed. 'It was.'

'It's no wonder it's so popular,' I said. 'I haven't enjoyed myself so much for a long time. I got quite engrossed by the end.'

'You tricked me,' she said. 'You've done it before.'

'No, never.'

She smiled then nibbled my nose. 'Then you're a promising beginner.'

'I did it all right?'

'Yes, Charlie. You did, Charlie mine.' And she stroked my back in a way that spoke sincerity.

This set me thinking. It's nice to find a new aptitude, especially one you enjoy.

'Well. . . . would you tell your friends I was good? Then they might be more willing. Would you ask Alice and Melanie?'

'You shit!' she said, and with more vehemence than mere pleasantry required. Then her slender arms pumped out like pistons to roll me out of the warm, crumpled sheets onto the chill tiled floor.

She poked her head over the side of the bed, regarding me sober-eyed. 'You're meant to say you love me,' she advised. 'A girl expects it. At the very least, you could mention my beauty.'

'You're perfect, Jenny.' And she was. Lots of men thought so. But I couldn't love her. I needed a flaw to stir my sympathy. A club foot, perhaps, or speech impediment, to fire my yearning.

'I am perfect,' she agreed, 'though I say so myself.'

'It's better than grated carrots. Or salted almonds.' I spoke my ultimate compliment. 'Having sex with you.'

Then she hit out, with a pillow and exasperation.

After sex come the complications — physiological, personal, social. It was a long list of woes.

Somehow, we were diminished. The easy amiability was gone. Jenny turned prickly and sulky.

'It was kind of you,' I said, 'to show me how to do it. I'll always be grateful. I didn't realise a plump body could be so attractive. Some of your lumps are lovely. And your smells are a revelation.'

'You're too kind,' she said, but there was a taint of sarcasm to it.

I wanted to ask her if she'd do it again. But I didn't want to contest the condition of her agreement – to do it just the once.

'It was fun. While it lasted.'

'That's it, is it?' There was a glare of detestation she'd never shown me before.

'Don't feel you have to stay,' I volunteered, 'You've probably got better things to do.' I knew I was treading on her sensibilities. And I didn't want to infringe on her Saturday night. She liked to go drinking with her boyfriend, John.

'I don't believe this,' said Jenny. 'I'm to go now, am I?'

She made me feel guilty – as though I'd been insensitive, or breached some special trust.

And her face told more besides. The blushing hearsay hints of her complexion bloated to livid certainty.

'Jenny! Look at yourself in the mirror.'

Her face and neck were blotched scarlet. I hadn't expected this. She'd come out in a rash. She'd an allergy. To me. The touch of my skin, or to the fluid deposit I'd banked within her.

Every species has its special sexual conventions. Humans make a virtue of complexity – weaving eroticism, power and affection into a tangled tale. I'd ventured in out of my depth.

I reckon that the seasonal hermaphrodites – like the Annelid worms – have the best system. They have sex once or twice a year or lifetime. They meet and mate on equal terms; or please themselves, if they're alone or taken coy.

Zebra finches do it when the monsoon starts. Rain is their aphrodisiac. That could save a lot of time, prevent frustration and confusion. If people knew there was a proper time, and could rely on the weather forecast.

Worst seems the convention of certain stick-insects. The

male's post-coital tristitia is considerably magnified as the female proceeds to chew off his head, once he's spilled the beans.

Of course, an ape gets a distorted picture. But can I tell you how I see it, from my side of the mucous membranes? For I've always met the same tacky problems, whenever I've been bestial with a person.

Animals do it with their parts. You use your imagination.

There's the rub. Though a couple entwine their bodies, their erotic parts can't tangle or touch. He cannot penetrate her imagination; she can't capture his; they can't fondle the other's fancy.

Sex is a moist civility. But you insist on dressing it up as you shed your clothes. You want an epiphany. You revolt against the banality.

I expect you close your eyes when you kiss. It's the usual precaution, the proper prophylactic. If you kept them open you'd see the other's face — the yawning pores, oily pitted skin, pimpled truth. And the optics are alarming. Their nose seems supernaturally large. It looks as though you could lose yourself, pot-holing up their nostrils.

Do you find another more alluring when scantily clad than naked? Can your imagining remedy their sorry flesh? You, not nature, can construct what lies beneath the cosmetic cover. Can you conjure mystery, instead of tussocks of curly hair over tumescent tissues?

So you often have sex in the dark — to conceal the gloomy business? At least your partner is hidden in the shadows. Have you tried imagining them different, or someone else entirely? I advise against light and sight, which only dispel delusions.

You could try screwing a mirror on the ceiling, then see outside yourself, and imagine those squirming bodies belong to others.

Yet it's hard to escape the conclusion. The transaction is a trade in flesh, a coincidence of desire, as one surface slides on another.

Those spasms shake a small part around a fixed point. They can't transport you.

The inside is only an outside folded back. There's no way

into the other or out of your self. Intimacy, a brief collision of slippery parts. Two privates on leave.

That's why, you sense, there's something missing — whenever you have sex. You ask too much of your bits and pieces. Byron took his on the Grand Tour and introduced them everywhere. But he could never teach his dick to compose epics, or speak a foreign tongue. And de Sade never found that evasive orifice through which he could bugger God. Casanova was diligent. He passed through hundreds of women but never grasped what he sought. He kept getting lodged up the same unlikely cul de sac, seeking a nameless, elsewhere thing.

You can't get to know another by scratching about on the surface. You'll only find a façade. It's no substitute for conversation, I reckon. Yet people seldom agree.

So I caused a deal of offence when I first took my healthy appetite to sex. I disagreed with women. I caused them irritation. And it wasn't just a blotchy rash.

I must make clear my complaint. I shouldn't say that the inmates of universities are more degraded than people at large. This is mere appearance, and superficial dazzle from the glossy patina of the academic's occupational skills.

Gomorrah was probably more dissolute than the University of Kniggle, even if the latter held more libertines, drunkards, addicts, conspirators, perjurers and psychopaths.

At university, I believe, people can realise their full potential, becoming human to the highest degree. Humans are a rhetorical, reasonable species. People are designed to think, speak and write, conspire and have sex. They are unhappy with simple, natural things. They blink in bemusement at raw reality. They will not sniff a flower. They'd prefer to write or talk about it, give it a name, pluck it, sell it, or slander it as a weed. Their crimes — against the natural world, against each other — are rhetorical, reasonable matters.

At university rhetoric and reason find their highest forms. So the crimes they conceal are greater. It is not that academics are naturally more wicked people. Indeed, they will say they are better than most; and earnestly believe it. It's just that in universities people are better at twitching their lips, to justify their acts.

Paul Walster, my tutor, explained it.

'People have simple physical needs — for food, water and warmth. Once a person has satisfied these, which doesn't take long in many societies, they have to find ways of occupying themselves. And there's nothing left to do but think, explain themselves, dress up, take risks, have arguments, haggle for status and prestige, read, argue, slander their acquaintances, spy on their neighbours, listen to music, try to fuck each other. . . . Oh, and explain to those around us that everything we do serves a moral. It's just a problem of filling empty time with the organs we enjoy best, which are the genitals and the mind.'

'Put like that,' I said, 'you must represent the highest form of human life.'

'I do my best,' he conceded.

'Can you justify everything you do?' I asked.

'I'll say. Try me. I bet you I can explain any action and sanctify it with a moral.'

'Disembowelling a cocker spaniel puppy?'

'Call it medical research,' he advised, 'to save suffering children.'

'Stealing from a church?'

'Property itself is theft,' he confided, 'and religion is the opium of the masses.'

'Killing yourself?' I thought I'd trap him on home ground.

'Don't be daft,' he said, 'I'm a degraded, vicious cheat. I'd be doing the world a favour by leaving it a cleaner place.'

'What have you ever done that's wrong?' I asked.

'Nothing,' he sniffed piously. 'I'm a deeply moral man. I always act from firm conviction.'

'But that's inconsistent,' I protested. 'You just said you were degraded.'

He shook his head with weary contempt. 'No one's consistent,' he said, 'not if they want to like themselves. And intend to get what they want.'

'No?'

'No. You've got to find the best rhetoric for each occasion.

Then you can do whatever you like. You have to be a conservative about your own property and a radical about other people's. You have to be Christian when you need charity, an atheist when they rattle the collecting-box. You have to be an existentialist when you want to do something, a determinist when you need an excuse. . . .'

My face must have shown some distaste.

'Everyone does it,' he said. 'Do you suppose Freud would have blamed the Unconscious if Jung had biffed him on the nose? "Workers of the world unite," said Marx. But he didn't want his daughter to marry a Jew. Professor Skinner says we act like rodents, but I think he excludes himself. He'd be annoyed if you called him a rat.

'God's as bad. He made us free to do as we choose and decide for ourselves. Then he threatens us with his wrath if we do. He says there'll be hell to pay.'

'Excuse me if I seem rude,' I ventured, 'but I think you're a cynic.'

'Only on Tuesdays,' he said. 'Wise-up Charlie. Don't be a hamster all your life.'

Suppose you have several sets of relatives. And you can't help noticing that one branch of the family is acting badly. They call on their distant relatives without an invitation, shoot them, eat their flesh and wear their skins as clothing. If they took prisoners, they'd torture them, and stick them behind bars. Well, you couldn't help taking sides. You'd lament the dead, sympathise with victims, and worry about the perpetrators. You'd wonder if the villains were quite right in the head. You'd ponder what they had in mind in place of morals.

I felt in a special position, with a particular responsibility. My perspective was that of a liberal ape. I could see both sides. I'd grown up with people. I'd seen they couldn't help themselves. They've got this fetish about others' blood. And a certain arrogance — that tells them that the rest of creation is a picnic hamper. But I could see how animals felt. They may not be as clever as people, but they still know it's better to live than be luncheon.

121

I had to do something, I knew. Yet I felt so small and insignificant — like a blade of grass in a field of wheat. There's only so much a solitary ape can do.

Whatever else you do at university, there's plenty of time to think. I pondered long and hard what my contribution might be. I sincerely wanted to help.

A monkey mustn't get disheartened. He mustn't suppose that, if he can't do everything, it isn't worth doing anything at all. Gorillas set a benign and heartening example. Gibbons show us how to have innocent fun. Chimpanzees point out how the personal is political. Baboons offer a cautionary show of the perils of personal vanity. I, too, would do my best to lead a good and moral life. And be a lesson to you all.

It occurred to me that I could make a contribution. I could offer a mirror to people to show them how they look to others. Perhaps I could shame a few to change.

And I could spread my gentle genes. By impregnating women. It'd be quite a task to make any appreciable difference. There was only one of me. I'd have to act with the vigour of ten.

I swear the world seemed a cheerier place, once I'd made my resolutions. Society seems more intimate when every passing woman might be mother of your child. Men seem less menacing if you believe you can reform them.

I was more ambitious and idealistic then. They were radical times. And I was young.

Thirteen

It was the high season for sexual liberation, a pregnant phase for promiscuity; but a barren time for fertility, for every girl seemed to be popping the pill.

The crutch was a radical crux. Sex became a radical act. Woman was willing. She spread herself for man; that he might casually enter in, casually slither out, and chuckle at his luck. It was to be a few years before the feminists woke their sisters, to tell them they'd been fucked.

Promiscuity came no easier to me than to other apes. I made a stuttering start. After Jenny, there was Melanie, Alice, Mary, Helen, Sheila and Jane. There was a recurrent awkwardness.

Women invariably found me more attractive when they were drunk.

'Charlie, yorra larf. Less hava nuffa drink.' Helen sways, lax-mouthed, spraying a golden rain. The droplets stain her blue blouse black. She has hiccups. 'I've heard sdoris – about you.'

'Nice stories? Funny stories?'

She leans over the bar table, the sheeny upper slopes of her chest glisten under the flickering lights.

'Scone fidential sdoris.' She nods soberly, narrowing her olive eyes. Her mahogany tresses swish forward, curtains to her head, 'Scone cerning private things.' Filaments flicker and quiver on her breath.

'You've got lovely hair,' I say, parting the central strands with a finger, to regard her shaded face. 'You're very pretty.' She hoists her eyebrows, smiling archly.

'Nuffa drink, Charlie,' she says. She'll ponder my purpose

through the advice of an amber glass. 'Wis-gee.' She finds me a diverting curiosity. 'Double, pliss.' She slurs. 'An aesthetic. Against life.'

'I've got a bottle in my room.'

'Naughty,' she observes. But she rises, after pausing to collect her thoughts and legs. We stagger out, shivering against the gusty night, staggering, arms locked in mutual support, across the neat cropped lawn towards the glistening mosaic of hall. Golden lights blink on and off as students come and go, in and out, till dawn.

I was quite taken by her pubic hair — which she'd had dyed a fluorescent green.

'Do you like it?' she demanded, fluffing it out with a finger. 'It says green for "go".'

Naturally, I wondered if she had the temperament to be mother of my first-born child.

Snuggling in, I lay my mouth in the warmth between her shuddering breasts, above her slumbering heart. I'm contented with regret. We are ravished. She jerks in her sleep.

Helen had confided. She takes the pill daily, when she doesn't forget. Even as she sniffles in her doze, man-made hormones are wafting down clandestine tubes, whispering to secret waving fronds, scotching the chance of our child. I cannot purloin this body for my private purpose. I delight in it anyway.

We had our moments. We briefly belonged. I betrayed myself — in a reverie that I was a man — as I squirmed about her hot, kind centre.

When she wakes she may feel a spasm of shame for spending her night in my bed. She may come to my room again but she won't want it known. I'll be cautioned to discretion. There's her status to consider. Her stock might fall, if it's known she sleeps with a proper Charlie.

Perhaps she'll have a rash. Jenny and Alice will eye her wryly or, giggling, ask her where she's been and whether she's had an experience.

I had a certain reputation as an experience, amongst a small group of cognoscenti. Mary told me so. Alice had recommended me; as though I were an Indian restaurant or avant-garde film. You wouldn't want to go every night, but it's certainly worth trying once at least. It's interesting to find something different.

'What do girls say about me, Mary?'

'Nothing nasty, Charlie. They're quite complimentary. They say you're kind and ...' she hesitated, in brief conclave with her tact, to elect an epithet '... stimulating,' she decided.

'Only, I've noticed this, Mary. The women that will sleep with me don't like to go out with me. Normally, fellows have the opposite problem.'

'Mm,' Mary considered the conundrum, biting her lip, her brow knitted, 'Perhaps it's because you look ... unusual.'

'Oh.'

'I think that might be it,' she advised, twining a curl of her honey hair around a twitchy finger. 'Interesting, but unusual. Nice eyes you've got, Charlie. A very young complexion. You could pass for fourteen or fifteen. Most men look much older.'

I found this a favourable judgement, and encouraging. At least *she* found me attractive. 'Would you like to go to the cinema, Mary? Tonight or tomorrow.'

'Sorry, Charlie,' she went into mute hiding, tugging her T-shirt back over her head, '... I'm busy this week. Seeing people ... Where are my knickers?'

'Oh,' I said, 'There. By the door, where you dropped them.'

An ape I may be. But we have a lot in common. For I'm an English, middle-class, public-school, university-educated, liberal ape. We detest vulgarity, don't we? We don't care much for loud, opinionated people — like Americans, say, or Latins. We prefer our pasta al dente. We know how to eat an artichoke without drawing attention to ourselves. We believe this matters. We dislike patterned carpets. Our walls are white or beige. We can recognise the music of Mozart. We know our arse from our hautbois. We know how to speak the names of John Paul Sartrer and George Louis Burgess. We'll tactfully correct a foreigner who mispronounces them. We are decent, at heart. The world would be a better, more decorous place, if other souls behaved like us. But then others haven't had our advantages or education.

On holiday, on the beach or in the kebab queue, we feel a certain unease. It's not just the dehydration and sunburn. It's that the world cannot see us for what we are — when we have no cover but a flimsy swimming costume. So we carry literary paperbacks. And talk rather loud. When we aren't sneering at the posers, complaining about the children, or enjoying an ethnic experience.

Our pretences are governed by tact. When we are desperate, we go quiet. Least said, soonest mended. Sometimes we feel a strain in our face, from forced smiling. Anger we find difficult to express; except when we are driving, or talking on the phone. If we have something nasty to convey, we prefer to write a letter. We're good at writing pointed letters.

Yet we try not to lose our tempers with people we do not like. Home, we feel, is the forum for anger. Friends and family are the proper targets. We have most arguments on weekends or holidays; for that's when we spend our time together.

If we hurt anyone, we tend to keep it in the family so as not to cause a public scene.

If we kill another, we kill lover or family. But more often we select ourselves. We aren't a nation of murderers: we aren't extrovert enough. We prefer suicide. This is our choice. We hate ourselves more than we hate our nearest and dearest. I suppose we have our reasons. But we're a mite half-hearted, if we ever try. There's a failure of will. Many aspire but few succeed.

Sex is a fine pretext to meet new people. After intercourse, with luck and goodwill, you can skip to intimacy. From 1971–73 I made 768 vain attempts, with thirty-six women, to make a baby. It wasn't wasted time. For I enjoyed the effort and relished the companionship. But I concluded — and sadly — that it was unlikely I should ever breed with a woman.

Lions and tigers have made ligers and tigons: the horse and the ass make mules or hinnies. But the offspring are themselves infertile. Different species can rarely interbreed. Humans and Xique Xique seemed incompatible. Else I, myself, was sterile.

In the spring of my third year, I laid aside my libido and set my mind to my final examinations. There was some ethnic pride to this. I wanted to better people. And it satisfied some sense of mischief that an ape should know more about human nature than most people knew themselves. I had a point to prove. I intended to be clever as a monkey.

I told Paul Walster, my tutor, that I wanted a first class degree. I wanted something worthwhile — and more than memories — to take away with me.

'I'd cheat, then, if I were you,' he advised. 'I always did. It never did me any harm. It got me where I am today.'

'Cheat? How?'

'Come on, Charlie! Use your initiative. There's no credit in it, if someone has to show you how.'

'I'd rather use my wits,' I said.

'Are you sure they're sharp enough?'

'I'll show you,' I promised.

It wasn't easy. First, I had to think — hard and murky — like a human. In the past I'd betrayed myself, showing unscientific sympathy for the animals on which psychologists wrought their work. I vowed I should not venture any conclusion that hadn't been written in a scholarly text. For the duration of my assessment I'd side with man against nature, and suppress my originality.

Then I had to study psychology: the psychology of my examiners, by placing myself in the head of the lecturers, to decide what questions they'd ask. Halliday knew only seven questions and asked them every year. But Marshall, Johnson and Beattie preferred a system of rotation. Some stony ground lay fallow on alternate years. Hargreaves always raised the issue of his last published research, six years old, lest it be forgotten. McGringle gave the game away, telling us the questions — in perverse revision sessions in which he discussed only those topics which would not appear in the exams. Paul Walster posed terse, flashily enigmatic questions — e.g. ' "You are your own fiction": discuss, demur or refute.' or 'Why bother?' — which were best parried by quoting from a thin paperback which, as chance would have it, he'd written himself.

There were eight exams and four questions to be selected in each. So I was required to learn thirty-two topics, before writing a model answer on each — two thousand words long. Even with the manic advice of amphetamines, this was as much as I could scribble legibly in the time allowed.

I took each exam three times: twice for practice in my room, before the challenge of the real thing.

Paul Walster gave me the news. He told me I was a first-class fiddler, and a credit to his tuition. For the first time in our three-year acquaintance, he bought the first round of drinks.

As we got drunk, I became maudlin. I was proud to be (to this day, to the best of my knowledge) the only New World Ape to gain a first class degree from the University of Kniggle. And I was choked that I must soon depart this fine place that valued me so well. I sensed that I might perhaps never again achieve so much. They had passed so quickly, in the flicker of my yellow gaze, those three golden years.

I feared I might never find such a fine room again as my small chamber in the Hall of Residence. And if I did, I doubted that I should ever find such pleasant neighbours again — like Jenny, Alice, Mary and Jane — who would call at any hour of the day or night for coffee, sex or friendship's sake.

I'd struggled to earn my four friends. And now we would be severed. I should have to start all over again.

And I was not an ape of independent means. I should have to work for a living. But I lacked any desire for human labour.

'Can't I stay?' I asked Paul Walster.

'And do what, exactly?'

'I could work as a gardener. Or in the cafeteria. Kniggle feels like home. And I'll miss the girls.'

'Don't be dumb, Charlie. You've got to move on.'

'I have?'

'Yes.' He was quite definite. He said I'd have to go. 'Sod off,' he said.

It was always the same. Whenever I'd adjusted to a place, people would make me move on.

When I sunk my face in his jacket and wept, he wriggled away with embarrassment, making a lame excuse to leave.

'Grow up, Charlie,' he said. That was his terminal advice, as he brushed my hand from his shoulder. They were the last words he spoke to me.

University had taught me a lot. I'd learned how to have sex with women, seduce, get drunk, pose, haggle, argue, deceive, cheat, smoke dope, act radical, wangle and wrangle. People were less of a mystery.

Much had changed at home, at Cloudesley Road, during my time at university. The first and most extreme transformation had been the accession of Dr James Cadogan. Like a Victorian explorer, newly arrived in Africa, he displayed a nonchalant possessiveness. No sooner had he set foot in the place than he called it his. It was his adamant conviction that he had been the first to discover each and every room in the house. It was as if the natives didn't count. And like an imperial explorer, he renamed any place at his whim.

When I'd returned for Christmas, he'd given me a conducted tour of my home.

'The lavatory's here,' he disclosed, opening the toilet door. He showed me the flush in the pan for good measure.

'I've rearranged the dining room,' he indicated the lie of the parlour with a wave of his pink palm. I wouldn't have been surprised if he'd pointed out the roof and called it Mount Cadogan.

'Then this must be your throne,' I said flopping into my armchair; the one I'd inherited from Dr Duckworth.

But he was deaf to irony. 'In a manner of speaking,' he conceded, 'so I'd rather you didn't sit there.'

For like a colonist, Dr Cadogan brought a new system of government in his wake. He told me of bye-laws regulating the use of the bathroom, explaining how these served his general good. There were statutes regarding the door mat, standing orders relating to the kitchen table, and some sensible ordinances concerning the closing of doors. Access to cupboards was a matter of tort. The electric fires were subject to curfew. Of course, I was free to use the stairs and corridors at all reasonable hours for reasonable purposes. I was to treat the guest-room as my own for the duration of my stay.

You needed an ordnance survey map to cross the sitting room, to find the narrow public rights of way through the private estate. It hadn't taken me long to realise that Dr Cadogan resented my stays in Jamestown. I overheard his mutters to Mother which suggested he thought me less than a man.

'He's like a child. He has to be told.'

'It is his home,' Mother suggested.

'In a manner of speaking,' Dr Cadogan advised. 'Until he goes.'

I could see his point of view. He'd married Mother, not me. I wasn't the sort of son he'd have chosen for himself. He'd have preferred a pink one, with better manners, who didn't imitate his lisp. And I suspect he begrudged me his wife's affection. It was as though he believed her heart a tin of peaches. He'd bought the can for his sole consumption. He feared I'd find an opener, gobble the segments then drain the syrup.

His profession didn't help either. A pathologist gets used to having his own way with people. The dead are tractable, if stiff. They don't compete, bleed or answer back. You can take them out when you need them. Or keep them stored and tidy in refrigerated trays.

When I returned after finishing university, he interviewed me in his study.

'Of course,' he smiled distractedly, 'you must treat this place as your home.'

'Oh, I do,' I consoled him.

'Until you find a place of your own.'

'My own?'

'You'll want to be independent.'

'I grew up here,' I said, 'with my mother. . . and father.'

'And now you'll want to fly the nest. It's only natural.'

'I think,' I advised, 'you're confusing me with a bird of passage. I'm more like a canary or budgie, that's happy in its cage.'

He smiled gently, with polite effort. 'And now you'll want to get a job,' he threatened.

There it was again — that human preoccupation with labour. People always ask 'What do you do?' And if you say what you like doing they smile with incomprehension.

'I suppose I'll have to be a psychologist. It's the only qualification I've got.'

'As it happens,' he smiled triumphantly, handing me a folder across Dr Duckworth's desk. 'I've been collecting application forms for jobs that might suit.'

'Mm,' I fingered the chill wodge of starchy papers.

'And I've found you a room you could rent.'

'Yes?' It struck me that he was taking his role as stepfather a mite too literally. 'You needn't have bothered.'

'Clapham. Ten pounds a week. Far enough away to feel independent. Close enough to visit. You can come over on Sunday afternoons to see your mother. She's fond of you, you know.'

'I'm afraid, I can't afford. . . .'

'I thought of that.' He nodded and curled his upper lip. 'So I'll lend you a few month's money.' He slid a cheque across the desk. Two hundred pounds.

'But, Dad. . .' I grimaced pitifully. It would have brought tears to sympathetic eyes. 'I can't. . . .'

'No, son. Take it.' He showed me his waxy palms, deflecting my mock protest with his fulsome fake generosity. 'That's what family is for. To help each other. . . . Now we'll go and tell your mother. She'll be pleased as punch you're showing some initiative. She worries about you, you know.'

'What can I say?' I pleaded.

Fourteen

I went up for seventeen interviews before seizing a job by the scruff. Prospective employers found me bemusing, despite my candour. Some even suggested I was odd. Being frank, I always agreed.

'Excuse me for asking,' they'd say, 'but would you describe yourself as eccentric?'

'Certainly,' I'd confirm. 'People always say that. It's one of the first things they notice about me. And it's not just my appearance. . . .' For there's no gainsaying face values, when six or seven people are ogling you with sincere surprise, 'but I've an unusual turn of mind. You'd be hard pressed,' I bragged, 'to find anyone else like me.'

They'd invariably ask me about my work-experience.

'Goodness gracious!' I'd say, 'I've never worked before in my life. But I'm willing to give it a whirl. Even if it means getting up early in the morning, or doing as I'm told.'

'Would you describe yourself as ambitious?'

'Oh, no,' I'd promise. Because I didn't want them to find me pushy. I knew a boss feels uneasy if a subordinate lets it be known they're after his job, before he's even started his own.

'What are your long-term objectives?'

'I'd like to grow vegetables,' I'd tell them, 'I want to save up enough money to buy a small-holding.'

At the end, they ask you if you've got any questions for them.

'How many days of the week would I have to come in?' The

answer was invariably five, but it was diplomatic to show an interest.

I finally struck lucky at Chelmstead Mental Hospital. There were only two interviewers and they smiled with approval at all my replies. They took me on as trainee psychologist.

'When can you start?' Dr Beccles asked.

'You'll have me?' My eyelids went all aflutter. I was stupefied by success. 'Are you sure that's wise?'

'Yes,' he said. 'You'll do.'

'Usually, people reject me,' I warned him.

'We need someone,' he said, 'and we can't pay a lot.'

'Thanks,' I said, 'But if you change your mind, I'll understand.'

Like Dr Cadogan, whose acquaintance she was, Mrs Colette Carmel McBride of 17 Clapham South Side, imposed stern house-rules. She pointed them out as she showed me the room. Indeed, it was difficult to avoid noting her strictures. She was more ambitious than Moses. For she handed down thirteen commandments. They were framed in the dank lino-floored hall, tacked on the back of the lavatory door, and sellotaped over my bed.

1. No drinking, smoking or hanky-panky.
2. Keep quiet. Mind your mouth.
3. Show some consideration.
4. Rent is to be paid weekly, in advance, on Fridays.
5. Breakages will be paid for.
6. No electrical appliances.
7. No visitors.
8. No music in rooms. No laughing in the common parts.
9. Management will inspect the rooms without warning.
10. No riff-raff.
11. House-meetings are compulsory.
12. No mischief.
13. Be warned. No excuses.

'You'll be my first coloured,' said Mrs McBride, 'but Dr

Cadogan says you're respectable. A Christian is a Christian. The deposit is fifty pounds.'

I was swept on a wave of nostalgia. Immediately, I felt at home. Disregarding the scent of cat pee, it was all uncommonly like boarding school. The house meetings were not unlike Assembly. After prayers, Mrs McBride would deliver a timely homily on the state of world or domestic affairs — advising us to vote Conservative, for example, or contribute to a Catholic charity named after St Michael de Pores — before calling her lodgers to individual account for their week's misdemeanours. Her sanctions were shame, or withdrawal of privileges, though, rather than corporal punishment. Beneath her gaze, we shuffled around in timid apprehension. Behind her back, we held her in derision and awe; calling her, in whispers, the Headmistress. For it wasn't empty rhetoric for her to call herself the Management.

Rumour had it that Mrs McBride had once had a female lodger called Bernadette. It led to a carnal scandal, bringing disrepute to the bricks and mortar. Now she'd learned the lesson of Genesis, and was too knowing to mingle the sexes in her Eden. All the other boys were much older. I was the only resident under forty years of age.

To be at work for nine I had to rise at seven-thirty. Punctuality cost me a deal of time. Eventually I got the knack, with encouragement from my employers. Dr Beccles bought me an alarm clock out of petty-cash.

I was first assigned to the Lister Ward for long-stay mental delinquents. It ran on a token-economy. The inmates were awarded plastic tokens for good-conduct. At the end of the week they could trade them in for chocolates, toothpaste, cigarettes and soft-drinks. The rules of good-conduct were tailored to each patient's eccentricity, and decided and revised in our staff-meetings.

The problem with Herman was getting him to talk. For he'd prefer to rock mute in his chair, thumping his head gently on the cast iron radiator.

'Morning, Herman,' I'd say. But the only reply was clunk,clunk of his temple on the central heating.

'If you don't say "hello", I won't be able to give you a five-point token.'

Then sometimes he'd hiss, '. . . arsehole.'

'Pardon, Herman. I didn't catch that.'

'. . . stuff it . . .' he'd whisper, '. . . up your arsehole.'

Then, if he'd been fully audible, I could give him a counter. A blue-plastic five-pointer, for talking to me. The flaw in the philosophy was that he didn't want it anyway.

'. . . up yours,' he'd advise, the disc resting in his open palm. But he wouldn't turn to look at me, or cease banging his bleeding calloused brow.

Dermot felt compelled to display his willy. Our ploy was to reward him for reticence. So he'd keep himself buttoned up, as was the practice in discreet society.

I'd find him in the armchair in the recreation room, hunched, scrutinising his lap, calibrating his willy against a length of knotted string. The quantity surveyor wrinkles his face in alarm. However fiercely he tugs his willy, the string remains the longer.

He believes it's shrinking. As willies go — as this one might — few can have received such fastidious research. Dermot has three pocket books, charting the rise and fall of its private numbers. He measures its length and girth, erect and dormant, its angles of elevation. This makes his private part one of the most thoroughly surveyed natural features of Kent. He'll introduce it, on the flimsiest of pretexts, to whoever will show a passing interest.

'Not good, Mr Duckworth. . . .' He looks up frowning, as my shadow falls across him. He shakes the flaccid member, as if trying to animate a limp, dead pet. 'It's really going this time.'

'Keep it out of sight till lunch,' I promise, 'and you can have a ten-pointer.'

'Thanks, Mr Duckworth. But I can't risk it. We could lose another inch by then.'

His life is the sorry story of a dick. But it's his plight, and he doesn't flinch from the challenge. He's taken the offensive. And he can be very offensive. He'll slow the rot, halt the dwindling of his asset, by keeping it under permanent scrutiny. When he forgets it, it sort of withdraws. So he launches a series of impromptu audits — surprising the thing when it least expects it — at lunch, during Coronation Street, playing Scrabble.

Only Frank Long, the staff nurse, can ever dissuade Dermot. Whenever Frank is around, the item's out of sight. For Frank fancies himself a psychologist.

'If I see your prick again today, Dermot, I chop the frigging thing off.'

It's crude therapy. Yet it works. Dermot and Frank have come to an understanding.

Jack's problem is picking his nose. It's quite a compulsion. He takes the task literally. So his nostrils are widening as the surrounds depart. They've fitted him with a pink plastic nose shield, tied around his head by tape. The appearance so gained, from the large synthetic snout, has earned him the accolade of The Pig amongst his fellow patients. We reward him for keeping his hands off. You can tell if he's done as he's told. Then, there's no blood trickling down his upper lip into his gaping toothless mouth.

They were a colourful, unconventional crowd on the Lister Ward. I was their companion, watch-dog and pay-master. We played a lot of Scrabble and ping-pong. It helped to pass the time. Time weighed heavily on us all.

Each had his task in this country of the crazed. Some did all the worrying. Others had all the fun. Some had sex for all the others who, in turn, had the guilt for them. They were routinely dirty when not obsessionally clean. Bernard washed his hands one hundred and one times before breakfast, as if bearing the brunt of hygiene for each and all the rest.

I wondered about my patients; and how we differed, they and I. There were some elegant symmetries. They were incarcerated in a mental hospital, earning plastic counters to trade in at the end of the week. And I worked in a mental hospital for my salary, paid into my account at the end of the month. They were accountable for their conduct to myself and the other staff. I was answerable to Dr Beccles, Professor Gay-Lawson and Mrs McBride. They were professional madmen. I was a professional psychologist, and sanity inspector. It struck me as rum and wry.

'Monkey cure thyself,' thought I.

I suspected that the staff needed the patients more than the patients needed us. We could only be psychologists with their assistance, whereas they could be mad on their own. And I doubted that we helped them. For we treated their symptoms and not their disorders. If a man claws away at his nose with his fingernails, there's more at stake than an itch. If a fellow can't trust his willy to stay, he needs more aid than a zip.

I suggested as much to Dr Beccles.

'Couldn't we try and help them?' I asked.

He glanced at his watch. He looked as chicly handsome as the leading man in a vermouth advertisement. He fiddled with the knot of his tie, tweaking his charisma. The grey wool jacket alliterated with the designer Oxford bags that went with the cream silk shirt that rhymed with the egg yolk tie that affirmed — without bragging — that he was a man of strong, yet educated, sensuality.

He's no ordinary Beccles such as you might chance upon in the telephone directory when looking for another Beccles. He is Beccles Clinical Psychologist, and I cannot know his number, though he knows mine. I'm translucent to his amused humane gaze. Whilst he is ex-directory.

'What are you gabbling about, Charlie?'

'Couldn't we give the patients some sensible treatment?'

'The point about Beccles Therapy,' says Beccles, swatting an absent fly, 'is to calibrate all reinforcement contingencies against asymptotic response probabilities. . . . '

For he's devised and named the treatment. He's given conference papers on it. Now he's writing a book of the show, showing that Beccles Therapy bears scant resemblance to similar therapies devised by others.

Busy Beccles clutches his wrist to take his pulse to assess the stress to his system. A frown briefly trespasses upon his forehead. He releases a hand, so that a fastidious finger can purge a black speckle from the spine of his ivory desk diary.

Then his watch squawks a pulse of alarm. For he employs

a digital Japanese neurotic-obsessional to keep him abreast of appointments.

'Later, Charlie. . . .' he promises, 'I've got a twelve o'clock morbid auto-erotic, followed by a chronic dysmnesic.'

He pats me on the shoulder. I slouch back to the ward.

Jacob is busy scribbling.

'What are you doing?' I ask.

'Secrete?' he asks, his eyes roll slyly.

'Promise,' I say.

'Epizzle,' he shows me. He's writing a letter on toilet paper in green biro.

Dear Sir or Madam,
Whatever your gender knob/sexual camoeflage in juice extrusion fuck-practices and suck barrage-activationals. Excrecancies cannot concern our hollowed-out-belly-continents and loin-cave-pulsars, or can ooziform bile-ogical stains be eradicated in tubular sin-sibilities. Our past intercourse (with a small i in the venial concordat) do not re-seal your dog-hole-dung-mind which befouls our mental pavements, though rat-capped have become the burrows of your prick-squirt-puzzules which now stain the un-dergarments of our mindseyesears. There is no alternative. Send a task-faucet. I look fore-warned to your replay in full violation of endeaviour or orifice prototectives. . . .

'That's poetic, Jacob,' I say, handing back the wrinkled paper, 'Who are you writing to? Is it a love letter?'

'Puss,' he says, shaking his knowing head. 'Is this monster-mind? Are you dungating discs?'

I give him two blue and one red one. Generosity moves me. Anyway, it's Dr Beccles' currency, not mine.

'Silly money,' he chortles, 'psycho-pennies.' He slips them into the side of his mouth, so no one can steal them.

I make a note in my audit book. "12.13. Jacob discusses current affairs. Lucid, fluent and reasonable. 20 points."

Sometimes it struck me as hopeless. Their condition, yours and mine.

I was eccentric myself. But often I yearned for more orthodox company. When Dr Beccles had me to his house for supper,

138

I realised there were much richer, more fulfilling ways to live than by the thirteen rules of Mrs McBride.

It was all very nice.

Nice, adj. (ish). Fastidious, of critical taste, punctilious, particular, delicately sensitive, agreeable, well flavoured, kind, friendly, considerate.

We went straight from work in his nice silver Triumph sports car. As we skidded around the ambulance onto the road through the hospital gates, Dr Beccles invited me to call him Dougal. He played Bach cello suites on his quadraphonic stereo, at an agreeably moderate volume. When he overtook in the inside lane, he turned to smile, with friendly politesse, at the becalmed driver alongside. Then we surged past, the car growling its throaty approval. It was nice to feel mobile in life, and to weave such swift, intricate patterns.

Dr Beccles' wife was called Melissa. Long hazel hair framed an oval face of self-satisfied serenity. Chocolate eyes appraised me unblinking as if she'd been forewarned. I thought her very nice indeed. I said as much to Beccles, as I sipped at a fluted glass of crisp chill Soave, slumped in his oatmeal velvet sofa, my scuffed shoes tapping on his beige carpet.

'Very nice,' I observed.

'What?'

'Everything — the way you live.'

'I suppose....' He sighed complacently.

'All the colours match,' I observed, 'the sofa, your wife, the cat, the walls, your shirt and tie. An alliteration of creams and browns.'

'Yes?' He gave a quick frown, eyeing me cautiously, perhaps suspecting sarcasm.

'I expect you have an ivory bathroom suite with a bidet.'

'Yes, Charlie. How did you know?'

'And avocado dishes, fish knives, a vacuum cleaner and open-marriage?' I guessed.

'Yes,' he conceded, tapping his fingers loudly on the glass-topped coffee table.

'And those little forkettes for sticking in the end of sweetcorn?'

'What are you getting at, Charlie?' I think I'd begun to irritate him.

'Nothing,' I sighed. 'It's all very nice.' To stop myself talking, I began cramming my mouth with almond-stuffed olives.

The other guests — Oliver and Harriet — were very nice too. It was all jolly until the women went to whisper in the kitchen between the gazpacho and the main course.

'Are you going to stop it?' Oliver asked Dr Beccles. He'd cast a sidelong glance to check that the coast was clear.

'Stop what?'

'Fucking my wife. Sleeping with Harriet?'

'Look. . . .' Beccles soothed, gesturing to me, 'Later. . . .'

'Don't mind me,' I volunteered, 'I'm interested — hearing how people live.'

'It's not very *nice*, is it?' says Oliver. He knows how to hurt a fellow. 'You're a sly fucker, aren't you?'

'Look!' says Beccles, explaining his innocence. 'Your wife isn't your property. . . .'

They get very engrossed. They quite ignore me, debating personal freedom. To love someone, Beccles observes, you must respect their spontaneity and freedom. Freedom in limits is freedom enchained. To demand fidelity is to wish a person cold in aspic, with a decorative sprig of parsley. Harriet was just being Harriet. Dougal had been Dougalling. That was Dougal's view on it.

'You boys look serious,' says Harriet, entering clutching a casserole. 'Is there a cock-up?'

'There!' declares Melissa. She bears bowls of vegetables. She scans our faces for a clue to the frigid silence. She is sensitive. She can diagnose a ruptured rapport when she meets one. 'What's the matter? Don't you like veal?'

'I don't like flesh,' I say. 'I never touch cows.'

'Dougal does,' says Oliver, smiling slyly to his wife.

A fragrant steam rises from the courgettes. Molten butter trickles down a mound of new potatoes. The mange-tout are surmounted by a sprig of fresh mint.

'Yummy,' say I. 'You know how to live.'

Harriet smiles wanly and twitches her lips — perhaps in

preparation for speech. Her eyes jerk from her plate to Melissa, but she finds discomfort in both. Overwhelmed, she jumps up, toppling the coffee and cream striped canvas director's chair behind her. She holds both hands to her mouth and rushes for the door.

'What . . . ?' demands Melissa, eyeing us in turn.

'Dougal and Harriet are having an affair,' Oliver spreads his elbows, sliding forward to confide, '. . . on Tuesday and Thursday evenings . . . when you're at your woman's group or badminton.'

Melissa closes her eyes to consider the disclosure. She reddens blind. When her eyes flutter open they glisten moist.

Dr Beccles speaks no denial.

'You shit,' she tells him, more in resignation than anger. He smiles with sheepish regret. 'You scumbag,' she adds, in quiet lament.

She empties the bowl of courgettes over his head with a studied weariness, as if acting a habitual domestic chore.

I giggled. Because any boss looks different − and less authoritative − when he's wearing a mound of vegetables on his scalp. Lime green fluid trickled down his temples, dispersing into thin rivulets over his cheeks. He stroked some steaming pieces from his shoulders, scattering them to the Berber carpet.

'Really, Mel,' he shook his head, solemn and aggrieved. 'Let's be rational. . . .'

She arched her eyebrows high and froze her face to a chilling smile. She reached across to lift the casserole. 'We all have our reasons,' she sighed, ladling the veal, and its bubbling viscous juices, onto his lap, 'Don't we just?' Perhaps Melissa was attempting aversion therapy. She knew about this. She was a psychologist too.

'Aah. . . .' he whimpered, with a passionate inadvertence, as if surprised by an orgasm.

I could tell that supper was a lost cause.

'Look,' I volunteered, 'Perhaps I should go.' I felt I was intruding on the intimate business of long-standing friends. 'I'm not very hungry. I could get a sandwich at the station. You mustn't bother yourselves about me,' I said. So they didn't.

I rose and retreated. In the hall I found Harriet, the bone of contention, looking thoroughly chewed. She was sobbing softly, slumped on the stairs.

'Can you say "thank you for having me"?' I asked her, 'They're a bit preoccupied in there.'

The sight of her almost moved me to tears. I could see why Beccles loved her. She'd a touching squint, a very emotive snuffle and a deeply troubling grunt.

I walked two miles to the station in the pelting rain. The restaurant room was closed. The chocolate machine stole my change.

Dr Beccles never mentioned the evening, so I don't know how events were resolved. But thereafter he was a mite chilly towards me. As if I'd made some unforgivable faux-pas.

Fifteen

Folk seem surprised if I tell them. That I was once engaged. To be married. To a woman.

'*You?*' they say, 'Who to?'

Well, it's a long story.

Some advice, if you'll take it: don't try to consummate a physical union on Clapham Common at night. Think again. Take yourself somewhere else. Preferably indoors. Apart from the cold, dewy damp and dark, there are spectators to contend with. I lived to regret that night on the Common when I got caught with my trousers down.

I wasn't doing badly as a person till then, considering I wasn't one. I had a profession of sorts, and lodgings of a kind. Mrs McBride had given me garden privileges. We'd negotiated a premium on the rent so I could plant a plot in her back garden. I grew runner beans and leeks. My advertisement in the lonely hearts column gave me fleeting company most weekends.

There was a balance in my bank account, a spring in my homeward step from work. My clothes were modish. I could afford whichever fruit and veg I fancied, quite whenever I chose. It was the spinach season. No one had broken a bone in my body for eighteen months. Harsh words didn't bother me. Water off a Duckworth's back. When a chap's a monkey, most insults sound lamely inept.

There was something to Emilie's letter that set it apart from the others and sent me athrob with warmth.

Dear Yellow Eyes,

I am not English. Perhaps you are not English also. I am
Belgian girl. What man are you? Like you I am lonely
and sensitive. Some persons laugh on me because of my
curve back I must say in the beginning. Otherwise I am
gay. I am twenty one. My best features is eyes and nose.
Face is pretty. Size is petite. What are you? Do you adore
cinema? Especial musical? Do you enjoy to eat? In Brussels
I have friends and aunt. So without I am sad. Perhaps
you are too sad. We will make a liaison if you do not
take badly my hump. Please Christ. We are none perfect
in God Eyes. If you are sincere please ring house ask for
myself Emilie and tell your personal informations. I do not
mind you are yellow if you are kind. Perhaps we shall be
coming intimate. We may fabricate some happiness if we
like. I hope.

Emilie.

We were both nervous when I first rang. There was a frisson
and the heady scents of hope and passion. She was an au pair.
I heard her family chattering in the background. And Beccles
came into the office just as we began to speak.

'I am your yellow-eyes,' I gulped as Beccles cast his sideways
glance. That one that said 'I thought so.'

'We meet?'

'Please.'

'Ah. . . .' she paused on a contented intake of breath,
'We meet . . . public.' Now her hesitancy spoke a cau-
tion.

'Yes. Where? When?'

'Sunday. Gates of Buckingham Palace. Two of afternoon.'

'Yes.'

'Yes. You recognise my back.'

'Yes. You recognise my colour.'

'Good,' she sighed. 'What do you call yourself?'

'Charlie.' I said. 'Sunday. Very good.' I agreed.

I'd become fatalistic about such meetings which often didn't
take place. Sometimes the other didn't show themselves, having
glimpsed me first and made a retreat. Or they'd briskly make

their excuses. Sometimes, no word was spoken; we'd stare, shrug and part.

I scanned the crowd from the edge. Perhaps she was there. Or watching me from afar – as I looked for her.

Yet, close by the gates stood a jerky marionette: a short, head-bobbing figure, raven haired, hunched, in a sky blue pvc raincoat, strangling a small bunch of crocuses in her locked gloved hands. Her head bounced like a puppet's, nodding downcast then jerking up to look about. I suspect you remember them. Those plastic doggies, that sat on the back ledge of cars, nodding their heads with mechanical amiability.

I daresay we'd look a sight together. There was an appreciable difference of height. But we had our slouch in common.

I considered turning away. Then, at a distant of ten yards or more, her eyes caught and arrested me. She cast down her gaze as I slinked the final distance.

'Emilie?' I whispered down.

'Sharlee?' She smiled bravely up, her head held back, displaying her downy neck. She appraised my face and gulped.

'Walk?'

'Yes.'

She fell in by my side. Looking down on her, I watched the bounce of her hair and eager, trotting feet. As we mooched through St James Park she cast her inquisitive sparrow eyes sideways, to take in my arms, chest and legs.

We sat on a bench by the lakeside. Canada geese paced about our legs, squawking peevishly for bread. A duck pecked at my feet.

'There,' said Emilie. She passed the posy of crocuses. 'Flowers like your eyes.' And I felt a sudden shame to have brought nothing but a misshapen self.

'Pretty colour,' she advised. It was a husky quavering voice. Her hands wrestled themselves in her lap.

'Too kind,' said I.

We took tea in the cafeteria, sharing a slice of green and orange marzipan cake. We were twitchy and shy together. Being seated levelled our heights. The stigma of each was clear to view. We earned some whispers and stares from other tables. There were long silences. Our eyes seldom met. She spoke of her work. Then I told of mine.

'Sad,' she nodded. 'Mad persons. Hard life. Poor people.'

I watched the dregs of my tea awhile. She examined the white formica table top and fingered the rings of dried coffee.

'Go?' I asked.

'Together?' Her eyes flickered closed. She locked her hands together. 'Or alone again?'

So we went to see *Doctor Zhivago* in the Haymarket. It was her seventh time, she said. For me it was the first.

I did not touch her there in the dark. But towards the end of the film, when Zhivago ran after Lara's train, she rested her fingers on my arm. She sniffed and gently grasped my wrist. I laid my head next to her and felt the lukewarm tears on her flushed cheek. We tasted each other's mouths. It was desperate and sad, as if each had at last clutched a friend. I felt privileged and chosen. Though I'd slept with my share of women, I'd never kissed so long another's mouth. It was a very intimate feeling. And hers was a novel taste.

We held hands on the walk to the tube station. Her clutch was insubstantial, but a jerky finger played in my palm.

'Perhaps you like me despite. . . .' she observed, watching the tap of her dainty feet. 'On Wednesday night I have freedoms to go out.'

We locked arms in the hall between the platforms, till the train came to carry her North.

'Emilie,' I sighed to myself. My coy elfin. My bride. Emilie and Charlie. Charlie and Emilie. Oh, fatal couple. Hunchback and ape. Will the world let us slouch along together? What pain will come of this?

I concede we looked odd together, just as we looked odd apart. For this reason people were prone to stare and comment. Particularly in pubs. The world curled its lip at us.

'Ah,' said Beccles, when I'd incautiously confided. 'The Hunchback est votre Dame?'

I don't suppose he meant any hurt. He was merely displaying his portion of wit.

I don't think you mind deformed people. As long as they keep to their place. But some found the sight of us a difficult thing to stomach. We knew we were absurd. You left us in no doubt. So we preferred the cinema and dark.

'Scuse me,' asks a boy in the street, 'but are you making a film?'

'Fancy dress, eh?' snickers a man in the pub.

'What is . . .?' Emilie asks.

'A pleasantry,' I say.

'A girl?' Mother smiles enraptured. 'Can we meet her? What's she like?'

'She's hard to describe,' I say. 'She's called Emilie. And she's Belgian.'

'Foreign!'

'And she's got a lovely elfin face. She's very kind. She's short. She's got black hair. Beautiful smile, and a little. . . .'

Shall I say it?

'. . . hump. But it's only small. And it's very pretty.'

'Belgian? With a hump?' Mother's eyes glaze. Dr Cadogan looks heavenward. Neither can understand.

What does an ape care for parochial human prejudices about physical beauty?

I kept putting off the day. Yet I would have to tell Emilie about myself. But once she knew, I feared, she would flee with horror.

And I was becoming queasy at work. There was a lot of hammering, drilling and excitement. Beccles had installed video equipment to help us in our task.

We sit in his suite, watching the patients who are locked outside. Beccles seems calm and pensive, slumped in his padded leather swivel chair. But he's hard at work, scanning the bank of television monitors. There are three rows of four televisions — these are our twelve intrusive, electric eyes.

Wherever a patient goes, there a camera can follow, whirring its hidden scrutiny. There are cameras behind mirrors, ventilation grills, pictures, above beds. When the patients watch television,

television watches them through a slit beneath the vertical hold. In the shower, a spare nozzle peers down on them. In only two days we have seen happenings in shower cubicles that would make Hitchcock wince. In the lavatory, a wide angle lens follows the motions of the occupants, winking down from the air-conditioning box. This is revealing. People are most candid if they believe themselves alone; as they do in the loo.

In the beginning, Beccles had created the Beccles programme. But it was without form when he left the room. There was darkness when his back was turned. So he said, 'Let there be cameras.' And there were cameras, and hundred watt lighting. But at night he makes it dark, ordering that the lights go out, so that man and woman may sleep. And he brought all manner to his garden — hebephrenic, dysmnesic, paranoid, admitted he them. To each he gave a name. And each was as he called them.

And Beccles said, 'Lo, there shall be every convenience of a progressive borstal, privileges for good behaviour. But whosoever shall eat from the tree of disobedience shall lose their ten-point tokens.'

He rests a lazy arm on his desk, fingering the video console. He can pan, zoom, refocus, peer in the smallest cranny, chart the inner depths of an ear, or retire to mise-en-scène. If there is a crucial incident, he can record it for Science and Posterity.

Life on the Lister Ward follows its familiar grain. Dermot is measuring his personal part, scolding it to wake it from its slumber.

In the rest-room, bolt upright in her armchair, Mrs Tyler is muttering to Desmond who sits alongside, shivering in his sleep.

'I expect tonight there'll be cold soup and lesbians on television . . .' says Mrs Tyler. 'They need to bring back decency and throw away the key . . . Nowadays, it's all discos and sodomy, thank you very much.'

Beccles swings round in his chair to adjust the contrast on monitor 7, peers avidly, pressing his face to the screen.

'The new patient,' he tells me, 'A delusional Christ. I wangled him from Nightingale House.'

'Why?' I ask.

'I've always wanted a Christ,' admits Beccles. 'Now I've got one all to myself. Watch. . . .' He'll experiment. He's an experimentalist at heart. He coughs to condition his throat, then flicks the intercom switch.

'Martin, I must speak with you.'

The man looks around, his eyes misty vague. No sweat. Voices he can handle. He shuffles a circle. 'Who's there?' he asks. His voice has the familiar slur from Modecate or Largactil.

'I am the all seeing eye,' says Beccles, 'Above, before, behind.'

'Cool,' observes the Messiah. 'Hi.' He looks about the room and shrugs.

'You're Christ, aren't you?' Beccles coaxes.

'The words are yours,' the patient smiles; coy and sly.

'Aren't you Christ?'

'Christ, man?' he looks to locate the voice, then spots the loudspeaker by the coffee table, 'I'm Martin. I'm a vesselage of woe. In my corporality, man.'

'Shit!' Beccles slams back the intercom switch. 'They promised me a Christ, Charlie. Otherwise I'd never have swopped him for my Hebephrenic.'

'You can't always get what you want in life,' I observed piously. 'People are often disappointing.'

'You'd better get back to the ward,' he snapped.

Of course, I was worried. Now Beccles could watch the patients, he could likewise watch me. I'd have to start practising what he preached. I'd have to act a Beccles therapist, and be unkind to my charges, bribing and cajoling.

I'll bet I contemplated Beccles more often than he considered me. He represented something to me. He seemed the quintessential human being.

I was grateful to him, of course. He'd given me a job when no one else would. He'd invited me to supper — which was kind, even if the food never quite reached my plate. We'd worked together for two full years, yet he'd never hit me once. He patronised me in a thoroughly amiable way.

But I had my reservations about him. Sometimes, I thought, he veered beyond justifiable confidence. He could gain from a smidgin of self-doubt. And he was startlingly stupid, in a flashily clever way.

If a man encourages his wife to pour courgettes on his head, or arranges his home to resemble a furniture store, plays sex as a competetive sport, spies on people in the toilet, and still believes himself a charming sort, then that's his personal business. We all have our foibles. But you wouldn't trust him to tutor the mad and set the standard of sanity. No, ideally he'd be a gossip columnist, or hawk pornographic videos.

'Have you ever thought of doing anything else for a living?' I asked him. 'Something that really matches your talents?'

He took it amiss: 'No, Charlie. Have you?'

But I've noticed this about life; if one Beccles falls by the wayside, there's another to smirk in his place. Society is riddled with unlikely experts. Confident incompetence is the human forte.

There was a nineteenth century surgeon who, as a preventative procedure, ripped out all his patients' teeth. For he believed dentition was dangerous. And a later colleague cut out people's thyroid glands; till, within a year, he'd collected a ward full of cretins.

Then, there's that well known politician who says society doesn't exist: but wants to govern it anyway.

For my part, I prefer that bishop who doesn't believe in God but says we should still be nice to each other.

I'd like to hear more from deaf musicians, like Herr Beethoven, or stuttering orators like Demosthenes, and see more of the art of blind painters like that nice Mr Turner. At least *their* disability is patent. Their struggle is open and noble. You know where you stand with the legless. The crypto-cripples are the problem. Like Beccles, for instance.

I don't say you're a Beccles yourself. I wouldn't be so rude. But there are some similarities. You're only half a scoundrel. If you don't believe yourself at the outset, you do after a bit of rationalising revision.

'It's incredible ...' you say, 'I can't believe it. ...' Or 'Do you know what they did, then?'

Yes. I know what they did. They answered you back. They

borrowed your biro without asking. They mentioned that you were a fool. It's incomprehensible, but someone tooted their horn at you. There's an incorrigible villain who still hasn't returned your phone call.

'Who do they think they are?' you ask. 'Do they know who I am?'

I fear they do.

They know you're a skinful — like each of them.

You believe in a Just World. You believe it should be justly nudged in your favour. The misfortunes of others are often deserved. Your own plight is a wanton injustice.

Most times I visited Emilie in Highgate, but sometimes she came to Clapham. Then we melted into the shadows on the Common, and fondled under a tree.

I was frankly distracted. Even if I'd been alert to the approach, my mobility was hampered. For my jeans were riding my thighs. It was our business. I won't disclose what we were doing or why.

A torch lit our faces. 'Brown bastard,' a voice muttered from behind the beam.

'White woman. Brown bastard,' said another, in quiet lament.

'See what they're doing,' the third observed.

'Naughty.' The fourth chipped in.

They were quiet, saddened voices; censorious, but not unkind. A moral majority; aligned in an arc round us.

'I expect you want to hit me,' I spoke to the citizens of the dark. An ape has an inkling. He gains a feeling for these things.

'Too true,' agrees the voice behind the torch.

'Go,' I whispered to Emilie, 'Get help.' I pushed her down beneath the light. Hoisting my trousers, I shambled towards the torch, hearing the tread of feet on three sides. I looked over my shoulder and saw Emilie's bobbing retreat. They didn't stalk her. They seemed perfectly content with me.

They don't hit you right away. People. They need to warm themselves up. First they push and prod. I had lucid thoughts of the timing. In fifteen seconds or so, Emilie would have reached the road and escape. Then I could scamper too.

So I tried to gain time. I attempted reason and charm.

'Would you like some chocolate?' I asked, as one thrust me into the arms of another who smelled of stale beer and bacon grease.

'Bastard pushed me,' he said, aggrieved, 'Fucker needs showing his place.'

'Are you sure you want to do this?' I enquired, 'It can't be much fun if I don't fight back.'

One landed a kick on my coccyx, so my back began to numb. It was to soften me up, I supposed. For it wasn't hard enough to lame.

I could see their points of view. I was skewered on the prongs.

'I expect you feel alienated,' I suggested, 'dispossessed inheritors of. . . .' I'd have mentioned Hall's notion of youth-culture, but I was choked by a chop to my neck.

But that's why they wore boots and braces, I think. They were trying symbolically to reassert a nostalgic cockney culture, when men were men and white. And there were jellied eels, cholera, docks and clog-dancing.

'Black bastard.' One confirmed, twisting my chin in his soft, moist palm.

'Nig-nog,' said another, landing a belly blow that floored me.

'Look,' I said, 'you're mistaking me for a man.' I started to crawl through a gap between their legs. But, in truth, I wasn't going anywhere, for they stamped their heels on my hands.

After this it's predictable. They hack you in the ribs, kick you over your kidneys, boot you twice in the face and once in the groin.

Then you must lie doggo. Unless they've a fancy to kill you, it shows them enough is enough. As with every social encounter, there's a protocol to observe.

If you want to scare them, you stay absolutely mute and still. Which is what I did. I'd lost all sympathy for them, and cared not a fig for their feelings. Besides, a crimson curtain was closing across my vision. I felt all leaden and limp.

'Christ,' says one, rolling me over, 'we've killed the coon.'

But I wasn't going to disabuse them. Let them stew in their juices, I thought. So I held my breath to make them suffer. I wasn't going to help them wriggle off the hook. They'd only themselves to blame. 'Now!' thought I, 'I'll scare you. I'll make you flee in fear of me.' And sure enough, they did.

Then I took a sleep.

Everyone was kind and helpful at the hospital. A urologist saw to my kidneys, and a dentist fixed my teeth. My ribs felt mended in weeks. Emilie came several days, bearing flowers or fruit.

When I returned to Mrs McBride's she gave me a week's notice to quit. She said she couldn't risk tenants who got into trouble in fights. I could see her point of view, though I couldn't bring myself to share it.

Sixteen

I took new rooms in Highbury — a flat of my very own. There was a single rule — the weekly payment of rent to my landlord, Mr Christos Georgiades. I could just afford this gesture, now I'd been promoted to assistant psychologist grade IV.

There was a south-facing lounge with ornate cornicing, like the frosted edging to a wedding cake, a marble fireplace, and shutters to efface the sun. In the small kitchen there was a sink and a fridge large enough to hold cool and crisp a cornucopia of vegetables and fruit. A cosy windowless corridor led to bathroom and bedroom. The only mar was the choking stench of human juices. For the previous tenants had dribbled and leaked their redolent fluids and essences all over the soft furnishings. The vapours wafted up from the water-stained mattress, clung in the folds of the curtains, and impregnated the carpets. Yet, after a week of burning joss sticks, I'd overpowered the stenches of sweat, grease and urine.

Emotionally, it was a grand perch from which to watch my world. I was only eight minutes walk from Mother's. Any time of the evening or night, I could slink past her home and discern from the lights and curtained windows her whereabouts in the house.

And Emilie could catch a bus down the Holloway Road to visit me on her free evenings.

'Look!' I exclaimed proudly, on her first visit, leading her in by the hand, 'All ours.'

'Can't see, Sharlee. No light.'

'No light bulbs,' I explained. 'Better dark.'

She kept stumbling into my plants. Her night vision was poor and human.

I cooked her chervil soup, a nut-roast, with courgettes, Jerusalem artichokes, celeriac, and tarragon sauce. Then we had a dill sorbet, fresh mango, and fennel tea. Before we took ourselves to bed.

I stroked her bent back, licking her neck and chest, gulping in her tastes. Then our mouths met, clamping with the thud of coupling railway carriages, our molten tongues flickered, our teeth clinked together like porcelain. My tentative fingers took their tour of her. She opened moistly to me, splitting like a ripe tomato. I gorged on her.

It was a warm and fragrant evening. I felt very close to her as I lay jerking on her thin sparrow ribs.

'What is?' she asked, 'You all right?'

'Org-as-mm.' I explained. 'All-ways ... makes ... me ... st-st-ut-utter. . . . '

These were special occasions, those first times in bed. I was more relaxed than I'd ever felt on Clapham Common. We could loiter warm and naked. There was no fear of interruption. There was no risk of getting a good kicking from a disapproving audience.

We'd make love through the night and into the morning. Though Emilie was prone to lose her concentration and nod off into a drowse, even while I stirred inside her.

I had to compromise. She liked some light, so I bought her a torch so she could find her way around the rooms. Sometimes, like a cat that carries home its prey, she'd leave lumps of dead bird or thin slices of pig rib in my fridge. I'd find the stains of murder, spatters of coagulating blood, alongside my vegetables.

'Nuts are just as nutritious,' I'd advise. But Emilie was incorrigible. She had to sup the blood of beasts. So I'd try to stay sanguine, even if she chewed on the breast of a chicken, or spooned a gelatinous ovum into her mouth.

Sometimes she pestered me to keep the company of people.

'We go pub?' she'd plead, 'Watch people.'

'People can be cruel,' I'd warn her, 'They'll laugh at us.'

'No. People kind.' She'd pretend. But she needed to be amongst her own kind, so I'd go along with her, to the lounge of the

Grosvenor Arms, where the air smelled of fear, formaldehyde and vomit.

'We love?' Emilie would ask, eyeing me plaintively as she sipped on her glass of Pils. She was toying with a bag of pork-scratching. I could not bring myself to tell her that she'd been nibbling the deep-fried nipple of a sow.

'We love,' I'd confirm. It was a repetitive pattern of invariant question and answer. As if nothing could convince her, or allay her corrosive doubt.

'I ugly,' she'd sigh, 'bent thing.'

'Very, very, pretty.'

'No. You leave me. Find a girl without hump. Get married.'

'Never,' I'd protest.

'Yes.' Her eyes would well with water. She'd sniffle. Then so would I. And Jerry the barman would cast his caustic gaze on us. He didn't like his customers to sob. He said it cast a damper on his atmosphere. He preferred people to slur and snigger.

'It's a lovely hump, Emilie. Promise you'll never lose it.'

'I go hospital,' she said. 'Get straight.'

'If you do, you'll leave me. Find a handsome man.'

'Never!' she'd sob.

'Yes!' My eyes would brim with tears. 'You'd find someone else.'

'All right, woebegone and red-eyes,' says Jerry, glowering down at us, 'Cheer up or sod off.' He said it was a pub; not a funeral parlour.

'Sorry,' I sniff.

'You will be fucking sorry, if you carry on like that.' And he was right about this, as it happened.

One night abed I tried to tell her.

'I'm an animal, Emilie.'

'Not animal... but sometimes you hurt me with your thing. Too rough.'

'No, I'm a beast. My humanity is just a façade.'

'You're kind,' she pecked my cheek, 'but sometimes makes me sore. You do it too long.'

'You don't understand. I'm a monkey.'

'Yes! My monkey.' She laid her head on my chest and stroked the length of my thigh.

I lifted her head, staring down into her drowsy eyes. 'Listen. You're a human. I'm not. We're different.'

'Is joke?'

'No joke. It's serious. We're different sorts. I'll only hurt you. You understand?'

She jerked away, presented her back and submerged her face in the pillow. The bed began to quiver in rhythm with her sobbing head and flailing arms.

Her head twisting sideways, her mouth came out for air, 'You tell me go,' she mewled. 'You tired of Emilie. You get rid.' She howled, clutching my chest with frenzied fingers, and my skin opened, weeping beneath her nails.

Oh, how we howled, screeched and wailed. It was quite inhuman. As if we wept at the horror of life, by proxy for you all. But after the storm came the calm. The neighbours tired of banging on the ceiling. Emilie was worn down to a whimper. And I moaned soft and quiet, rocking her in my arms.

I asked her to marry me. She consented. But I feared it was all a mistake; that I could not make her happy.

I've never cared for doctors. I've always seen them as enemies. I've always resorted to robust health, or mute suffering, to keep myself from their pink-pawed clutches. They'd expose me, I feared. They find a name for everything. I didn't want them to devise one for me. Then, there's their arrogance. It's an enigma that a group of specialist plumbers, prone to drug-addiction, alcoholism and suicide, should believe themselves our betters. Perhaps it's a matter of life and death. If a person's negligence or incompetence can kill you, you'll treat them with polite respect. And if they're privy to your naked surfaces, grope your intimate orifices, and snip around beneath your skin, you'll want to believe them caring and skilful. Then they get carried away by your esteem. They think that because they can untangle a colon, they should likewise straighten your morals.

They get very irritated by the human mind, doctors do. They think it should pull itself together. They believe it should

157

behave itself like a self-respecting organ, like a gall-bladder or pancreas, and obey the firm corrections of their scalpel or pills.

There's nothing wrong with the human mind that some lithium tablets, short sharp shock, or snip in time can't cure. If you get depressed, and find it hard to start up in the morning, they put electrodes on your temples and give you a jump-start. They used to treat schizophrenics by cutting the connections to the prefrontal lobes of their brains. But twenty years experience showed this was a cruel, unhelpful cut. It's a rude organ — the mind — to refuse medical advice. It still won't do as the doctor tells it.

When they first spied Emilie, Mother said hello, and Dr Cadogan said 'Kyphosis'.

'What is?' she asked.

'Spinal curvature,' he said.

'Can cure?'

'Traction,' he said, 'a firm mattress. Physiotherapy to build up the muscles. I'll arrange an appointment for you.'

'Please!' Emilie beamed. 'If you please.'

'No!' I muttered. I didn't want a doctor to steal the hump that marked her special.

'Tea-time,' said Mother.

After crumpets, egg and cress sandwiches, sponge-cake and trifle, Dr Cadogan steered me by the elbow down the steps to the garden.

'Do you really intend to marry a cripple?' he asked.

This nudged me close to anger. I'd always been too polite to mention to him that he was an obese, bald bigot who tainted my air with his stench of stale Brie. I didn't see why he should make free to cast a disapproving eye over Emilie, defaming her pretty back.

'I don't believe we could straighten her out entirely.' He added, 'and there are children to consider. The defect might be hereditary.'

People are like that. They clutch a single piece of the jigsaw, then start describing the entire picture.

'Then there's culture to consider. Mixed marriages are difficult.'

I'd thought of this already. An ape engaged to a human being would have considered compatibility.

'Is she one of us?' he asked. 'What do her parents do?'

'One of us?'

'Decent? Cultured?' he explained.

I'm not a nice beast. I get troubled by vicious urges to vent a violent spleen. 'Piglet,' I thought, eyeing Dr Cadogan's pink fleshy face. Like him, pigs believe their own sty is a nation entire unto itself. They'll sniff out an intruder and nip it on the rump. They won't tolerate another that hasn't wallowed in their dung.

'Don't rush into anything you might regret,' Dr Cadogan advised. 'It's not too late to back out.'

'I *love* her.'

'She isn't pregnant, is she? If so, there's a chap at the hospital. . . .'

'No.'

'Take a tip from me . . .' he said. The urge was irresistible.

I reached out and tweaked his nose.

I believe he never forgave me for this. I must have tampered with his dignity when I touched upon his nose. Nor did he keep his promise to arrange an appointment for Emilie at his hospital. No, she arranged that for herself. Despite my wails of protest.

There was a new treatment. They arranged a grid of tiny electrodes across her back. Pulses of charge fired her muscles at alarming rates, exercising them to strength, tugging her spine straighter. Every Tuesday afternoon Emilie presented her hump for this correction. Alternate weekends, for two days, she suffered the inquisition of traction. When I visited her, she'd be hanging, crimson faced, in a rotating frame with lead weights strapped to her ankles.

'Make me pretty, for my Charlie,' she'd wince.

'Emilie, they'll spoil your lovely shape.'

You can be sure I noticed the slow but inexorable changes. Within months she seemed merely hunched. Autumn stripped her of all but a slouch. There was a new bounce to her step. She held her head higher and looked strangers in the face. A whole evening might pass without her once apologising for herself. The second glances she gained in the streets were no longer those of pity or curiosity. Twice, I heard men whistle at her. It went to her head. She began to court the company of vanity. I'd seen her smile at herself in the mirror. She submitted herself to fashion.

I knew our time together was ending. She was deserting me to join the ranks of people. Once, I swear, she tried to get me to go dancing. And one Saturday I arrived home to find the flat blazing incandescent. She'd drawn all the curtains open and fitted electric light bulbs in every socket. So I locked myself in the bathroom and wept.

She tapped on the door. 'Charlie, what is . . .?'

'I feel very orange today,' I whimpered. 'I'm depressed. I think it's my period.'

I knew she could sympathise with this; a shared discomfort. And, in truth, it was that time of the month. I get headaches. I feel weak, jittery and apathetic. My ankles swell from water retention. My nipples feel raw. My vision blurs. And my nose bleeds without warning. People seem vicious. I worry for my skin.

'Carrots, Charlie,' she whispered through the keyhole. 'I've made grated carrots. With apple and raisins. . . .'

So I let her coax me out. It always made her happy to see me enjoy my food.

'I know what,' Emilie passes me a mug of nettle tea, smiling through the steam, 'we could have friends around for supper.'

'Friends?' I wailed, 'People? Here?' Well, I had no intention of turning my home into a cafeteria for human transients. They can loiter at Victoria bus station instead. I do wish them a safe journey through life. But it wasn't my task to provide a waiting room till they caught their next connection.

'Yes,' says Emilie, smiling smugly, 'I know nice peoples.'

She was the gentlest, kindest being I'd known. Yet she was transmuting into an alien thing, a foreign body, a thoroughly human being.

It was no longer enough for her that we were together. She

wanted to show her face to the world, coax me out, correct my inhuman foibles. Her loyalty was turning, ponderous and sluggish as a tortoise, away from me. I watched it turn its back. I saw its stumpy tail receded from me, carried away by a remorseless waggling tread.

The elastic of our affection was straining with the stretch. Soon, I feared, it would snap.

I had to spend my days with people. I didn't wish to come home to one. For I needed time to rest, recoup and recover.

A person won't leave you alone, you see. They'll keep pointing out your oddness, naming and numbering your deficiencies, then advising how you could become every bit as fine as them.

'Sleep on bed, Charlie,' says Emilie, 'Not under ... be like proper person.' Or: 'Come out of wardrobe, *please.*'

My answer was always the same; but she could never understand my sensitivity. 'I like the shade,' I'd say. For it was hard to find a restful gloom, now she'd had the flat flood-lit.

And Emilie carried a radio from room to room. So there was the insistent screech of song, human chatter or the unkindness of laughter. There was no dim quiet to be found; unless a beast slithered through the trap-door into the roof space, closing the hatch behind. But even there, soothed by the squeaks and scuttling pad of mice, he'd hear Emilie below, opening and closing cupboard doors, calling him out of his hiding, coaxing with promises of roast parsnips or steamed red cabbage.

People are all of one family. The geneticists have shown this. All humans are related to an African Eve, a common great-great-grandmother, who lived ten thousand generations ago. Because every living person has similar genetic material in their mitochondria — those portions of a cell that produce energy.

When a human embryo is conceived, a sperm and ovum fuse, mixing their genes. But the mitochondria come from the ovum: so the mother alone provides these. In the history of people, only one mother produced a daughter, that produced a daughter that produced a daughter etc, in an unending matrilineage to this day. She is the common mother from whom you are all descended. Every human is related to every other. You are all

161

of the same African descent. I believe you should bear this in mind, before you start squabbling again. Though I daresay it's none of my business. Only, often, an outsider can see things that brothers and sisters can't.

But perhaps you Africans can understand how alone a South American feels when the flickering flame of his family has been snuffed out. Every man and woman is your relation. Yet I am the last Xique Xique; solitary and sterile. My species dies with me. It was enough to make a chap weep in his loft, aloof in Islington.

Seventeen

I didn't pride myself on being a moral animal. I had neither the pride nor the morals. So I stayed a simple beast.

All I could claim was a reflex empathy. And since it was a simple heart jerk, involuntary as a wince or sneeze, I could claim no credit for it. Without wishing to — and how I wished I didn't — I shared the sorrows and joys of others. I would not knowingly hurt another beast. For that hurt me. And when I pleased another, as I sometimes managed to, it was to please myself.

You are welcome to your Scriptures and strictures, credos and doxies, pieties and dogmas. To my nose they're fusty or rotten. Give me a carrot any day. Or, failing that, a parsnip. Your ethics are too sour and bitter for my taste. Besides, they always bemuse me. Riddles and rhetoric aren't my forte.

Sometimes I have stolen. That's to say, I've filched something — because it is shiny, or tasty, or otherwise tempting — without simultaneously pinching a pretext. You seldom do this. Instead you take what is rightfully yours, claim, discover, appropriate, liberate, redistribute, confiscate, so teaching a salutary lesson; so as to align your act to an ethic.

It's all so ingenious. I watch it with wry admiration. There seems a moral for every misconduct. One selfish shit I knew prided himself on the honesty of his deceits.

'I may be a lying bastard,' he conceded, 'but at least I'm honest about it.'

He was scathing about the Nazis; because they'd fibbed about what they'd done. 'You've got to have the courage of your convictions,' he advised. For he was a sucker for courage, too.

Did you hear of the American girl who shot her parents because they were always fiddling with the TV knob, changing channels without asking? She must have been a democrat, valuing consultation and consideration above all other niceties. Condemn her if you will. At least − like you − she had a moral purpose, a favourite virtue and colour.

So far as I can discern, you have at least five moral principles. They are incisive instruments. You keep them sharp as butcher's knives.

You rechristen your offence, so it becomes an innocent or generous gesture. You rename the victim a villain, so it's clear they deserved what you gave them. Or you call the hurt a kindness. Failing that, you disown responsibility, or howl that your critic's a crook.

A crime is a moral act seen from behind, by a man who'd rather see a bum than a face. From any other perspective, the beast seems more sanitary. Then, a murder becomes a restitution, a liberation, an act of nobility, a fearless blow, a kindness. The poacher only shot the deer because it was looking sick.

And a victim is merely a suspect falsely accused of an inno-cence. Stalin knew this. Anyone with half a wit will understand, if they can only find a scruple.

Besides, a person is only a person if they earn that designation. They could be a thing or an animal. If you call them inhuman. Or they might be no more than a number. Then murder's no more than subtraction. Some are no more than expendable units − like a dollar, or calorie. Spend a penny, wash your hands, cash a life, burn a therm. It's not so much a moral issue; more a linguistic nuance. Words can quite erase any unsightly, unethical stains. Language washes whitest.

A hurt, an injury, is no more nor less than a lesson defamed or denied. Being robbed teaches us to share. Pain shows us how we have hurt in our turn.

If you can't wriggle out, it helps to be helpless. You needn't carry any morals at all if you haven't got the strength. Call yourself the victim. Your life hasn't been easy either. People should understand.

It's the fault of your early conditioning and your genes. Your parents — who gave you both (and so rarely understood you) — are obviously to blame. Men are hapless victims of their nature; women are victims of men; all are stooges of indoctrination, pawns of capitalism, dupes of advertising, façade of a crazed unconscious, infected by original sin.

Anyway, who are *they* to call you names? You could tell some tales about them.

You got carried away in a moment of weakness. It could happen to anyone. Everyone does it. They'd admit as much — if they were honest. Those hypocrites. It's just bad luck getting caught.

Anyway, to err is human.

'No one's perfect,' said Waldo Kremer Junior, 'The bottle sorta coaxed me to drink it. Then the devil got inside me. He laid the knife in my hand. I sorta lost all sense of right and wrong. When I woke up, God opened my eyes. So I buried them decent. Said a few words to the Lord. It seemed cleaner that way. Cos it was a hot day — no shit — and the bodies had started to stink. I'd have got the cops. But my phone had been cut off and the car was out of gas. Then after a day, I kinda forgot. You know. Outa sight, outa mind. They were some-mean-mother-fucking-godless-bastard-pimping-spics but, God knows, I'm sorry now. An' I never meant to waste them.'

Everyone can be blameless. In their own eyes, at least. It's just a matter of finding the logic to fit. I can't believe there's a human perversity that can't be fitted in ethical fancy-dress. There isn't any viciousness that rhetoric can't cure.

Myself, I'll stay dishonourable. I've never been bothered to find the morality to blend with my clothes, or agree with my occupation. Nor have I bought beliefs off the peg, dyed them to match, shrunk them down to size, or tailored them to fit. So I remain a shameless, guiltless beast — a thorough psychopath, an unprincipled ape — bred for mischief.

You have my sympathy, for what it's worth. It can't be easy, being yourself. You've enough on your back already, without being saddled with a conscience and the impudent jockey of guilt.

*

When I found Ludwig on my steps — withered, wall-eyed, cringing, vicious, incontinent mongrel — we became a three-some. Emilie resented this from the start.

'Ugly dog,' she observed, wrinkling her nose, brushing at his hairs which clung resolutely to her skirt.

'That's his beauty,' I agreed. For it was impossible not to love such a hound, unblemished as he was by any virtue, grace or charm. 'He's completely despicable, bless him.'

'Put him out,' she demanded.

'Emilie! He needs us. Without us he'll starve.'

He became quite a conversation piece when we were together in the evenings. Often he came between us, especially in bed. For he'd sprawl shivering on the duvet; snarling if either Emilie or I reached out a hand to touch the other.

She kept a ruthless account of his flaws and foibles, making no fair allowance for the instincts, whims or aesthetics of a dog. Every night she'd give a vehement speech for the prosecution.

I'd noted with sorrow that her sympathies were becoming twisted as her spine was growing straight. It was as if she'd forgotten how it felt; to be degraded and deformed.

'This dog, Charlie ... he piddles on the floor. He shits on the sofa. He snaps. He smells nasty. He barks when we kiss. He leaves hairs on my Jaeger trousers. He steals from my shopping bag. He chews my shoes. This dog is impossible. . . .'

'Isn't he just, the little rascal!' I'd pat his snout. And though he'd raise his lip, he'd never nip me.

So there we were together — a woman, a New World Ape and dog. A menagerie à trois. Once a couple acquires a third party, the balance of opinion twists, the community of interest shifts. Majorities emerge. There are accusations of favouritism. Minorities are singular, and sulk. I didn't have everything my own way. The other two were carnivorous, censorious and snappy.

But Ludwig and I disliked visitors, so Emilie gave way on this.

'How can I have peoples?' she demanded, 'When dog bite their legs.'

Every day saw a succession of byzantine conspiracies. Emilie would lure me away, trying to get me to intrigue with her and collude against the dog. She argued a favoured status for herself, a special relationship, on account of being human and the longer-standing friend.

Emilie would give the dog a bad name. Worse, she'd thin-edge-of-the-wedge-ify. It was her vehement opinion that a mongrel, once allowed to pee unchecked against the leg of the kitchen table, would feel sufficiently encouraged to proceed to destroy all decency. She'd start ends-justify-the-means-ing: proposing that some solid suffering by Ludwig would serve a human abstract.

'Hit him, Charlie. For God's sake.'

'I can't . . .' I wailed, 'It hurts.' I had to speak up for Ludwig. He couldn't answer for himself. 'Emilie. . . .' I sought to soothe her, 'Love me, love my dog.'

'No, thank you.' She was adamant.

'No?'

'You must choose, Charlie. . . . Dog or person. Ludwidge or me.'

This I knew. But I tried all manners of delays and prevarication. To hold our family together.

Ludwig didn't help his cause. He wolfed a box of her rum truffles, then retched them up in her Italian handbag. Every day, he contrived to exclude her, lying watchful on my lap, snarling at her scowling approach.

I was jostled by the jealousies; sorrowful that we three could not live peaceably as friends. It was all unnecessary pique. For my affection for the hairy did not diminish my love for the smooth. I felt no lust for Ludwig; nor he for me. And Emilie had no interest in chasing sticks or hoarding bones. If we fancied a walk, I knew which to take by the hand and which to put on a lead.

The selfish, sensual part of me favoured my human lover over the dog. Yet my sympathetic impulses were steadfast for the mutt. Ludwig would be lost without me. Emilie would be found. In my fantasy, I saw her eloping with a man.

'Either that dog goes or I do,' Emilie screeched.

So the final, fatal words were spoken.

Ludwig snarled at Emilie. He lowered his leg from the cocked position, stepping fastidiously over his puddle as it drained steaming into the carpet.

I didn't sleep at all that night. I paced the streets, Ludwig trotting morose and dogged at my heels, all the way to Dulwich and back, pondering the awful choice.

Ludwig depended on me. He was a manic-depressive; with a phobia about strangers; he was innocent of pedigree or charm. If I passed him on, or let him go, he'd be gassed by a vet within the week.

As we stood shivering on Blackfriars Bridge, dampened by drizzle, dawn divided the elements, dispelling the confusions of night.

The luminous grey sky arched up from the charcoal buildings. The oil-black river lapped the columns. Emilie's air rose above our earth and water, signalling our parting.

A tug on the Thames sounded its foghorn, blaring the decision as a long rude fart of fate.

I suppose I'd decided at the outset − by taking the whining dog for a walk, instead of following the whimpering woman to bed.

I took Emilie an early morning cup of tea, with two slices of buttered toast, and answered her ultimatum. We exchanged red-eyed glances.

'Where is honey?' asked Emilie. For she liked bee-vomit for breakfast.

'Here,' I said, 'but Ludwig stays. . . *He* needs me.'

So, faithful to her promise, Emilie packed and went; taking all she'd brought, leaving me five last words − innocuous individually, yet viciously combined.

Though she sounded hurt and surprised, I knew it was for the best. She would have left me anyway. Ludwig was a pretext. It's a dismal thing to remember.

It wasn't a decision. It was the decision. To choose between people and good. To submerge myself in morality, and so abandon life. Or keep good faith with another, needy, beast.

I knew what a Brazilian would do, and Beccles or Dr Cadogan. So, in truth, there was no choice. In honour of my family, I could take no other course.

It was chilling to watch Emilie pack. With her went my love of people and my last, lost chance. I felt humanity turn its back on me as she spun away from a final chilling kiss.

'Be happy,' she said, 'alone with dog.' It was as though she'd spoken a curse.

When the door slammed closed behind her, I was entirely shut off.

Ludwig padded forlornly to the door, sniffed at the crack, whined and scratched. I believe he'd grown fond of her, by the end, in his own gruff doggy way.

It was my tragedy. She left yawning holes in my head and heart. With her went all warmth. My fire went out.

It was the cruellest, coldest time. I was forced to choose between them. But both were gone in a week.

They were the two beings I'd loved most. Both, like me, were torn between the bestial and human; sharing features of animal and folk.

The bent Emilie of old had been a flittery, frightened, feral thing; cowed by human approach. And she'd awarded me her animal love — fevered and obstinate, unconditional and unreasoned.

And Ludwig was such a human dog — pessimistic, phobic, deranged. Like a person, he was seldom ashamed of the messes he made. 'Like you, I have my reasons,' said his brazen, sullen, hauteur. 'If you accuse me, I shall defend myself,' said his quivering muzzle, unmasking his china teeth.

He never frittered his fondness like a promiscuous puppy. No, he'd stow his surly tail between his leg, disdainful as a commuter, flinching from his fellow travellers, fearful of intimacy, smiles or talk.

There's a lot of disdain about, have you noticed? Not to mention a surfeit of blame.

Would they mind being happier? Or do they just love to loathe?

I've had some unlikely accusations levelled at me.

One night in a pub in Kentish Town an Irishman accused

169

me of causing the potato famine of 1846, then evicting twelve thousand families in 1886.

'Look. . . .' I stammered, 'I am sorry. But that really wasn't me. I'm not that old. Perhaps you know my face from somewhere else.'

He considered this, closing his downcast eyes, blowing on the froth of his stout. 'Bastard Englishman,' he said at last. Then he raised his head from contemplation and butted me in the face. I knew from the sharp snap and dull pain, he'd broken my nose to spite my race.

And when I once declined to buy a copy of a magazine outside the Angel tube station a man accused me of promoting apartheid and betraying the working class.

'No,' I protested. 'Surely you're confusing me with someone else.'

But he was adamant. 'Scab,' he shouted after me, 'Traitor to your race.'

Then there was a pleasant looking woman in Islington library who turned nasty when I held a door open to prevent it swinging back in her face.

'Patriarchal prat,' she spat.

'Me?' I asked, all innocence, in case she was muttering to herself.

'You,' she confirmed. 'It's taken thousands of years, but now you've been found out.'

She had good grievance, of course. She'd mistaken me for a man. It would have been too convoluted and lame to explain I was just an inconsequential ape.

I didn't know which of you did it or why. It made me recall a thing I'd learned at university — an ambiguous sentence beloved by linguists which goes:-

THEY ARE HUNTING DOGS
They/are hunting/dogs
They/are/hunting dogs

The single sentence has two distinct meanings. Whichever the sense, the morality's a mystery to me.

As Ludwig padded ahead across Grosvenor Avenue, he gave

me a morose sideways glance. I was to value the gesture later. It was a sort of adieu.

The pink Cortina accelerated to meet him. He saw it coming and broke into his loping run. Whatever his suspicions of people, he didn't sense the worst. Perhaps, in my way, I killed him by teaching him some trust.

Dogs bark but the caravan goes on.

The car slewed, then swerved to intercept him. Its wing flicked him up, somersaulting through an arc. I knew from the dull thud of his landing, he wouldn't rise again.

The driver sounded Colonel Bogey on his horn and waggled his car in a victory salute. A face looked back through the passenger window, leering its delight. Then with squeals of wheels, the car swung round the corner into Highbury Grove.

Dead dogs bark not. I buried him in Highbury Fields.

I couldn't understand it. Why were they hunting dogs? There's always some good reason. What people do, they can invariably sanctify with some spare ethic.

I'd never had his photograph taken, so I drew a variety of sketches whilst my memory was sharp. There was so little left to know him by — a chewed blue plastic bowl, a collar worn shiny, and his tartan blanket. The blanket was best; covered in his fine fawn hairs, redolent with the thick brown smells of him.

I slept a lot, wrapped in his blanket, and he was with me in my dreams.

Some days passed. Then the phone rang. I lifted the receiver. Beccles said 'hello', his voice clotted with pique. So I replaced the hand-piece on its cradle.

I didn't want to see people. People could see each other, I thought. It seemed the best arrangement.

Yet people wouldn't leave me alone. They kept phoning, alternate days. So I cut the connecting cord.

People tried the doorbell too, until I snipped the wire. Once a person hammered on the door. But a pillow over my head kept the voice at bay.

When I found a razor blade, I cut long gashes into my back, chest and legs.

The pain came as quite a relief.

The blood dried to brown crusty threads. I looked like a train map of Europe. All twisting intersecting lines. I often pondered these; winding routes across my skinful.

One day, I stood at the fridge door, nibbling a flaccid, wrinkled carrot. The black blighted edges to a lettuce woke me to the realisation that weeks must have passed since Ludwig got carried away. Grief is such a distraction.

Eighteen

Fear went lasciviously with fact. Together they bred nightmare.

I dreamed that Dr Cadogan gave me an autopsy, as Emilie and Mother watched. He crunched through my ribs with surgical shears, before pruning my internal organs. This was a painful operation, for I was paralysed yet awake. He sensed this, winking at my open eyes, as he remarked upon my pancreas.

'See!' commands the pathologist, 'Variegated spongiform islets.'

'So he isn't human?' gasps Mother.

'So he doesn't matter?' Emilie sighs her relief.

Cars were also to the fore in my dreams, as were dogs and bones. So, I preferred to rest awake. And keep a cold hold on my mind.

Time ran like a long coil of celluloid film, through the gate of my mind. There were empty sprocket-holes of day, through which I saw rectangles of light edging the curtains. Then dark-light-dark-light. . . flickering across my vision.

I knew it would end, but let it run its course. It came unwound with a clatter when the front door was ripped screeching from its hinges, falling flat in the hall. The dark silence was broken.

My blinking eyes knew more light than they could comprehend. I heard shrieks and grunts from behind the blinding golden aura.

A hand tore Ludwig's blanket from my frozen body. I started to tremble and shiver. I heard the curtains being torn back at the windows. My ears — unused to the hurts

173

of speech — crackled to guttural blasphemies and squawks of surprise.

Laying my hands across my eyes I saw, through the strips between my fingers, three men stooped to watch me.

Mr Christos Georgiades, and his brothers Tassos and Nikos, had come to evict me, in the nicest possible way.

'No pay, no stay,' said my landlord, kindly with regret. 'Rent spent.'

'No money,' I said blankly.

'Sorry,' he pats my bony shoulder, 'business.'

'Do you hit me now?' I asked, for Nikos was clutching a crow-bar, eyeing me with distaste. It's nice to know what's due to you, so you can prepare for it in your mind.

'No hit,' said Nikos, pained by the accusation. Instead, they lifted me from the couch, led me wobble-legged across the room and leaned me against a wall. As my eyes regained the power of sight, I watched them pack my books, clothes, bedding and plates into my suitcase.

'Here. . . .' says Christos Georgiades, rustling two five pound notes between finger and thumb, 'Go quiet. No trouble.'

'No,' I protested. In truth, it was I that owed him.

By some crafty conjuring, two more notes sprouted up, crackling persuasively between his twitching fingers. 'Twenty,' he warned, 'is most I give.'

Well, I felt very orange and disconcerted in the light of day. There were things I'd need to buy. So I sniffed my thanks and took the money.

'Good man. . . .' I winced, 'too kind.'

'Don't take piss with me,' he warned, gruff with grievance.

'No!' I said. 'I've only been evicted once before. . . . but you do it with more kindness.'

'OK. Is business, see.' He swallowed and looked downcast to his feet, 'Bye, bye,' said he. 'No come back.'

His brothers led me out and down. Each had me in an arm lock. Their touch, though firm, was fair. They barred my way at the front door as I turned for a long, last look back to the dim hall and gloomy stair-well. Then the door was shut with a decisive thud in my face.

174

I couldn't face Mother or Dr Cadogan. I felt too feeble to explain myself, and also unworthy. I knew where I must go to make myself safe. But I was an orange ape, loose on the streets. I needed camouflage for my journey.

In a second-hand shop on the Holloway Road, I bought a wig for six pounds. It was a luxuriant, tangled mop of thick black strands, centrally parted with long back and sides. There was more hair to it than I'd ever wished for. It lent me the look of a rock musician.

From a chemist's shop two doors along, I bought heavy-duty face-powder smelling of attar of roses, and a pair of gold-rimmed, mirror-lensed sunglasses. In a side-alley I dusted my face and hands with the powder, admiring my distortions in the curved reflection of my shades.

Of all the people I've ever seen, I most resembled the pale-faced lead guitarist of a renowned rock and roll band. He was famous for several habits. Some suspected him of a sympathy for the devil.

You can be sure I took particular care crossing roads. There's no telling which motorist was out on a journey and which had come hunting for game. I'd wait for someone else to cross, then scamper alongside, using them as a shield betwixt myself and the traffic. I turned my head away when anyone cast a curious gaze upon me. My pallor was blanched as bread, a radiant white lie; but beneath I smarted orange.

As I trudged beneath the arched gateway to Chelmstead Hospital, I wilted and relaxed. Now, I believed, I'd be saved.

Maureen, Dr Beccles' secretary, seemed dismayed when I shuffled up to her desk, though she was used to unlikely sights. I let my suitcase fall by her white stilettoed feet.

'Yes?'

'It's me,' I smiled, and felt the crust of powder crease and flake on my cheeks.

'Name?' She cocked her head and blinked, like a disconcerted parrot.

'Charlie Duckworth,' I said, 'to see Dougal Beccles.'

175

'We used to have a Charlie Duckworth. But he's. . . .'
'Back where he belongs.' I said. 'Reporting for duty.'

'You look different, Charlie,' Beccles said drily. He wasn't overly friendly. There was a sour taint of irony to his speech that seemed an unfortunate barrier. 'You look. . . .'

'Like a person?' I suggested hopefully.

'Well . . .' he trailed off, staring blankly. He took his spectacles off and began polishing the lenses with a tissue.

'Mel well?' I asked, 'And is Dermot still up to his tricks?'

'Look, Charlie. . . .' He leaned back in his chair, to widen our divide. 'You stay away for a month, without a word. . . .'

'A month?' I gulped, 'As long as that?'

'And then you stroll in . . .' his voice went starchy '. . . looking like . . .' his nostrils arched unpleasantly. 'And think you can just start work again.'

'Please,' I pleaded. 'Don't be harsh . . . I'm feeling delicate.'

'Delicate!'

'They killed my dog,' I said. 'Now, they're after me.'

'Who?'

I looked around, to check that no one else was in earshot. 'People,' I whispered. 'Softly, softly, catchee monkey.'

'Save the jokes,' said Beccles. 'You're fired.'

'Look!' I said, 'I haven't come for my job.'

'No?'

'I've come to stay. As a patient . . . Look. I've brought my suitcase.'

'You must be mad,' the psychologist tells me. Only, he says it with impatience and contempt. Which seemed harsh in the circumstances, and considering his profession.

'Yes!' I agreed. He was beginning to get the gist of it.

I unbutton my shirt to display my proof. He leans closer to look. Then he asks why I'd done it — criss-crossed my chest with razor cuts.

'I don't want people to cure me,' I say.

'Cure you of what?'

'Cure my skin,' I explain, 'to use it as leather.'

'That's an unlikely worry, Charlie.' He's curious now, giving me a long considered gaze before returning his scrutiny to his finger-nails. But I've got him properly interested now. He's never met this condition before. 'Why should anyone think they could use your skin as leather?'

'I'm an animal. People use animal skins as leather. Look. There. . . .' I point to his bull-hide loafers, his suede jacket and then to his executive, number-locked, pig-belly briefcase.

'Why do you think you're an animal?'

'I am. I've been a beast all my life. I've only been *acting* human.'

'We're all animals, in our way. It's human nature.'

'I'm different,' I said. But then most patients believe themselves special, think their problems are unique.

'What kind of animal are you, Charlie?'

'Homo ridiculus duckworthensis. I'm the only remaining specimen. I was discovered in Brazil. By my father.'

We paused here, exchanging embarrassed glances. It was time for him to reach a provisional conclusion.

'Are you still seeing your girlfriend, Charlie?'

'No. She said I had to choose between her and the dog.'

He asked if this was a joke. I told him that I could understand his point of view. I could see that I might seem a joke. I didn't mind him pointing it out. 'It depends on one's perspective,' I said, 'whether you're inside my skin looking out, or outside looking on.'

'Do you ever feel suicidal, Charlie?'

'Only when I'm depressed.'

'And that's when you cut yourself up with a razor?'

'It seemed a sensible precaution — at the time.'

'To prevent people using your skin as leather?'

'Well. . . .' I gestured to my thin frame with my bony fingers, 'Nobody would want to eat me, would they?'

'No,' he agreed, 'they wouldn't.'

'Except as cat food,' I suggested. 'They put any old offal in cat food.'

177

'Cat food?' He hoisted his brows in polite surprise.

'Surely, you've noticed? At the check-outs in supermarkets. Everybody's buying cat food. To eat themselves,' I explained. 'It's cheap you see. I know people eat it. I can smell it on their breath.'

'I hadn't noticed.'

'Well, you eat babies and buttocks yourself, don't you?'

'What?'

'Veal and steak,' I explained.

'So what do you eat?'

'Not a lot recently,' I said, 'I've been on a diet. . . . But I don't think you can beat carrots or parsnips.' I went on to mention cauliflower and courgettes, swedes and turnips, cabbage greens and spinach. Talk of vegetables brings me out of my shell, renders me rhapsodic.

'What are we going to do with you, Charlie?'

'Observation, first,' I advised. 'Then a full clinical interview. We could do the Rorschach and Kelley's Repertory Grid tests — and take a stab at a diagnosis.'

I didn't believe myself mad. Madness is relational. To qualify, I'd have to think differently from others of my kind. And of these there were none. I was not to be judged by human standards. As the only surviving Xique Xique, I was an epitome of normality — the sole average and standard.

Yet I had been sick. Now, I'd recovered from a delusion of complacency. I'd believed myself safe amongst people. Then, the killing of Ludwig had disabused me. So I'd scampered to a sanctuary. I found my asylum, as an emotional refugee.

They did not know what to make of me, my colleagues and co-conspirators.

Dermot sidled up to me, all zipped-up and chirpy. 'Aren't you working, Mr Duckworth?'

'No,' I said. 'I'm a patient, now, like you.'

'A likely story,' he smiled, and tapped his nose confidentially. 'Aren't you going to give me some tokens?'

'They haven't given me any yet, Dermot. They haven't worked out my programme yet. I'm still under observation.'

'What are you in for, then?' he challenged.

'Who knows? Delusions? Paranoid schizophrenia? Manic depressive psychosis? . . . I'm waiting for an expert opinion.'

He pats my shoulder to reassure me. 'If it's any comfort, I always knew you were a bit of a loony.' he says. Then he slips two blue counters into my hand. 'There, Charlie. Take them. In case you want some chocolate.'

Beccles was bemused and apologetic to address me across the barricade, from the safer side of sanity.

'OK, Charlie?' His manners can't agree. They haggle among themselves. They're torn between friendliness and detachment. His gaze is glassily distant, but the tilt of his torso is amiably forward. But his folded arms are a barrier signal. Though his tone is coaxing. 'We could transfer you to another ward if you like.'

'I'd rather be here, amongst my old friends.'

'Anything you need?' He hoists his glasses and rubs at his eyes. Perhaps I'm an illusion, caused by a speckle on his cornea which he can just wipe away.

'Just treat me like the others.' I propose. 'I'd be grateful for a diagnosis. Then a treatment and cure.'

'What do *you* think is the matter with you?'

'I've developed a phobia about people,' I told him, 'they're cruel and vicious. I believe they want to hurt me.'

He scribbles this on his clip board, then smiles disarmingly. He waves his open hand at the other patients in the day room. 'But you feel safe here? With them, and with me?'

'It's the sane people I worry about. And you're almost harmless. . . except to your wife and close friends.'

There was a tangible chill. He went all frosty and formal.

'Right. . . Charles. Can you remember when you first felt that people meant to harm you?'

So, I began to explain, telling him my partial truths, which tumbled from my wearied mind. They were easier than lies. I felt safe. I trusted him not to understand me.

*

Beccles-business is the person-perplex — untangling the knots of human nature. He has a keen and eager nose for your nature. He writes about you — without your consent — in the *Journal of Abnormal Psychology*. You'd be peeved by many of his observations. He mentions your bedroom behaviour.

Beccles believes in a universal and constant human nature. He tries to disregard the interfering hiss of history and crackle of culture. These distort his picture, making him reach for the vertical hold. Point to differences if you will, but Beccles knows that Homer, Mozart, Einstein and Marx all suckled at the breast; albeit with varying satisfaction. Beccles has his suspicions about Mamma Marx, for her lad grew into such a materialist. All were toilet-trained, weaned and disciplined. And from those universal experiences did Newton, Machiavelli, Plato and Thatcher learn the separation of self and the world, shame, power, subtraction and addition, generosity and empathy. Insist that each is different, but Beccles knows better. Each is a multi-modal-information-processing-device, equipped with a corpus callosum, ascending reticulate arousal system, bi-cortical brains, united by our dismally short span of attention and leaky, acoustically-confused short-term memories. We are man in general, as are women.

Individually, we are particular instances of the person in general. So if you were to cite two people — Jesus of Nazareth, and Joseph Goebbels of Munich, for instance — Dr Beccles could talk indefinitely of the features they had in common, without exhausting his fund of facts. This gives an insight into knowledge and the nature of infinity.

As therapist, Beccles lends his insights to his patients. He wants us to lead good lives. He believes we could, with effort, lead lives that are as productive as his own.

He's both eclectic and original. He knows he has to be flexible, for people are so variable in their sameness. Albert Camus was a very self-aware person. Beccles could have talked him through his depression. But with someone less self-critical — Joseph Stalin, say — he might have tried some informed psycho-drama. Beccles would deploy behaviour therapy to coax John the Baptist out of his attention-seeking rituals. But for a person like Adolf Hitler,

Beccles would use social-skills and sensitivity training, to help the blinkered fellow see the other person's point of view.

'Do you believe you can help me?' I asked him.

'I'll do my best.' he promised.

I had no definite plans or strategy. I just wanted to keep alive, rest and recover my strength. I needed to rethink my position with people. I'd got tired of always being underneath and lying on the damp patch. In time, I'd find some remedy.

There was food, warmth and safety. During the day we had Conversation, Therapy, Scrabble and Ping-Pong. In the evening there was Television, Ping-Pong, Scrabble, Conversation and Visitors.

The first to twenty-one is the winner. Then you start over again. You get a double score for some words.

Beccles wanted me kept alive, and could watch out for me on his video screens. Aside from any residual affection he felt for me, I was an engaging patient. He'd had a Satan, Napoleon, Virgin Mary, and Wolfgang Amadeus Mozart before. But never a Bald Animal.

The deluded characteristically opt for more powerful or prominent identities. It's rare to find a psychotic who claims to be a hedgehog, say, or the reincarnation of a solicitor's clerk. This made me an unusual and valuable specimen. My humility gave me my stature.

Beccles had started writing about me — for one of those learned journals to which he subscribed and confided. I'd found this out when I'd taken my curiosity to his desk, to read through my personal file. His article — 'If you pay them peanuts you get a monkey: a case of delusional identity' — had shrunk my life to six lucid pages. Beccles had found a wealth of reason in my madness. But the reasons were his, not mine.

Nineteen

My fellows on the Lister Ward were pleasant enough and harmless. The mad are not less human than the sane, but more so. They are humanity writ large, for the hard of understanding — like those library books written in simplified language, printed in very large type.

Dermot still insisted on displaying his willy. Like you he confused his parts and his whole. He took a pride in his appearance and feared its decline.

Like you, Henry Spatwit had trouble with his memory. But he was less selective at forgetting than you. He could remember nothing new. As though he'd learned too much of life already. Every day he'd introduce himself, as if we've never met before.

'Henry Spatwit,' he beams and extends his hand. 'Don't I know you from somewhere?'

He doesn't remember he doesn't remember. His past and present have parted company. They got in a huff and can't be reconciled. Now, they have the decree absolute. He knows he is thirty-four. He has known as much for the past four years — whose passing he hasn't noticed. If he looks older, more care-worn, puffy perhaps, in the shaving mirror each morning, he puts it down to a hard night. He supposes he got drunk. He woke in a strange bed this morning, in a shabby hotel. Perhaps, he should check-out and go home. The maid is surly. The waiter — a spiv called Beccles, wearing a white coat and supercilious smile — has just refused to bring him a gin and tonic.

Henry is reading a Raymond Chandler novel — as he has been for three months now. He never gets past page 12.

By then, he's forgotten how it started and has to begin again.

"'I ain't seen Velma in eight years,' he said in his sad voice," says Henry, "'Eight long years since I said good-bye. . . .'"

Audrey hunches on the sofa, opposite Henry and me. Her knees are drawn tight to her chest. An avid mouth sucks a raw thumb. The taut fingers of her left hand clutch a magazine to hide her pale, creased face.

Like you, Audrey is worried. But more so. She dedicates her days to anxiety before nightmares come to claim her. Her body is her problem — that and her mind. The magazine doesn't reassure her. I've looked at it myself, for a fellow gets tired of *Country Life*. In the first four pages there's dysmenorrhoea, stretch marks, jogger's nipple, varicose veins, facial hair, intimate hygiene, white-heads, split ends, foot-odour, pot-noodles and constipation. And that's only the advertisements. I can see how far Audrey has read. Craftily, with a sideways peek to check we are not watching, she slides a finger beneath the arch of her foot and, quick as the flick of a snake tongue, draws it back, then sniffs at it suspiciously.

Audrey sits near Henry. She likes to keep him in sight. Sometimes, during evening Recreation, they have sexual intercourse in the laundry cupboard. Audrey and I know this, but Henry cannot remember. If he wants to do it again, he'll have to seduce her afresh. It's pleasant for her to have a lover who finds her a perpetual exciting novelty. He never takes her for granted.

Martin and Mrs Tyler complete our party in the rest-room. Bolt upright in her arm-chair, Mrs Tyler declaims to us, on behalf of all sensible people. She warns us that the television set is watching us and listening — even when it's switched off. On Sunday evenings she likes to wear a clean dress; so Cliff Michelmore will see her looking her best.

'Don't slouch, Charlie,' she cautions me. 'Not when the Home Secretary is watching us. It creates a bad impression.'

'Sorry, Mrs Tyler,' say I. 'Sorry, Roy Jenkins.'

She's in a nostalgic state, telling me about her youth. 'We didn't have orgasms when I was young . . .' she shudders, 'we took ourselves hiking or camping. . . .'

183

'Really?' I ask.

'Now you get fornication on the National Health ...' she looks first to Audrey – who should know better – then to Henry. Both disregard her. 'And there are degenerates on the television. ... In my day, we had Black and White Minstrels and Wilfred Pickles.'

'That's a shame,' I sympathise, as best I can.

'Do you know what we need?'

'No?'

'Corporal punishment.' She nods soberly.

'You'd like a fair crack of the whip?' I guess.

'I have the stigmata,' says Martin. He holds his palm out for us to see. There's a white button scar in the centre of his right hand. But he'd inflicted the wound upon himself. Having nailed his right hand to the wall, he'd been without the means to fix the left. And had dropped the hammer teasingly beyond reach.

We were a varied lot on the Lister Ward. Not a minute passed but someone said something interesting or provocative, pertinent to the human condition.

Beccles gave me the Repertory Grid Test. I had to name the people and things that were important to me. I volunteered my father and mother, Dr and Mrs Duckworth, Emilie, Ludwig, Kafka, Mozart, apples, bananas, truth, and assorted vegetables.

Then the game began. I had to say how two of these might be similar to each other, but different from a third. The answers I gave showed how I thought of my world, the concepts I employed in giving order to my life.

'Tell me, Charlie, how do your father and Mozart resemble each other but differ from a courgette?' He kept a straight face as he asked this.

'I never knew my father. . . or Mozart.'

'Yes, what else?'

'They weren't vegetables. . . .' I offer lamely. I watch him scribble down, "never knew" and "not vegetables".

'What else?'

'They died young. . . .' I sniff. 'They were misunderstood, and sensitive – and devoted to their families – ugly sounds made them ill – they had yellowish complexions, whereas a courgette has a dark green skin — they were sympathetic, easy-going, gregarious — but they kept bad company — they were too trusting. That was their undoing.' Somehow, this test of Beccles' was getting under my skin in a manner I hadn't expected.

A week later, he gave me a proper talking to, alone in his office.

'This notion of being an animal, Charlie. . . .'

'I know the notion you mean,' I said.

'I think it's just a metaphor, isn't it?'

'How's that?' I asked.

'It's a way of saying you feel inhuman, vulnerable. . . isolated, lonely, hunted, abused.'

I nod my sorry head. 'So I'm not really an animal at all?'

'Of course you aren't.' Beccles winces his exasperation.

'That's a relief,' I say. I couldn't help admiring his confidence. 'How do I get better?'

'Learn to take people on their own terms. Mix more. Talk to the others. Be more assertive.'

There was sense to this, I knew. Piss not against the wind. Better bend than break. Howl with the wolves. If you can't beat them, join them. Say as men say, but think to yourself.

It's no good posing as a person. To get by you have to believe it.

There's no short-cut to getting human. It's not as crass or easy as it seems. There's a lot more to it than acting callous, snuffing animals, sniggering, bragging and dressing-up.

At first, I tried to discern the coherence; till I realised there wasn't one. It's a complicated recipe. Take the lump of flesh and sear it in the oil of pain. Then leave it to stew in its own juices. Mix in a teaspoon of kindness in a cup of cold indifference. Thicken the mixture with conceit, until it turns opaque. Reduce it till it coagulates. Spice with shames and guilts. Baste it in anxiety. Then glaze it with deceit. A sprig of wit doesn't come amiss.

I sat out spring on the patio, outside the rest room. Summer, I spent in the garden, tidying the flower beds; or lying in the grass, learning *Hamlet* by heart. In autumn I collected the fallen leaves and made a compost heap. I spent winter playing scrabble and reading Samuel Beckett.

I watched my fellows. I observed myself. I bided my time.

Within a year, I felt rested and ready. I'd lost my reflex flinch and wince by then. If I heard someone enter the room, I'd trust them not to harm me. I could bear footsteps close behind me, without a backward glance.

I knew what I had to learn. I'd made a list of it all:

get callous

kill animals

find some ethics

borrow some reasons

keep thoughts apart from feelings

stare back (scowl if it helps)

forget this (and that)

eat gore (muscles, entrails, vital organs)

learn more excuses

pretend nothing's wrong (whistle etc)...

I started one afternoon, in Occupational Therapy. I was making a raffia tea-cosy for Mrs Duckworth. Perhaps it was Providence. When the pupil is ready the teacher arrives. A large mottled moth alighted on my raffia-work. I knew the question this throbbing pretty parcel posed of me. It wasn't easy, but it had to be done.

It had six legs. After I'd plucked off two, I felt nauseous. But I closed my eyes and swallowed. Then I plucked the remaining legs. And the wings for good measure.

No one was impressed by this when I showed them. Mrs Tyler remarked tartly that a child could have done the same. Perhaps. But it was a big step for me. We develop at our own speeds. And, frankly, I'd been retarded by my maudlin feelings.

Within days I'd recovered. I felt strong enough to stamp on a toad in the garden. It croaked and belched as I ground my foot down on it. There was a muted, liquid popping sound as its belly burst, and entrails erupted through the split.

'Are you a man or a mouse?' Dermot asked, when he found me retching over the splattered beast.

I didn't take this in at first. But later it got through to me. Gave me human ideas, to tame my bestial spirit.

I took to trapping mice and voles. It's easy. Rodents are fucking stupid. And they spread diseases. I'd put them out of my misery by tapping their heads with a half-brick. It was hard not to think of Molly as I did this. I had to stifle my sentimentality. Dermot remarked that I was as good a mouser as his aunt's tortoiseshell moggie; which I took in good part as a compliment.

It wasn't long before I felt fit enough to try the taste of a sausage. The knack is to approach the task with an open mind. If you think of pigs squealing in the abattoir, immediately you're lost.

It's all a matter of clutch control. You must disengage your thoughts and your feelings. Else one will snare the other.

Mrs Tyler told me she blamed the blacks. I could see her point of view, once she'd drawn it out from the scabbard of her decency.

'Do you think I should blame them too?' I asked.

'Lots of respectable people do,' she advised, 'like that clever Mr Powell, who spoke to us on Thursday, during the news.'

'I expect it's very convenient? Blaming other people?'

'I find it so.' She nodded soberly. 'It's never done *me* any harm.'

'Who else do you blame?'

So she told me about Jews and Catholics, Irish and homosexuals, estate-agents, communists and masons. She explained that the Queen hadn't helped matters — marrying a Greek and breeding half-castes.

I told her I blamed the Brazilians.

'That's a good idea, Mr Duckworth,' she said. 'I hadn't thought of them.'

She seemed such a decent, sympathetic, respectable old lady. The simple dignity of her camel-hair twin-set complemented the sincere directness of her words. She reminded me of Mrs Duckworth.

*

Of course, I never thought to fuck *her*. Respect is one thing. Fucking is quite another. You mustn't confuse your interests, otherwise they get tangled. That's my fourth commandment.

Anyway, she was dried up and wrinkled as a prune. She was sixty if she was a day.

But I tried it on with Audrey. Never mind if she was miserable and flat-chested. She was the only young skirt on the ward.

For want of better, I really fancied a poke with her.

It wasn't easy. It wasn't difficult. It was a matter of patient persistence. I had to tell her I loved her. She wasn't going to unhook her amber, sweat-stained bra, or wriggle out of her purple winceyette knickers for less than three full words. Everyone has their price.

'Do you *really* love me?' She looked at me so wide-eyed and plaintive. As if I'd tell the truth. Her blue eyes went watery. Or perhaps they were brown.

'Yes,' I said, 'we could be alone in the cupboard.'

Fuck that for a laugh. She was always wet about the eyes. But dry inside. You never knew such a tearful cling-on. She was always trying to make me feel guilty.

Henry Spatwit kept us entertained. I used to kid him that Beccles was a waiter.

'Order me a pint of lager, will you? Ring the bell for room-service.' I'd point to the fire-alarm.

The prat would always do it. No harm done. You've got to laugh. Otherwise you'd cry. Got to keep cheerful.

I could always get around Henry. It wasn't hard, the dickhead could never remember. He set himself up to be taken.

'Hey, you owe me a fiver,' I'd tell him.

'I do? Sorry.' And he'd fumble about, searching his pockets for a wallet. Fat chance. Last seen four years ago.

So I'd do a deal with him. A swap. Fags or chocolate his brother had brought him. In exchange for the money. Not that it mattered, if I looked after them for him. Because he never noticed. Had a memory like a sieve, that man.

Only I had to be quick about it. After he'd had a visit. Otherwise Dermot would fleece him first. That's why I never felt guilty.

If I hadn't done it, someone else would. You've got to get the jump on the bastard. Or some other bastard will get there first.

'God help them that don't help themselves.' So Dr Cadogan used to advise me. For he was an advocate of enterprise culture, before it became so respectable.

Mrs Duckworth came alternate Sunday afternoons. Sometimes she'd drag along Dr Cadogan. The ponce. I was always pleased to see them. I'd beam away like sunshine. I tried to appeal to the best in Dr Cadogan — his guilt, confusion, self-doubt.

'I used to think you were a right jerk,' I told him. 'I thought you were a selfish, bigoted bastard. I didn't understand things, then. Now, I know better.'

'Yes?' He'd flush, blinking, and twitch his lips.

'No offence, mate.'

'None taken, I'm sure,' he'd mutter.

'You've got to look after yourself in this life,' I observed. 'If you don't no one else will. Can't let people get you down.'

'Well . . . you have us. Your family.'

'Thanks,' I'd pat his clammy hand before he could retract it. 'I was going to mention that. Can you lend me some money? To buy stuff from the shop.'

It always worked, that con — playing on his guilt. You could see he resented it. But he always paid up like a good 'un. Five or ten, if his wife was listening. I'd sussed him and no mistake.

Beccles told me I was getting better. Said I was on the road to recovery. But I should carry on taking the Largactyl.

'It's easy once you've got the hang of things,' I conceded. 'I'm more confident in myself. I'm learning to handle people.'

'Quite a transformation,' he beamed, 'I can't believe my eyes.'

'It's all down to you,' I told him. 'You've made me the man I am today.' I thought I'd butter him up. The poof. But the truth was I'd worked it out for myself, with a little help from newspapers and television.

'You've still a little way to go,' he warned me.

'I know,' I'd conceded. 'But I'm working hard on it. I've just got to control my anxiety, suppress some inappropriate feelings. . . and adjust myself to my morals. And try to think less — about things.'

'Have you decided what you're going to do? When you leave?'

'I'll have to look after myself, won't I?'

Dr Beccles nodded soberly at the wisdom of this.

'I'll buy a new wig, and a leather jacket,' I assured him. 'I've learned by my mistakes,' I promised.

In the end, they were well pleased to be rid of me. Beccles himself signed my release.

'Does that mean I'm normal and sane, squire?' I asked.

'Well. . . sort of.' He went into a pedantic rigmarole of tangled reason. '. . . It means you can function in society.' That was his conclusion.

'Can I have a copy of the certificate?' I asked.

'I could give you a photocopy.'

'Thanks, chum. I'd be proud to have it. I can have it framed for my room. If anyone ever doubts me again. . . .'

'Yes?'

'I can show them my qualification.' Somehow this certificate of normality seemed more important to me than a first-class degree in Psychology from the University of Kniggle. I suppose I'd had to work harder to earn it. I'd been struggling for it all my life.

'I hadn't thought of it like that,' Beccles smiled. 'And now you'd better be getting along. You've got a new life to lead.'

A brand new life to lead, I thought. I'd take better care of this one, and keep it on a tight leash.

Twenty

I believe my cure has cost me something. Everything has its price. I've lost my sense of sympathy. But, then again, I don't give a fuck what other people think.

I am not the joke you take me for. 'Look at him,' you snigger to your partner. 'Is he wearing a wig. And make-up?'

So I saunter up. Gaze down upon you, behind my mirrored shades. You see your own reflection, where my eyes should be.

'Anything amused you?' I ask with a crisp and formal concern. 'My appearance, perhaps?' You shudder in my shadow.

'No,' you gulp.

You don't frighten me any more. I've learned to call your bluff. I can look you in the eye without a flinch or blink. If I stare at you — in the street, on a train, or in a supermarket — it'll be you that looks away first. You know I've found you out. I can see through your tricks. You blush. You daren't confront me. Behind that oily smirk, you're weak, like me.

And when I walk Ludwig, my Alsatian, you worry about us both.

I gave him a good beating when I first got him as a puppy. To teach him I was boss. Once you've drawn blood, you reach an understanding. Then you can afford to relax and be nice.

But he's a mean dog, Ludwig, bless him. His bite is worse than his bark. It shows in his eyes. He's been trained to handle traffic and cross a road with care. He's been taught not to trust people. Men, women, children, they're all the same to him. He doesn't like them at all. Far be it from me to criticise, but he's a bit of an misanthrope, my pup.

At night we walk the streets. We used to keep an eye out for a pink Ford Cortina, until we found it parked in Balfour Road. We waited seven hours for the owner. He helped me with my enquiries, concerning a mischief I promptly repaid — with no more than stealth and a half brick. Ludwig had a dog's chance — and chewed him about a bit.

Well, I wasn't going to go bestial and mad again. So, I got coolly and humanly even. Revenge is a dish best eaten cold, as a famous moralist once remarked. Nonetheless, I often have to count backwards by threes — to forget the dull crunch, and reluctant acquiescence, of skull yielding to brick. Frankly, it left me shaky. It was all quite disturbing. I'd never make a habit of it. I'll never be the sort of person who can commit a violence every day.

When we get back from our walk, I often sit down and attend to my correspondence. I prefer writing to talking. It's less intimate, and more rational. It helps me to tidy my thoughts, and keep them apart from my feelings. Also, I can correspond with all manner of influential and famous people with whom I have certain concerns in common. I write to the very top —

Dear President Saddam Hussein,
When I was a vegetarian I had some difficulty understanding your seven points of view. Now I eat meat and know better.
    I realise that the Iranians have a special place in your heart, but do you intend to let the Brazilians off the hook? As it happens, I have a personal interest. . . .

or

Dear Mr Scargill,
Can I consult you? We have the same problem — viz, how to reconcile a wealth of personal vanity with a poverty of hair.
    When you comb the side hair over your scalp (to cover the central bald patch) how do you get it to stay there? It looks all crinkly, so I suppose it may be woven.
    Have you tried a wig? I wear one myself, but a brisk wind or sudden movement can. . . .

I have several replies from prominent persons thanking me for my involvement in their affairs. Occasionally, there are small gifts. When I wrote to the Reverend Doctor Paisley — concerning some hatreds we share and enjoy — he sent me a religious tract, in which he marked certain passages for my attention with a red biro. The President of the Ford Motor Corporation sent me a key ring bearing his company's insignia. An eminent actress (I shall not betray her confidence by giving her name) replied to my enquiries, concerning the size of her talent and teeth, by enclosing a publicity photo of herself inscribed "To Charles Duckworth, a darling and my greatest fan". This hangs in a frame above my bed.

The morning's mail always promises some surprises.

I have a first floor flat at 122 Hermit Street. Ours is a special and curious household, maintained by Christian Fellows for the former inmates of mental hospitals: an asylum from asylums. But not all are cured who lodge therein. Josh on the ground floor, and Derek on the second, are both prone to hearing voices, muttering mischief.

Derek laughs along with the whispers in his head. He laughs regularly — at thirty- to forty-second intervals, all through the night and into the morning.

'You dirty bastards. . .' he chuckles, '. . . filthy rascals.' He giggles, stamping his feet with delight.

His voices are lewdly amusing companions. Whereas Josh's mental chorus tease him something rotten. They cast vile aspersions.

'Faarkin wankers . . . cunts,' he howls. '. . . stop calling me filthy names.'

This is pitiful. Also paradoxical. For the neighbours — unable to hear Josh's inner voices — believe it is *he* who starts shouting the dirty names. They whisper about him in the street. Sometimes they call the police. Which makes him howl the wilder.

The neighbours don't like Derek's outbursts either. It's disconcerting to hear his staccato laugh at the very moment you've dropped your pants, or started picking away at a pimple. It's as though he's privy to your intimate moments. You think he's laughing at you. And nobody likes a nosey smart-arse.

Just as I am lodged between Josh and Derek in the house, so I am perched between them in life. There is a correct balance — a happy compromise — I believe, to be struck in our human existence between those twin extremes of incessant howling and hysterical laughter.

This is my goal in life — to find the golden mean of the middle ground, then pitch my tent there, above the waterproof groundsheet of my indifference.

I, too, hear voices in my head — the Drs Duckworth and Cadogan, Paul Walster, Mother, Beccles. Oh, and my lost love Emilie. I listen with cold politeness, as they speak to me from memory. Though I wish they'd go away, I neither laugh nor howl at them.

We're carnivores, my dog and I. Meat-eating hasn't come easily to me: flesh is an acquired taste.

Ludwig is partial to chuck steak, ox liver or the entrails of pigs. Sometimes I give him boneless rabbit for a change. On Sundays and holidays, I buy him a box of chocolate drops.

It's a wonderful thing — giving pleasure. Even if it's only to a dog.

My joy is classical music. I collect cassettes. Currently, I have two hundred and seventy, arranged alphabetically by composer. Each is a small, discreet box of emotion. So I can pick and choose my mood. The Ms are best. Requiems are calming. Best stay clear of Bartok, if you'll stand advised. Never let him bend your ear.

I tend to buy orchestral and choral works. Aside from aesthetic considerations, they're much better value. You can get a tape of an entire orchestra, and massed choirs, for the very same price as you'd pay for a solo violin. Berlioz is the best of bargains. Sometimes he'll give you an orchestra, brass band, two choirs and a cannon. But against this you must offset the noise.

Mozart is my favourite. That man was a god. When I wish to cry I play the Ave Verum Corpus. To rejoice, I listen to Exultate Jubilate, K. 165 (Salzburg version). I invariably prefer Emma Kirkby to Kiri Te Kanawa, and Hogwood to Davis, amongst the contemporary recordings. Harnoncourt is a wanker. Foreigners tend to misunderstand Mozart. It's odd because, although he was technically a kraut, he's a particularly

British composer. Like me, he spent his happiest times in London.

Le Nozze di Figaro holds a special place in my affection, having been my father's favourite. Otherwise, I prize K. 220, 259, 317, 626, amongst the choral works. It is a wonder to me. That I so love the human voice in song, when I cannot abide its chatter.

The music relaxes me after work, and provides me with pleasant emotions. It quite restores my feelings.

Though the remuneration is fair, it is a thankless task recovering debts from forgetful creditors who don't wish to pay. Sometimes, it is necessary to speak harshly. But we are a respectable company. We never show malice. We keep our hands clean. If we can't convince a creditor, we sell the debt to someone more persuasive. What the eye does not see, the heart does not grieve over. I wish grief on no man, least of all on myself. I expect you're the same. It's only human.

Except on certain evenings, I keep myself to myself. You know where you stand with yourself. You make your own bed and you lie on it.

Even in the pub, I keep to myself. I go to the Empress of Russia. The clientele are English, if you understand my meaning. They are a pleasant crowd to stay aloof from. It is understood by the regulars that a certain seat is mine. This is by the alcove, next to the clock, facing the door, where I can watch the passage of people and time. There's a time and place for everything. Every person has their use, if you'll only take the effort to find it.

I get quite philosophical, sipping my Guinness. Then I have to stop myself thinking too much. Because I don't want to tax my mind or tangle my reasons. The chloropromazine helps; especially washed down with Guinness. But some disturbing thoughts still visit me.

We have a plight in common, we people. It isn't pleasant being the hyenas of creation. We plunder nature, then turn on our own. We prefer things dead. Our aesthetic favours still life. We cast our dismal shade. Life flees from us in panic. For the beasts find us beastly, as do the fish and the fowl.

Sometimes we worry there'll be a justice and judgement beyond our own — like Nuremberg or God. We must weather the storm and hold our nerve. We are what we are. We have to be brazen and bold.

Well, can you imagine what would happen if a leopard changed its spots, and went vegetarian? It'd go all morose and mangy. Some satirical zebra would prance up and kick sand in its face.

We may be bullies, but we have our feelings. We whimper and suffer. We are lost waifs, whistling against our dark, swaggering to scare our shadows.

You aren't so bad, yourself. Compared to certain others. Take comfort in that at least. Off the top of my head, I could name thirty-six well-known historical characters compared to whom you seem kindly. And I could name twelve species of animal that — though they do less damage — are arguably more vicious than people.

We all have our furtive secrets, don't we? — those intimate things we'd rather not mention. And our misdemeanours. For we've cracked a few skulls in our time.

Can I offer some advice? From one person to another. I have my moral commandments. But perhaps I'm preaching to the converted.

Don't let them laugh at you, or take advantage of your sweet nature. Give credit where credit is due. Nor a lender be. If you take good care of your cash-flow then it will take care of you. Don't struggle to understand another's point of view, for they won't strive to see yours.

There's a fucker born every minute. Don't let the bastards get you down.

But always keep your hair on in public. Home is where the heart is. Keep your snout out of other people's troughs. Try not to be sentimental. Do your best to like yourself. Your first responsibility is to yourself and your own. But don't forget your dog. Take the tablets, if they help. Don't think too much — it causes confusion and saps your confidence. Don't get your interests in a twist. Keep your thoughts apart from your feelings: or they'll fight like cat and dog. Don't feel guilty.

You had your reasons.

There's always an explanation. Be firm but fair. And stay out of mischief. Then everyone can be happy. That's my morality.

You live and learn. You make a contribution. Before you die.

If I come into the Empress of Russia and find a stranger seated in my place, I explain that the chair is mine. I am fair but firm. I try not to make a fuss. Usually, they will move for me, because my height and expression command their respect.

Sometimes, we get foreign tourists coming in. I keep an eye on them. Call me a patriot if you will, but I don't see why they clutter up the Empress of Russia when they've got places of their own: tavernas, bars, bistros and such. Besides, there's only one urinal. And we've only got seven tables. Sometimes the regulars are forced to stand.

Maxine comes home with me on Wednesday and Saturday night. Then I fuck her.

Well, if I didn't, someone else would.

We have an understanding. Though I had to hit her when I first got her, to convince her who was boss. She knows how I like our business done. As always, I take pride. My firmness is fair, my fairness firm. She has no cause for complaint. She knows I take care not to bruise her. I never tie the knots too tight.

My life isn't all a barrel of laughs. Every cherry in the bowl wraps a stone. It isn't all valium and skittles. We all have our problems. Sometimes, I feel my old sickness coming over me. I feel I want to cry. So I take a firm hold on my feelings.

Sometimes, I fear, I lack the strength and discipline to stay sane, healthy and wholesome. I'm like a reformed addict or drinker. One sip of sympathy, from the cup of kindness, and I'll be in the abyss again.

I see one man twist a broken beer glass into another's face. A toothless man sits on a park bench, his face contorted by the challenge of chewing a toffee. Or I watch a fur-coated lady shop-lift in the Army and Navy, furtively pocketing a padlock.

I wonder why people do these things. I am touched by the perversity and pathos. There is something precious and poignant in people, if you discount their façades — faces, characters and manners.

For pity still stirs deep within me — like the wriggle of

illicit desire. Beggars and destitutes move me, till I'm forced to look away.

A scowl in time saves nine.

Life is hard enough, without borrowing other's woes. You have to be harsh, to be kind to yourself. I prefer to stay indifferent. I can't bear another's burdens. Lately, I'd sooner not know. I don't care to be concerned.

If my tenderness ever threatens to overwhelm me, I knock myself out with pethidine. The next day I feel strong.

What helps me most is to think of you. I don't mean to be sycophantic but it's people like you that have taught me all I know.

I wonder how you'd act. An image springs to mind. Then I know what to reach for — snigger, blank mask, sharp word or blunt instrument, whichever the occasion demands.

Of course, I'm still a novice — only an apprentice person.

I have my unfortunate foible still. People can see the space between my ambition and attainment. Sometimes, when I imitate people they think I'm mocking them.

I do my best. I get better as I improve. The world can't ask for more.

My stare and sneer are near perfect now; and I'm practising a smile. I'm with you. Human. Kind.